Shattered Dreams

A Dark Tale of Love, Loss & Betrayal

We All Fall Down Series
Book 1

CJ Warrant

Disclaimer

This book is intended for mature audiences, 18 and older, due to harsh language, graphic violence, sensitive subject matter and sexual content.

Cover Design: Sara Cunningham PA

Images: Adobe Stock

Editor: Rebecca Aksdal

Paperback Edition ISBN: 978-1961685-16-1

Digital Edition ISBN: 978-1-961685-15-4

Dear Reader,

It's been a while since I've delved deep into the dark side of my writing. But I love the outcome of this book and the journey I went through with Regina, Krew and Decker.

Now some of you may say this book isn't dark, which I have to agree. I've gone much darker in some of my other books. Shattered Dreams dips its toes into the dark pool. But buckle up, readers, it will only get darker from this point on. I will have Decker and Krew's books out in the near future, which touches on matters of different traumas people endure.

For those who have triggers, please be warned there are several that needs to addressed in this book.

Sexual assault off the page. Childhood trauma. PTSD. Depression. Emotional and Physical assault. Self-harm. Sex, including crossing swords and other delicious stuff. Graphic violence. Murder, by gun and knives. Love and loss. Morally gray. Foul language.

Through all this, I truly hope you enjoy reading these childhood best friends and their journey in finding love and happiness.

Smooches,

CJ

Everyone suffers at least one bad betrayal in their lifetime. It's what unites us. The trick is not to let it destroy your trust in others when that happens. Don't let them take that from you.

— Sherrilyn Kenyon

Prologue
Regina

Every frantic, stumbling step I took through the dark woods was one step farther from *him*—the asshole who'd ripped away my innocence—my soul—with every brutal thrust, he stole a piece of me.

I swallowed, trying to rid my mouth of the coppery taste of blood, but with the tortured motion only worsened the pain. It felt as if dull razor blades were scraping the back of my throat. Vivid memories assaulted me—how he'd clamped his filthy, calloused hand around my neck and squeezed until his blunt fingernails dug into my skin. How he'd repeatedly punched me in the face to stop me from screaming.

I swiped my swollen tongue along my split lower lip, and a sharp sting made my eyes tear up even more. But I couldn't let myself focus on the pain. I had to get away.

As I continued to hurry through the trees toward an open clearing I'd glimpsed a minute ago, desperation filled my gut, warning me to keep looking back over my shoulder for any sign of the monster who was chasing me. I prayed the bastard wasn't following.

Finally, I came to the edge of the woods and found an old corn field. I choked out a relieved sob as fat tears blurred my vision and slipped down my cheeks.

Clutching the ragged edges of my torn shirt, I hurried on, oblivious to the rows of stubs left over from last year's harvest. The sharp remnants of the old stalks were like dull knives cutting into the tender sole of my left foot, but not the other. One of my favorite flip flops was still on my right foot—it'd stayed on by some miracle, through the attack and even during my escape.

I was oddly grateful for the sting in my left foot, a it gave me temporary relief from thinking about the throbbing pain between my legs.

Keep moving, I told myself as my heart rate ratcheted up and the pounding in my ears got louder. No matter what, I had to run faster. Had to find a hiding place before *he* saw me out in the open. Because if he caught up with me, I knew I'd be dead for what I had done to him.

He'd raped me, but I'd fought back. And for certain, the gouges I had made with my nails would permanently scar his face.

The cool spring wind and the sliver of waning moon in the dark sky added to the horror and dread flooding my veins. I didn't want to think about that—think about *him,* or what he could do to me— not when I had already endured hell.

Noise from behind had me dropping to the ground and stiffening like a statue. My heart thundered furiously against my ribcage, the hammering in my ears intensified, and stars burst across my vision. Even though I felt like passing out, I refused to close my aching eyelids.

I swept a cautious look along the field and found loose husks rustling along the uneven ground. Then I saw them. In the distance were twin lights. *Headlights.*

There was a road. That meant my phone might finally have

enough bars and I could call for help. Hope caused the panic that was piercing my chest to withdraw just a bit.

I heaved myself back onto my feet and ran as swiftly as I could in the direction of those headlights, still glancing over my shoulder every few steps to check the edge of the woods.

My anxiety was a knife's edge and so was the hatred swarming in my blood like killer bees ready to attack. But I kept on running even though I struggled to breathe and the pain intensified with each jarring step.

Every few feet, I glanced down at the cell phone clutched in my left hand. There were no bars. Yet. Even with dread creeping back in, my choice was to keep moving. I wouldn't die here—not here—not where he could find me.

Clinging to a thin thread of faith, I finally reached the ditch by the roadside and decided to drop into it and hide. But I tripped and tumbled down, face first, before rolling onto my side into the muck at the bottom. Pain wracked my entire body, making me dizzy.

I placed my right hand between my legs and put pressure on my throbbing crotch, hoping to ease the ache there.

When the dizziness finally cleared, I pulled my hand away and tapped the screen to unlock my cell to check for bars again. That's when I saw it—blood, which was illuminated by the meager light from the phone screen. Absolute horror engulfed me at the red coating my fingers.

I had been so focused on running and finding a safe hiding place, I hadn't realized that I was bleeding. A soft cry tore through me as I tried to block out how I'd gotten into this mess. Instead, I fixated on the cracked screen. I straightened the best I could and prayed I got reception.

"Two bars," I uttered in relief, and then quickly pressed my thumb down on the button, and shakily uttered, "Siri, call Maya's cell…"

Please answer, Siri answer. I repeated the mantra in my head, while my heavy breaths sawed in and out of my exhausted lungs.

Three full seconds passed—an eternity for me—before Siri robotically answered, "Calling Maya's cell."

I held my breath while the call connected, clinging to the hope that Maya would pick up right away.

"Girl, do you know what time—"

I wept louder at the sound of her voice. "Maya... I need—"

A shout of rage echoed through the night air, and I froze, the cell pressed to my swollen cheek. I didn't know what direction the scream came from, but I immediately plastered myself to the cold, damp ground. Fear spiked like a lightning bolt and I began to shake uncontrollably as the thought of being raped again shredded my soul.

I forgot in that moment that Maya was on the phone. I was so lost, frightened and filled with anguish and pain that I didn't hear my best friend yelling my name.

"Regi! What's going on?" Her voice ultimately cut through my living nightmare. "Where are you?"

"I... need, help," I whispered hoarsely, all my energy suddenly seeping out from me.

"Let me call your par—"

"No. Please, don't call them. Just come and get me," I pleaded, as a torrent of tears blurred my vision once again.

"Hold on," she said. "Don't hang up. I'm seeing if I can locate you... Jesus! How did you get all the way out to Dixon County Woods?"

I didn't even know where that was. "Hurry," I frantically uttered as I pulled the phone away and listened harder for more sounds, then whispered, "before *he* finds me."

"Who—who is after you?"

"Please," I cried, not able to say his name out loud.

"Okay... Hang tight, girl. It's going to be a bit."

"O-k—." Then the phone went dead.

No! I silently screamed. I tried shaking it, but there was no reception, no light came from the screen. It was dead. And so was I. Maya was never going to find me.

I curled myself into a ball, my dead cell phone cradled to my chest, and I shut down.

The moment Decker, Krew, and I climbed into his brother's car, my beautiful day was shattered into a million shards.

Deep down in my soul, I'd known the second I had taken off and left my guys that my life would never be the same again. Ever.

I didn't know how long I lay in that ditch, plagued by the cold that was slithering into my body. It had to be quite some time, because I was numb down to the bone.

Hallucinations rattled my mind, and when a voice called my name, I thought *This is it. I'm dying*. The angels my mother had told me about during church service were here. They'd come to take me away from my family, from Krew and from Decker.

Or so I thought, as I lay in the dark, hiding in the cold, wet ditch. I even bet myself that the cops wouldn't find my body until I was decomposed. I actually smiled at that macabre notion. At least *he* wouldn't hurt me again.

Then I heard my best friend's voice, which startled me out of my morbid frame of mind.

"Maya," I croaked. I summoned whatever energy was left in my body and launched my arm upward as a bright light swept over me. It might as well have been the sun shining down, because now I had a real reason to hope.

"Jesus fucking Christ, Regi—Who—Oh my God..."

Using nothing but pure grit, I dragged my tired and battered body up from the ground. Despite the blood, the sweat and the mud, my best friend hugged me.

Regina's Diary

*May 2**, 2008*

Dear Diary,

This is the worst Wednesday ever. It's Terrible with a capital T.

Maya passed me a note in math class. She asked me, 'Who do you like more and who do you want to kiss? Krew Gatlin or Decker Moss?'

They are the two most popular seventh graders in Granger Middle School, Diary. All the girls—including us fifth graders, like them.

I thought my best friend's questions were fun. So I wrote back, 'I like them both.' I never answered the kissing question, Diary, because I really don't know. I never kissed a boy, ever!

When I passed the note back to Maya, Mr. Trince—the jerk, grabbed it out of my hand and started reading it out loud in class. Do you believe a teacher would do that, Diary?! I was so embarrassed. I covered my face with both hands and wanted to cry. But I didn't.

Thank goodness, Krew and Decker weren't in my class, but I was afraid they would hear about it anyway.

And I was right. The kids in my class blabbed during lunch hour today and Krew and Decker found out. They scowled at me from the across the lunch room. I know they hate my guts now. Maya feels bad for passing me the note, but it's too late.

I'm never ever going back to school again.

Love, Regina

Chapter One
Regi

Present Day

"I don't know how you talk me into these things, Maya." I glanced up at the steel girders running along the high ceiling of the abandoned warehouse. This seedy building was in a less-than-reputable section of Chicago and had more holes than Swiss cheese. Just standing there gave me the heebie-jeebies. "Are you sure this place is safe and legal?"

"Safe? Yes. But legal..." She pursed her lips and shrugged.

"Jesus," I snapped, folding my arms across my chest. "You aren't serious, are you?"

"Stop being so damn naïve. You worry too much, Regi. Jess told you when he dropped us at the door that it's all good—we're safe here," my best friend hyped, avoiding eye contact with me.

Her attention was solely on searching the crowd for her current boyfriend, her flavor of the month. it had been a few months and Jess Duncan was still around. Although, who knew if he'd last the rest of August.

"I don't care what Jess said, I want to leave. This isn't my type of place to hang out, Maya, and you know that." I gripped her arm and tried tugging her back toward the doorway we'd entered through.

"Damn it, Regi," Maya admonished as she pulled out of my hold.

"I want to leave." I took a step back from her.

"You're not leaving, Regi. For Christ's sake, girl. It's Saturday night, and you never go out. Stop acting like some fucking nun. We're here now. So, let's have some fun and enjoy ourselves." Maya clasped my hand and yanked me through a crowd of well-dressed people.

Most of the men were in expensive suits, but the women—including my friend—were glitzed up. They looked as out of place as I felt in my black babydoll dress that Maya had insisted on me wearing.

She'd actually walked into my closet and pawed through my clothes until she'd found it. Maya was adamant that it was her duty as my best friend and roommate to make sure I was *appropriately attired*—her word, tonight.

Everyone was dressed up and acting like this was an exclusive nightclub and they were here to drink and dance the night away. But this place was like no nightclub I'd ever been in—or would go to.

"Fun?" I hissed in her ear. "Watching two people beat the crap out of each other isn't fun, Maya."

"Then close your eyes," she said with a sneer, before she replaced it with a toothy smile that didn't reach her brown eyes. All of her angry bravado was gone. "Stop being a bore, Regi. Besides, maybe you'll meet somebody here. Get laid—anything to get that old lady stick out of your ass."

"I don't have a stick up my ass," I huffed out. And what the heck did she mean by old lady? "And I'm not old."

Maya swiveled back around toward the crowd. "Yes, you do

have a stick up your ass," she threw over her shoulder at me. "Ever since you took over the manager's position at the salon, all you do is work and sleep. I'm surprised you even had time to put on makeup and do your hair tonight. All work and no play makes Regi an *old lady*."

I snorted. Maya was ridiculous. "If I hadn't done my face and hair, you'd be bitching up a storm about *that*. At least..." I bit my lower lip to keep from saying anything hurtful. But maybe she was right and I needed to loosen up. It had been quite some time since I'd last gone out and had some fun.

Maya got in my face. "Say it," she hissed. The glint in her dark eyes displayed a warning I knew all too well. My best friend didn't play nice, especially when she was pissed off. And since she was my ride...

"Nothing." I backed down. There was no point in arguing with her. Maya had been there for me at the most horrific time of my life, and throwing trash back in her face wasn't nice. It wasn't me.

Now that I'd given in, the ire slipped out of her eyes and the familiar warmth of friendship reappeared.

"Girl, it's been ages since we let down our hair—or what hair we have left on our heads." She ran her fingers through her new pixie cut. "This will be fun—and we don't have to stay long. I promise."

Dang it, I hated when she gave me the puppy dog eyes.

"Fine, I'll stay," I grudgingly agreed. "Talking about hair, why did you cut yours off? I thought you were growing it out. And did you match my color too?"

"I loved your color and cut so much I wanted the same. Is that okay?" she asked in a chirp.

"Yeah, it's okay. The cut is actually cuter on you than me," I admitted, brushing the bangs out of my eyes.

One of the stylists at work had suggested three months ago that a modern pixie would look good on me, so I went for it. While the style was cute, the cut wasn't for me, and I decided to grow my hair back out to shoulder length. For now, I'd just have to deal with the fact that we looked almost identical.

"Thank, God. I thought you'd be mad." Then she circled her fingers around my wrist like an iron manacle and dragged me further down a surprisingly desolate corridor, deeper into the bowels of the building until we entered another hallway, partially filled with people.

With the crumbling cement walls, holes in the floors and ceiling, and rebars protruding out here and there, I wouldn't be surprised if someone who wasn't paying attention got hurt, or worse. As Maya yanked me up the stairs, I stumbled and proved myself right.

"I think I see Jess." Maya released me and called out his name. She took off toward her boyfriend. He was what Maya called a gym bear—or was it a muscled bear—whatever the term was, Jess was certainly tall. And muscled.

As I neared a large, rectangular doorway, echoes of cheers and jeers bounced off the walls. From the volume of noise, there had to be hundreds of spectators down on the main floor, surrounding the cage. I wanted to cover my ears, but I was too stunned at what we'd stepped onto.

We were on a walkway—made of steel. One side hugged the outside perimeter of this gargantuan space. The other side—except for the metal handrail, was open to the center of the building. Fear skated along my spine at all the ways I could get hurt up here.

No sooner had Maya left my side, then a sea of human bodies pushed their way forward and I was mashed up against the metal railing, my body bowing slightly forward into the open space. One skinny railing determined my ultimate safety or demise.

An overwhelming queasiness swamped my stomach as I precariously stared down at the lower half of the warehouse. People milled around the outer periphery of the large, octagonal cage in the center of the floor. Some had their faces right up against the galvanized chain links, screaming their heads off.

Between the bloody fighters in cage and the rising shouts from the bloodthirsty people crowding the arena, my head spun and it was a real possibility that I was going to lose my dinner of chicken and potatoes all over those people below us.

I needed to get away from the railing, but I was wedged in tightly, with no room for escape. Falling from the second floor of this building wasn't how I wanted to die, so when the crowd of watchers disbursed down the spiral gangplank that led to the lower level, I squeezed past the few enthralled spectators that remained.

Once free, I plastered myself to the cement outer wall, taking deep breaths until my heart stopped thrashing against my ribcage, and contemplated if I should just leave.

"Regi!" Maya shouted my name over the roaring screams of the spectators.

I glared at her, silently conveying *This is far from fun.*

She gave me one of her smirks, then her eyes shifted to the left. I followed her gaze and my annoyance grew into utter frustration. The last person I wanted to see was standing next to Jess.

Kane Maxwell. He was one of Jess's closest friends. Three weeks ago, Maya dragged me to his penthouse, where he was hosting a lavish party. Want to talk about pretentious?

Kane obviously thought highly of himself, because he'd made it extremely clear that night that all he wanted out of me was a fuck, and I could be one of the lucky ones to have his dick down my throat and in my pussy—his exact words.

By the look on his face, Kane was surprised when I had told him to drop his dick in the piranha tank that was displayed in his living room, and then I left the party.

When Maya came home the next morning, she said Kane thought I was being coy and he refused to believe I wasn't interested in him or his offer of sex. Apparently, given the wide, evil grin currently pasted on his somewhat handsome face, Kane Maxwell still didn't believe I had been disgusted by his advances.

If I were a desperate woman, I might have taken him up on his proposition to ride him like a champion bull—his words again, not mine. But I wasn't that kind of girl.

Besides, he set off my creeper alert. And I learned a long time ago to follow my instincts with guys like him. Or any man.

"Regina, I'm so glad you came," Kane said as he approached me like we were the best of friends. *Gah.* I was going to kill Maya for using my real name in front of Kane. Besides, how hard was it to say *Regi.* Two simple syllables.

"That's not my name."

Maya and I needed to have another chat about her loose tongue. If I wanted people to know who I really was, I wouldn't have gone to the trouble of making up a fake past and started calling myself Regi Martin.

"Regi," he said, as he began to reach for me. I halted, just out of range of his long arms. The man had a body—I'd give him that. Thicker than a runner's build and quite tone. But that was all I'd give him. His personality left much to be desired.

"Kane," I replied evenly while keeping my narrowed eyes on my best friend, who was fake smiling at me like there was nothing wrong—even though she knew better.

I gave her the *You're in trouble* glare. She gave back her *I didn't know he was going to be here* eyes. I returned her stare with *You're a liar*.

"Since we're all here, how about we head down to the main floor and take our seats. The next fight will start in ten minutes," Jess suggested, before he wrapped a brawny arm around Maya and planted a hard, quick kiss to her mouth.

"Great idea. Can we get a drink first, baby?" Maya bounced with exuberance.

"You ladies can have whatever you want at the bar. It's on the house," Kane said and winked at me.

On the house? Gah. Is he for real?

I wasn't going to ask what that wink meant. Instead, I followed the three of them down to the main floor. We got our drinks, then headed to a set of seats in the front row, where the view of the fight was—unfortunately, unobstructed. Maya squealed in delight at how close we were. Me, on the other hand...

We were so close that I could see the blood splatters on the edges of the gray mat in the cage. And were those broken teeth? My stomach churned up, and I quickly looked away. I wanted to get the hell out of there. Even more than I had earlier.

I swallowed down the acrid taste in the back of my throat, along with some of my Southern Comfort and soda—heavy on the Comfort, thank God. I welcomed the burn. All the while, I attempted to ignore the brutal fight that was taking place in front of us, where one fighter made mashed-meat of the other fighter's face.

We sat boy-girl, and, for some unlucky reason, I got stuck between Jess and Kane. I wanted to tell Kane to move over since he was practically glued to my side. During the two minutes we were sitting there, however, he scooched even closer and then Jess did the same. I was literally sandwiched tight between two men I had no desire to know. For Maya's sake, I clamped my mouth shut, kept my eyes straight ahead, and slowly sipped the rest of my drink.

I wasn't a person that got off on watching two people beat the shit out of each other for money—I didn't find it the least bit titillating. Actually, it turned me off.

Maya though? I hadn't known she was so bloodthirsty until she was cheering as the bigger boxer railed on the smaller fighter, who stood there and took every blow.

I couldn't watch this—neither the fight or the people around me hyped up on booze and blood. "Where's the bathroom?" I asked Kane.

He pointed to the far side of the wall through which we'd entered. I nodded and got up, and Kane stood up too.

"I can go to the bathroom by myself, Kane," I said with barely-there civility.

"This is a dangerous place for a beautiful, single woman like you. Appease me, sweetheart," Kane said with sugar lacing his tone. Like that was going to make me cow to his whims. *Not.*

"I'm not your sweetheart. And I can take care of myself." I didn't wait for his reply and stalked off toward the bathroom. Luckily, Kane didn't follow me.

The bathroom was bare bones, with two stalls and a single sink. Though, it had the privacy I needed and no view of the fighting.

At least there's toilet paper.

I took my time and did my business. Even though the thick concrete walls dampened the shouts and yells from the crowd, the echo of noise still jabbed at my nerves.

I stepped out of the stall, went to the chipped sink to wash my hands and noticed the other stall in the mirror Its door was wide open and a woman in it was snorting something. Our eyes met, and she smiled. "Want some? It'll help take the edge off."

Edge off of what?

"No thanks." I shook my hands and walked out. As much as I dreaded returning to my seat, I'd rather deal with Kane than be caught with drugs like cocaine. That was idiotic thinking on my part, though—there was no way cops would be here at an illegal underground fight just to bust people for narcotics.

When I got back to the seats, Kane was absent. In fact, Jess wasn't there either. With a quick glance at the cage, relief washed over me that the fight was finished.

I dropped into the seat next to Maya and scowled at my friend. "I'm leaving. Are you coming with me or not?"

Maya opened her mouth, but she was cut off by the announcer's voice booming through the sound system. We both swiveled toward the cage and I immediately spotted Kane and Jess, standing with a huge beast of a guy in black shorts and a white robe that hug open and exposed a chest covered with hair and his black shorts. The fighter was jabbing his meaty fists in the air in quick succession.

Before I could repeat my question to Maya, the cage announcer spoke again.

"All eyes to me, ladies and gentlemen," he said, and then he patiently waited for the noise to die down. "We have a special treat for you tonight. First to walk into the cage is none other than Forest Sulley, the current UGF middleweight champion. With six consecutive knockouts, two first round knockout wins, and a total of twelve straight wins."

The roar of the crowd was deafening. Maya was bouncing in her seat while I put my hands over my ears until the noise ceased. My eyes darted from my friend to the announcer, wishing I was home in my bed instead of here with her.

"His competitor is no stranger to the world of fighting. With seven knockouts, five first round wins, and a total of twenty wins under his belt in the underground circuit, let's welcome middleweight competitor, Krew Matthews."

My entire body stiffened at the name the announcer had spoken. *Krew.*

That wasn't a name parents typically chose for their sons. The last name wasn't familiar either. Or...

"No. That can't be," I whispered and immediately stood. Facing the cage, my eyes swept the interior, and the other fighter was gone. I asked Maya if I heard the announcer correctly, but she was screaming at the top of her lungs and paid me no attention.

Then I caught sight of a tall, not-so-lean fighter, striding toward the cage. He had on a black robe, with the hood pulled forward, it covered most of his face. I couldn't determine if it was Krew. *My Krew.*

"Regi." I heard Maya calling my name, but I was so focused on seeing this other fighter's face that I didn't realize I moved and was standing at the cage. My fingers clamped onto the fencing, my face mere inches from the links.

The thrashing of my heart drowned out the cacophony—all the hoots and hollers around me. I held my breath as my anticipation rose. I needed to see *this* fighter's face. I wanted to deny that Krew Matthew Gatlin, the boy I fell for—the boy and the life that I ran from years ago, was here.

Life couldn't be that cruel. Could it?

So many years had passed since I last saw his handsome face and the intense colors of his unique eyes. If Krew was the fighter, the last place I would want him to be was in that ring.

"What are you doing, Regi? You can't stand that close." Maya tried to yank me back, but I refused and pushed her hands off me. I wasn't going to move, not until I saw the fighter's face. I had to be sure it wasn't Krew.

The fighter turned his back to me, pushed the hood off his head, and turned, shrugging off his robe.

His head was shaved, and it was glistening with sweat. His skin was covered in ink. Black and colored—too many tats to count. When he slowly turned around, my stomach bottomed out, and so did my heart.

Those eyes, and that all-too-familiar face.

My Krew.

Tears of the past were reborn. Anger, heartbreak, and fear slid in like a landslide trifecta, as memories from the last few days I had with Krew and Decker filled my head—those days before our lives imploded.

Then our eyes locked onto each other. Shock froze his features for a brief moment before he physically shook his head and turned to face his opponent.

I couldn't catch my breath. A whirlwind of emotions clogged

my throat, and I stood there as my lungs demanded more oxygen. This couldn't be real. *He* couldn't be real.

Maya had a death grip on my arm, and she finally pulled me away from the cage.

"Regi?" Maya tugged me to our seats. "Look at me."

I swiped the tears away and uttered, "That's Krew up there—my Krew."

Maya glanced up at the cage and an odd look crossed her features. "I know," she said somberly. "I'm just as shocked as you are."

But was she really? The look on her face didn't reflect her words.

And I was sure she had seen the line-up of fighters earlier. Maya was talking about a few of them on the ride here. She even admitted that she'd memorized the schedule and who was fighting tonight.

I turned back to get another look at the man I had missed so much, and my entire being turned to ice when I saw the bastard standing next to him. Another set of memories—dark and intruding, poured in, flooding my synapses. My mind scrambled to release the words clogging my throat. "I—I have to go."

"Regi." Maya cast another glance to the cage and frowned. "Go," she urged, never looking away from the monster who had changed my world to black.

I didn't respond as I tore out of her arms with only one thought in mind.

Run.

Chapter Two
Krew

W*hat, the, fuck.*

I thought I was seeing things, with how the adrenalin was running rampant through my body. My heart was pounding and a new kind of feeling—a nervous excitement, was filling the spaces between my ribs. I was ready to fight until the last person I expected to see in this place fractured my focus.

Regina K. Morton—my Regi was here.

Regina was one of the past loves of my life. The one I lost years ago.

She might be grown up now, and her features were slightly different, but I could never forget Regina's beautiful face.

Her hair was short, a rich brown instead of the honey wheat blonde I remembered. And those eyes; they belonged to only one girl.

It had been years since I'd seen her—not since that sorry day when Decker, Regina and I climbed into a vehicle my brother Teke had stolen—though, we didn't know it at the time. We'd figured out soon enough, when the cops started chasing us, but by then it was too late. That was the last time I saw her, or Decker.

To this day, I hated Teke for irrevocably tearing away the people I cared about the most in this world. Now here I was, fighting at the whim of the brother I despised, for money my father needed for his healthcare. Win or lose, Dad would get what he needed and I would walk out of here with empty pockets and a shit-ton of bruises.

Still, it was a shock seeing Regina here, in this abandoned, crumbling concrete building, amongst the elitist and the rich, the snobs who paid good money to watch us fighters beat the hell out of each other.

By the time my brother drew close and blocked my view of Regi, I completely lost my pre-fight focus.

I had no choice but to redirect my attention to Teke, who was glaring at me. My brother's eyes were both the same golden shade as my right one. My left eye? It was hazelly blue shade with a small brown spot on the iris. I suddenly remembered Regina used to say it made me special.

"Focus," Teke grated out and flicked my forehead like he'd done since we were children.

"You do that again and I'm going to cut off your fucking finger. Now, get out of my way. You're blocking my view," I growled.

"Of what?" he scoffed. "I want you to focus on knocking this guy out—not some cunt—do you hear me, Krew? He needs to go down this round."

"Regi's not a cunt," I leaned in and growled.

Teke stiffened, and a frown slid across his face as he quickly looked around. He then turned back to me and shook his head. "It's a fucking mirage. Now get your head out of your ass and into the fight. We'll make bank tonight when you win."

Not *if*, but *when*. And *we'll* make bank—*ha!* I knew my cynical, egotistical brother all too well. Most of the money earned from this fight would go into his pockets.

I wanted to knock the shit out of Teke for calling Regina a cunt. Yet, punching him right now wouldn't give me the satisfaction I needed to curb my ire.

Besides, Teke wouldn't have a problem starting shit in this ring. The bastard was stubborn, selfish, and downright surly—a real fist-up kind of asshole.

I was the opposite.

I shoved Teke to the side and glanced back to where I'd seen Regina, but she was gone.

Teke clamped a hand onto the back of my neck and shook me. "Focus, or this bastard will clock you first. Do you want to lose all that money for Dad?" Even though Teke sounded earnest, I knew he pocketed most of the fight money.

I shifted my eyes to the fighter, who was notorious for his hard, right upper cuts. Though, that was all he had. I was stronger, faster, and s fuck-ton meaner. "I'll win."

"Are you sure?" He tapped hard at my temple with the edge of his coke-fingernail, purposefully cutting my skin.

"Jesus Christ." I yanked my head away, but I still felt the dull bite of pain.

I'd dealt with Teke's verbal and physical jabs for years. It was how I learned to fight. From the day after I turned twelve until I was sent to juvie at seventeen, my brother regularly beat the shit out of me. My father used to set us against each other for bare-knuckle fighting, solely for his enjoyment. It might have been fucked up, but I learned. I survived. Maybe I should thank them— at least, I was well prepared for juvie and my two-year stint in prison

The announcer called us fighters and our managers to the center of the mat.

"Knock the motherfucker out," Teke repeated, then backed out of the cage.

I ignored my brother and centered my focus on the beast of a man across from me, who was getting his own last-minute pep talk from his manager. My opponent looked like he had hams for hands. There was no doubt his hits were going hurt. Even so, I was determined to walk out of this cage the winner.

Forget Teke. Forget the crowd... But Regi. Forget her, too.

I shook her image out of my head, knocked my wrapped knuckles together and growled, "Let's do this."

Chapter Three
Decker

From my vantage point on the roof, I spotted my target. The smug bastard had no clue. In less than a ten minutes, he was going to die. I couldn't help but smile at the notion.

I surveyed the back metal staircase to the open roof access, making sure no one was coming up.

Suddenly, the noise of the spectators tripled and my entire body buzzed to life. I always trusted my gut and shifted to scan the main floor below.

My vision zeroed in on the fighter who just entered the cage. I looked through my scope and froze.

"Krew," I breathed his name.

My best friend in grade school. My lover since high school, until unfortunate events had put us on two different paths so many years ago.

How had I not realized that Krew was part of this fighting ring? I recalled the names on tonight's roster. There was a Crew—spelled with a C—not a K. Still. My eyes moved to his side of the cage.

Fuck, Teke's here, too. I owe you a bullet between the eyes, asshole.

This was a complication I hadn't foreseen.

I glanced at my watch. Less than six minutes left before the job expired—no time to reminisce or wallow in past hurt. My focus had to stay on the target. I wasn't about to lose this big paycheck—not over that fucktard.

This kill-contract had an expiration date. One hitman had twenty-four hours to make the kill. If the mark wasn't terminated within that time frame? The two hundred and fifty grand were forfeit and someone else got the chance.

Tracking down the scumbag wasn't hard, but the prep work had taken some of my time. I was down to five minutes.

Hmm... Maybe two for the price of one? Kill the target and Teke Gatlin.

Sadly, my morals cock-blocked my need for revenge. I shook off the desire to shoot Krew's bastard of a brother once I'd taken out the mark, and looked through the scope again.

Right before I trained my barrel on the target, I saw Krew's body stiffen. His head tilted slightly to the right and his eyes laser focused on something. I shifted my focal point to the crowd and my heart practically leapt out of my chest. My brain seized in disbelief and I sucked in a silent breath.

Different hair and a fuller, more hourglass figure than I remembered her having, but her face hadn't changed.

"Regi," I whispered in a barely-there breath, like a prayer that needed answering. What the hell was she doing here—in a place like this?

My mission tonight was clear cut. Find my target, eliminate him, and then get the hell out of Chicago. So in what fucked up universe would the two people I had loved, planned to spend my life with, and then lost be here—in the same place and at the same time?

Glancing at my watch again, I had only a minute left. Nothing —not even Krew and Regina, would deter me from my goal.

Returning my attention to the target, I saw my mark was standing next to the other fighter like a fucking proud peacock. I altered my position a hair until the sight through the lens landed just where it should be. I concentrated on my breathing as I looked through the scope.

I angled my head a millimeter, while still keeping my eye trained through the scope. Then I took a slow, deep breath and waited a solid three seconds as the mark stepped out of the ring.

"Okay, birdy. Stay still for me," I whispered into the cool night air.

Clear head shot for the win. I released a breath, my finger pressed the trigger a millisecond later, and my mark hit the floor. A bullet through the middle of his forehead.

Done.

Regina's Diary

July 27th, 2008

Dear Diary,

Guess what happened today? You won't believe it. I hung out with Krew and Decker for the first time. I was at the park waiting for Maya, so we could go to Lion's Pool to swim. But she didn't show up. I'm kind of mad at her for blowing me off. Anyway, I was going to head back home but then they rode up on their bikes, with Krew's older brother, Teke.

Diary, I didn't like the way Teke was looking at me. He always creeps me out, and today was the worst. He kept touching my long hair and told me never to cut it because it was blonde and beautiful. Teke's so strange. But Krew is not like his brother, and I'm glad. Because I like Krew. I like Decker too. They are like the big brothers I never had, but way cuter.

Krew and Decker told Teke to stop touching me. He got mad, and flipped them the finger and said some nasty stuff I won't repeat and then left, which made me happy. I got to talk to Krew and Decker. They are nice. They even joked with me about that note

Maya wrote back in May. I was soooo embarrassed but they didn't care. They thought it was sweet. And Diary? Even though Maya never showed up, I ended up going to the pool with Krew and Decker and had so much fun. And I know we are going to be best friends.

I can't wait to hang with them again. Without Teke.

Love, Regina

Chapter Four
Krew

One second, I was bouncing on my toes, stretching my neck from side to side, trying to clear my mind after seeing Regi again, then all hell broke loose.

My opponent was standing there in front of me, mimicking my movement as his manager, Kane Maxwell, stepped out of the cage —and then crumbled to the floor.

Within seconds, screams echoed off the walls. I dropped into a crouch at the edge of the cage, making myself as small as possible to avoid being shot. I couldn't chance it if the shooter was out to kill random people.

I quickly scanned the row of chairs where I'd seen Regina, but she was gone. A measure of relief coursed through me, knowing she had left and was unharmed. I hoped.

After a good minute, I cautiously rose just enough to rush to the cage door. There on the edge of the outer mat, blocking the door, was my brother. Teke was in a fetal position; his arms covered his head as though that would protect him. *Fucking idiot.*

Just beyond, Kane's body lay lifeless. No doubt about it, he was executed and it sent a clear message.

I didn't know any of the shit the man was into, other than what little Teke had told me about the fight manager. Only that Kane Maxwell was in some nasty business with big players. I wouldn't be too surprised to find out my brother was tangled up in the dead man's affairs.

I nudged my asshole brother with my foot. "Get up." When he didn't move, I pushed the door open and exited the ring, leaving Teke still lying on the mat.

I assumed the cops would eventually come, so I hauled ass toward the makeshift locker room where my clothes were stored. I had to pass Kane's body and got a closer look at the bullet hole in the middle of his forehead. I didn't stop, though, and focused on getting out of the building.

I changed and was sliding my feet into my shoes when Teke rushed in, oral guns blazing.

"You left me out there to fucking die." His white-knuckled fist cocked back and swung, nailing the side of my head. "Do you want me dead?"

Teke wanted to fight. I wasn't going to give him the satisfaction —not now. He'd gotten in a lucky hit. Normally the strength of his punch was like a mosquito bite. No power. Yet, he landed good this time, and the pain radiated from my temple.

"Do you want to go at me now?" I bit out, wishing I could rub the ache away, but I wasn't going to give him the pleasure of knowing he'd hurt me. Teke would take advantage of my small weakness and attack. "I warned you, Teke, if you hit me again, we'll go rounds and we both know who'll win."

I glared at my brother, at the fury in his eyes, and knew instantly he was hopped up on some shit. Teke must have snorted something before coming in here. I lowered my gaze and there it was—a telltale dusting of white around his nostrils.

Choosing to ignore him instead, I turned away, which only incited Teke's anger more and he barreled around to stand in front of me again. But I didn't give a fuck. I wasn't in the mood to be my brother's punching bag tonight. I wanted out of this building, and if possible, to track down Regina before she disappeared on me. Again.

"Get out of my way," I demanded, towering over Teke by a good four inches.

"No," he hissed, holding his jittery hands up in clenched fists.

"The cops are coming." Those were the magic words. Teke dropped his hands and quickly looked around. "Do you want to be caught with shit in your pockets, while at an illegal underground fight, where a guy was shot in the head?"

That did it.

His eyes widened. "Fuck. Kane."

"Yeah, Kane," I snarled to reinforce his panic.

Teke swiftly spun back toward the doorway and raced out like hellfire was licking at his size ten shoes.

I grabbed my bag and hauled ass, but not before I quickly looked around again for Regina in the melee. Though, it was a wasted effort.

Outside, there were people still exiting the scene. Some getting into vehicles, while others were on foot. I rounded the building on the west side, looking for Teke and didn't see him. I should just leave him. That bastard pulled me into this fight with no regard whatsoever to my feelings. I was done being his damn meal ticket and money for his drugs.

I decided right then I'd leave his ass here, when I saw Teke trying to climb into black BMW where two blondes were sitting inside it. Stupid son of a bitch. Did he forget we drove here?

Teke drove off with the women.

Since I had Teke's car keys, and with a felony on my record for grand theft auto, I got the hell out of there rather than risk being caught by the cops.

I took shortcuts between buildings, not caring where exactly I was heading. I avoided the busy streets, weaving through alleys and lit up sidewalks. It wasn't until I was nine or ten blocks away from the chaos when I finally slowed my pace.

With another four blocks under me, I found myself at an intersection with no street signs. The streetlamp blinked on and off in an eerie way, which gave the derelict area even more of a creep factor. And I felt like I was being watched.

"Show yourself," I called out, ready for anything.

A man stepped out of the shadows. Lasering in on the long slender case that hung around his left shoulder, I quickly realized that this guy might be the one who killed Kane.

I swallowed hard and straightened to my full height, hoping to disabuse him of any notion that I was an easy target. For a moment we stood there, neither of us moving until I broke the standoff. "I have no beef with you, man." I took a step back, holding both hands up like I was surrendering, but I was poised to fight if I had to. Even to the death.

"Are you sure about that, K?" His tone was condescending, as he cocked his head slightly to one side.

Any moonlight was obscured by the clouds, leaving only the intermittent light of the funky on-off blinking streetlamp. I couldn't fully see his face, but that voice. So familiar—wait. *K?*

My heart stalled for a full five seconds until recognition finally penetrated my brain. "D-Deck?"

I dropped my hands. My body went numb as every memory of my friend—my best friend I hadn't seen in years, filtered through my brain.

"Who else calls you K, numb-nuts?"

Between the darkness and the flickering streetlight casting shadows across his face, I still didn't believe who I was looking at. "Is that really you?" I moved within a yard of him. So close, yet the space felt like a mile.

"Is that all you're going to say to me, asshole?" he asked as he bent to place the large case by his feet.

Without hesitation, I closed the gap and pulled Decker Moss into my arms. I wrapped him in tight, feeling him down to my bones.

Yes, this was *my* Decker. I sucked in his smell—though different now, it still eased the ratcheting panic cloistered in my chest. He reminded me of all the good things of home. And the bad that had separated us.

For a brief moment, Decker's arms were like iron bands around me, which gave me comfort in ways I didn't know I needed. Just as fast, he dropped his arms and stepped back.

The distance between us was now only inches, yet the gap felt like the Grand Canyon to me, especially with the way he stood there, rigid like a pole. Like we were strangers.

My eyes shifted to the case at his feet. "It was you, wasn't it? *You* killed Kane."

He dropped his chin, his face now fully hidden by the dark, before he lifted his gaze to me and nodded his head. "Krew." My name came out sharper than before.

"Why?" I took a small cautious step toward him. "You killed…" The words dropped off as I stared at the man I had once cared about—loved.

Decker hadn't known how I truly felt back then. I never had the guts to tell him.

I never told him how I treasured those stolen moments between us. Or how I had craved his touch—his mouth—his body connected to mine. That he had owned me from the day he took my virginity in the back of his father's Cadillac.

This new reality smacked me hard across the face. Decker Moss was a killer.

"I need to go," Decker said, as he looked over my right shoulder with a calculating eye. "So should you."

"So, it's true. You killed Kane Maxwell?" For whatever reason —even if that man was a dirtbag, I had to know the truth.

Annoyance flashed across his face as Decker took several steps back and then something—a look I couldn't decipher, slipped in, and he frowned. "I don't know what you're talking about."

"Don't lie to me. You took a man's life tonight. Why?"

His deep grunt of irritation echoed off the building before he grated out, "I haven't seen you in what... in twelve—thirteen fucking years, and you're standing here, demanding that I talk about shit you're not part of? Not, how are you, Deck? What's been happening with your life, Deck? How was the military—or maybe, I missed you, Deck?" Decker's voice dropped to a low growly whisper, but his words were a blow to my solar plexus.

"Decker." I took a step toward him.

He quickly backed away from me. "No. I can't do this with you right now. You know, I thought this would be different—thought of seeing you up close would be different." He shook his head. "You gotta go."

"A person was murdered tonight. And then you surprise me by popping out from the dark like some damn ninja with what looks like a gun case over your shoulder. What do you expect me to think?"

Even in the shadow, I saw the smirk on his handsome face before it evaporated into nothing. Whatever had happened in Decker's life changed the guy I remembered. And all the mischief we got into as kids was now only a blur of memory. The person before me now wasn't that boy anymore. I didn't know this man. He was a stranger to me.

"Me not asking you *Where the hell have you been* doesn't mean I don't care or that I didn't miss you," I replied earnestly.

"You could have fooled me." Another bite of ice.

"Fuck off, Deck. If that's how you want to play it, I'm out of here."

When I turned to leave, but Decker grabbed my arm and stopped me. "Wait."

He dropped his hand and didn't make any move to touch me again. And like a damn glutton, I stood there waiting... Hoping—for what? I sure as hell didn't know.

"Decker," I repeated his name, willing him to hear the earnestness in my voice. The want I had in my heart.

"I know it's no excuse, but you have no idea how hard it is for me to stand here," he breathed out, like it pained him to admit that.

"Me too." My heart ached at the two words I spoke.

"You saw Regi." It was a statement, not a question.

Relief flashed through me that Decker had also seen our girl. "Yes. I thought... I was seeing things. Guess I wasn't. Did you keep in touch with her?"

He shook his head. "No." There was so much emotion in that single word, that it cut me deep. "You?"

"No." This whole time, I thought I was the one left out. But I was wrong. None of us kept in touch.

"I thought... This entire time, I thought you and her..." Decker turned away, as though he too was affected by the news.

Relief hit hard, tangled with sorrow and the images I'd painted in my head of Regina and Decker living life without me. But the truth was worse—we'd each been alone in this miserable world, and that somber thought made me tear up.

"God, Deck. After all this time, you two pop back into my life— on the same night. It's too damn coincidental. I don't know what to think. It must be double whammy day," I admitted, turning away and swiping at my wet eyes.

"Double whammy day?" With a soft snort of laughter, Decker faced me again with a smile so genuine it melted my trepidation. "Look at you. I don't ever remember you looking this beefed up back then. You look good, K." He pointed up and down my body.

I wanted to preen at his compliment—at the familiar nickname only he had called me. But this wasn't the place to get reacquainted with my best friend. "Why don't we get out of here. There has to be a place where we can get something to eat. I'm starving."

"I don't think so, K," he said mindfully. "All together again, in one city, after all this time? You're right. This is too coincidental for my liking. I doubt the three of us being here was by chance." The semi-easy banter Decker had spouted moments ago was gone, and replaced with a cold, hard resolve. "You came for a fight. I came for a mark. And Regi was here... Why?"

That question hung in the air like a stationary pendulum, waiting for the right answer to bump it into motion again, and that answer suddenly clicked in my head. "She lives in Chicago."

"Most likely," Decker chimed in, his agreement raising a red flag.

"Who would organize something this elaborate, just to bring the three of us together?"

And yet, if I thought about it hard enough, with the situation that had separated us so long ago, I could accept that sliver of coincidence, and that we were here together purely by chance.

Sirens in the distance cut off my thoughts. We both went stock still and listened. While I looked to my left, Decker scanned toward the right.

"Go," Decker ordered with finality, reaching into his zipped-up hoodie and pulling out a handgun.

"The cops won't look here," I rushed out with certainty. Yet, I couldn't ignore the niggling fear in the back of my head since being released from prison years ago was pushing me to run.

"You don't know that. Take off and I'll call you in a few days."

"But I just got you back," I protested, not wanting to lose sight of him again. "You don't even know my number."

"You don't have me back." Decker stared at me for a long moment, his icy glare sending shivers down my spine.

"But—"

"Fucking go, before the past repeats itself, and this time your ass *will* end up in jail," he growled.

A chill ran along my skin at the horrible repercussions I had once endured, the part of my life Decker didn't know about, yet I didn't move.

"Decker—" My words were cut off when he aimed the handgun at me. I felt the blood drain from my face, leaving me shocked and then angry. I grabbed hold of my rage and said through gritted teeth, "You point a gun at my face? Where's the Deck—"

"I'm not that Decker anymore. The sooner you get that through your head, the better. Now, get the fuck out of here."

I wasn't afraid of the gun in Decker's hand or the man standing in front of me. No. What I feared most was never seeing my best friend again. "Why do I get the feeling this is the last time I'll see you—promise me, Deck, you disappear on me for good."

"I make no promises. Now go, before the cops find another body." Decker closed the gap and the end of the barrel pressed into my forehead. "Now go."

Clearly, *this* Decker Moss wasn't the boy I knew. That guy was gone. The sooner I accepted that fact, the better. "Fine."

"Good," he spat back with disdain.

I took off, and without bothering a glance back to see if Decker was still there, I somehow knew he was already gone.

I pulled out my cell phone, located where Teke's Toyota was parked, and ran the three blocks west from where I was. With the keys in my hand, I was ten feet away from the rusty, piece of shit Corolla, when a guy jumped out from behind a truck and tackled me to the ground. The asshole was on top of me, rendering my hands useless as his knees anchored them to the broken concrete sidewalk.

"Give me the fucking keys," the guy growled, a knife at my throat. On any given day, I would have handed over Teke's keys to his piece of shit. Tonight, I was too pissed off at Decker to think straight, and I let my anger at him fuel the fire that coursed through my veins.

The point of his blade nicked my neck, and my only reaction was to attack.

With all the energy I could marshal, I freed my right hand and punched upward, knocking the guy off of me. The tip of the knife cut deeper into my neck as he fell away, but I didn't give a shit. I wasn't feeling any pain. Only rage.

I rotated my body and punched out again, and the bastard dropped the knife as he flew backward. Before he was able to react, I was in a crouch position, ready to launch myself at him. The guy must have had a few working brain cells, because he took off without stopping to grab the knife.

Before I got into another confrontation with some other bastard, I picked up the knife and slid into Teke's car. I took off in the direction of the cheap motel we were staying at just outside the city limits. I wondered if Teke had found his own way back to the motel—and then remembered I didn't give a shit.

I wasn't sure how bad the cut on my neck was, but I could feel the blood trickling down onto my collarbone. I ran a finger along the neckline of my black t-shirt and it came away wet. But I kept on driving.

As I drove on Route 64, my thoughts slid again to Decker. "Jesus." I hit the steering wheel as anger and confusion rolled around in my gut. *How dare he point a gun in my face?* He knew better, especially since he'd seen how my father and Teke had treated me.

Maybe my memory of Decker had been pasteurized by the years of being alone, locked up for what Teke had done. How I hadn't heard a word—not one fucking word, from Regina or Decker while I was in prison for those two miserable years... My heart would never fully heal from their betrayals and I promised myself that I would never let anyone in. Never again.

I closed my eyes for a second, as heartbreak sliced through me like a jagged blade. After the years I'd spent stitching my life back together, my chest was ripped open again and the old-familiar ache was back.

So much time had passed since then, that these old, warped feelings shouldn't still be congealing in my heart. I've told myself at least a million times that neither Decker nor Regina was ever mine, and that I had to let them go. Tonight, I learned that they were never together. Now I wondered if all my memories were skewed. Delusions.

As I drove, I kept mulling over Decker's words. My head kept was reminding me that it would be best to walk away, but my stubborn heart refused—it desperately tried to convince me that I would see him again.

But what of Regina?

Chapter Five
Regi

Even after my apartment door slammed shut and I flicked the deadbolt home, the pain in my chest didn't ease up. The entire Uber ride home, I sucked in one calming breath after another, while I kept looking through the rear window, half expecting to see if someone was following the vehicle. To see if Teke was following me.

I knew I was being stupid. That bastard couldn't have seen me. There was no way, not with so many people crowding the main floor. But still, I couldn't clear away the notion that I was being followed.

Sweat soaked my dress, and it clung to me like a heavy, itchy blanket. I had to get it off, and quick. After stripping out of my clothes, I rushed to the kitchen, grabbed a trash bag and shoved the dress into it. Because I didn't want a reminder of this night, I crammed the bag into the garbage can.

I then got into the tub and drew the curtain snug from wall to wall like a protective cloak. The bathtub felt like the only safe space I had—oddly reminiscent of the ditch I had nearly died in.

My body was shaking so badly that I slid further into the tub, wrapped my arms around my bent legs and tucked my face to my knees.

"I'm alive. I'm safe. I'm here," I whispered the mantra repeatedly to myself, hoping to fool my racing heart and keep it from beating its way out of my chest. I pulled in another deep breath, but it was lodged in my throat.

How could it be, after all these years, that it took only one glance at the monster, before I crumbled into nothing again?

Then my eyes caught sight of Maya's old-fashioned double-edged razor she left lying on the tub's rim. The glint of its silver casing was like a beacon, and I reached for it with shaky fingers. I twirled the base of the handle until it opened fully and exposed the blade.

I removed it and the thin metal was like soft butter between the pads of my fingertips and its matte finish was still pristine.

I straightened my legs, and my eyes sought out the spot where I had last cut myself.

It had been years since I'd put anything sharp against my skin. The moment I placed the blade's edge on a portion of unmarred flesh on my right thigh, a sense of peace settled over me. I pressed gently on the blade and drew it smoothly and slowly across my skin. The sting was familiar, like a long-lost friend back returned to demand my attention. I tipped my head back and hissed in greeting.

As I returned my gaze to the blood seeping from the small slice and the bright, red droplets that splashing onto the stark white of the tub's base, the realization of what I had done to myself yanked me out of the dark space in my head, and I dropped the blade in horror. I'd thought I had overcome my cloistered desire to bleed. Apparently, I was wrong.

"Oh my God." I dropped the blade onto the lip of the tub as the enormity of what I'd done hit me. I covered the small wound with one hand and turned on the faucet with the other. Once the water was hot, I stood and pulled the button to re-route the water to the shower head.

Under the scalding spray, I watched the blood disappear down the drain—as did the red trail down my thigh, until all of the evidence of my lapse was gone.

As the sting along my cut skin ebbed, I reached for the hanging washcloth, soaped the hell out of it and scrubbed my body until every inch of my skin was squeaky clean. If only it was that easy to wash away the fear that crowded my sanity.

After shampooing my hair and conditioning it, I stood under the strong stream, hoping the pelting water wash away the rest of the memories that clung to me. It was a long time before I felt safe enough to step out of the tub.

The movement caused my wound to re-open and beads of blood formed. I grabbed some toilet paper, placed it over the cut and pressed hard, not caring if I was still dripping wet. Once the bleeding stopped, I quickly dried off, bandaged the wound and then dried my hair.

I moisturized my face, slathered a good layer of lotion onto my body—my normal nightly routine. Long ago, my therapist explained that routine was good for me, especially when I was stressed. Along with the mantra I usually repeated in my head. *I'm alive. I'm safe. I'm here.*

There one more item I needed against my skin. I rummaged around the bottom drawer of my dresser and pulled out a Nirvana concert t-shirt that once belonged to Krew. I stole it years ago because I loved his smell. His scent immediately calmed me.

Even though Krew's smell was long gone, every once in a while —especially after I woke up from a nightmare, the comfort the well-worn material soothed me back to sleep.

With his t-shirt on, I popped two Valiums with a few swigs of water and climbed into bed. After turning off the lights, I closed my eyes and waited for the pills to kick in.

I tossed and turned, forcing my eyes to stay closed. And yet, sleep eluded me. Still on edge, I reached into the drawer of my nightstand and pulled out my rabbit.

Why not get off while the pills kick in?

On my back, I spread my legs—slowing my movements a bit when the cut and the bandage on my right thigh protested the change in position. I pressed the end of the vibrator against my clit and turned it on. Its steady hum calmed me immediately and drew my focus to the pleasure slowly building within my core.

A groan left my lips as I moved the pulsating tip along my slick folds and then back up to the tiny bundle of nerves. My hips instinctively gyrated, as pleasure notched higher and higher.

"Krew," I whispered into the room and imagined the man as he looked at the fight, so different than the last time I saw him. "Decker," I moaned, trying to imagine what he would look like now.

My head began to fill with images of my men kissing me, kissing each other. Their mouths—separately, together, and between my legs. Me on my knees, my mouth on their most private parts.

In all these years I've been running from my past, I remained celibate. I had never wanted anything to do with sex—especially with men. Period. But one look at Krew, and I'd give up my celibacy in a heartbeat and go down on my knees before him to make one of my fantasies a reality.

Then Teke's ugly face popped in, destroying the glorious sensations stirring between my legs. His appearance reminded me why I wasn't with Krew and Decker.

My heart ached, and I lost the motivation to continue with my self-gratification. I threw the vibrator in frustration, and it clattered against the opposite wall.

I rolled onto my side in frustration, staring into the darkness of the room. My thoughts gravitated back to Krew and his face, envisioning the man I was still in love with—well, one of them.

After seeing Krew enter that cage for a fight, I questioned if I had known him at all. Was he willing to pummel another person for money? Did he enjoy it?

The intensity on his face belies the quiet embodiment of a boy I once knew. The hard line of his tense jaw and the cold glint in his beautiful eyes was of a man who been through hell and back. His hardened exterior was molded into a beast of a man. The ink on his sculpted body told a tale—probably many, that I desperately wanted to know.

Was he still tender hearted and quiet? I didn't think so. What did his voice sound like now? Soft and gentle, or hard and commanding? Would his kisses be the same? Loving and generous?

Don't go there, Regi. I shut those selfish emotions right down.

It didn't matter, if Krew was even more gorgeous now than in his youth. My heart yearned to see him again. To learn how his life had turned out without me. I began to tear up.

My thoughts suddenly detoured—if I hadn't run away, what would my life be like now? Would I have stayed with them? Let Krew and Decker touch me? Let them love me? I had no answers, because I didn't have the guts to face the truth. If I had somehow found the courage to confess to them that Teke had raped me, they wouldn't have wanted me anymore.

Over the years, I had thought about Krew and Decker. A lot. Where were they? What were they doing? Were they together, like I had always known they should be? If not, did they have partners?

I immediately shook that thought out of my head, not wanting to know. Jealousy was a salty bitch. The idea of my men having sex —touching someone other than each other or me, ignited my anger. Frustration cut me to the bone, at how I was driven to live a life that wasn't of my own doing. That was why I kept the thoughts of Krew and Decker in an iron box, and locked them up in the dark recesses of my mind.

Then there was Krew's monster of a brother.

I shuddered with absolute terror. Thinking his name aloud had me looking around in the dark with utter horror, as though he were about to magically pop into my room.

"I'm losing it." I flipped onto my other side, bunched up the pillow, and laid my head down. Then I did my best not to think of the events that had destroyed my life.

Exhaustion eventually won, the pills took effect, and I fell right into a fitful night's sleep.

Teke yanked my head back by my hair—the pain scored through my scalp like a thousand stinging hornets. But the agony was nothing compared to his brutal punches to my face.

I saw stars, the taste of copper filled my mouth, and blood dripped from my nose until I couldn't breathe.

I clawed and scratched—tried to fight my way out from under him, but Teke was relentless.

He captured both of my wrists in one of his hands, his grip as strong as a steel handcuff. He ripped my underwear off as though it was made of paper.

Then Teke forced my legs apart with his knees, and the whole damn time I couldn't look away from his eyes—both of them—eerily similar to the one so precious to me.

I screamed as he bit my—

"Regi, wake up." Maya's fearful tone pulled me from the dark. She shook me. "Regina!"

I jolted upright, a scream lodged in the back of my throat.

"It's me," Maya said in near panic, cupping my face in her hands. "You're safe."

I scrambled out of the bed, not wanting to be touched, and scurried to the kitchen, switching on the hallway light. I tried to swallow the knot in my throat, but my mouth was too dry. "Water."

I snagged a glass from the drying rack, filled it to the brim, and choked down half the contents before the constriction in my throat eased.

"Are you okay?" Concern etched the corners of Maya's eyes as she cautiously approached me.

"Yeah," I croaked out the lie and finished the water.

"Want to talk about it?"

I shook my head, not wanting to voice the nightmare, fearful that it might happen again if I talked about it.

Maya studied me through the speckled red-framed eyeglasses that she never wore in public, before she turned her eyes back to the wall clock. I followed her gaze, and to my surprise, it was only four minutes after three in the morning—I'd barely slept at all.

She blew out a heavy breath. "Okay. Then I'll tell you what happened after you left the fight. You have *no* idea." She dropped onto the sofa and tucked the small, gray rectangular throw pillow under her chin.

"What is it?" I asked, welcoming the change in topic. I sank into the chair next to her, curious on what went on after I left the fight, especially if it involved Krew.

Threading her fingers repeatedly through her messy hair, Maya's teary eyes appeared haunted. I'd never seen her so distraught. "Kane was murdered. Someone shot him in the head."

"What?" My spine snapped straight. "Who shot him?"

"I don't know. The second Kane hit the ground, everyone scrambled out of there so fast, I lost sight of Jess. I ended up huddled behind a damn folding chair like that piece of metal was going to protect me from a bullet."

I placed my water glass on the coffee table, moved onto the sofa next to my friend, and hugged her. "I'm sorry. But I'm glad you're safe." And I was.

However, I was a bit baffled at Maya's extreme emotional reaction to Kane's death. Being upset at witnessing a murder was normal, but I thought she hated the man. Maya often said she wished him dead, and described different scenarios how it was done.

"Why are you sorry? You didn't pull the trigger. Besides, Kane was a jag-off anyway. He probably deserved it. But Jess..." she choked out.

"Is he okay?" I hugged Maya tighter, since she was trembling in my arms.

"I think so. He was in the cage with Kane when... I don't..." Maya burst into tears, while she kept talking. "He sent me a text message an hour ago." Maya didn't explain further, and I didn't push.

"Were the cops called?" I doubted it—who would do that at an illegal underground fight?

"I don't know. Everyone was in crazy panic mode, trying to get out of the building. I'm just glad the cops didn't show up before I left."

"So, the cops were called in?" I asked in surprise.

"Yeah—I think so. I heard sirens when I was a few blocks away from the warehouse." Maya dipped her chin down and sniffled. "I was so afraid, Regi. I should have gone home with you."

"How did you get home?" I asked, as guilt at leaving my best friend in that terrible mess swamped me. But I'd had no choice. Not when *he* was there.

"After I realized Jess wasn't coming for me, I ran until I was several blocks away and then called an Uber."

I wanted to tell her that her boyfriend was an utter douche bag for leaving her alone there, but I kept that opinion to myself.

"Tell me what you were dreaming about." Maya straightened

and moved away from me. "I need to think about something other than the bullet hole in Kane's skull, or if Jess is safe."

"I... umm, don't remember now," I lied.

Maya's watery eyes narrowed on me. I was sure she knew I was lying, but my friend didn't call me out on it.

"Okay." She hugged me and got up. "I'm going back to bed since I have to work tomorrow morning. Whenever you want to talk about it, you know I'm here," she added with a slight touch to my arm.

"I know," I replied calmly. "Get some rest. And don't worry about Jess. I'm sure he can take care of himself."

Maya's brown eyes flashed with a hint of ire. "Yeah. That bastard just left me there." She went to her room and closed the door.

I didn't say anything. Though, I'd called it. Another boyfriend bit the dust.

I guess it was a good thing I left the fight when I did. I certainly didn't need another violent incident in my life. Seeing someone shot—someone I knew personally... Even though I thought Kane was a certifiable ass, I hadn't wanted to see him dead.

I sat there in the shadows thrown by the hallway light, trying not to envision Kane with a bullet hole in his forehead. Then the darkness of my nightmare crept back in, which left me shivering. I slumped back against the sofa cushions, covered my mouth with both hands, and silently cried until I had no more tears and their tracks had faded away like ghosts.

It had become crystal clear that, no matter what I did to make myself feel safe, I was never going to really *be* safe, now that Teke was in my city.

Glancing at the wall clock again, I drew in a long, tired breath. I got up and refilled my glass, then headed back to my bedroom. Desperate for a few more hours of sleep, I pulled open my underwear drawer and rummaged around inside it until I found the bottle of prescription sleeping pills.

Normally, I didn't mix medication, but tonight of all nights, I needed the extra kick. I uncapped the bottle, took out a pill and popped it into my mouth, then chased it down with water. "Dreams, dreams go away. Never come back another day."

Chapter Six
Decker

I knew Krew was wrong about the cops. Someone would call the Chicago PD, and once they discovered Kane's body, they would have every patrol car canvasing the area for persons of interest.

Since Krew refused my direct demand to leave, my only choice was to point the gun at his head. The anger and shock on his face had cut me to the marrow, but it was for his own damn good. He went to juvey for his piece of shit brother; I still cared too much for Krew to see him embroiled in this fucking mess.

I watched Krew disappear into the dark shadows of the alley. My soul screamed for him to come back. Instead, I bit my tongue until the outline of his perfect form vanished from my sight. Then I fled on foot toward the vehicle I stole yesterday and parked in a dark alley a block away from here.

A nondescript minivan, with dull red paint and heavy rust on the bumpers—the vehicle was old, but it ran. For added insurance, I had switched the plates with those from a different minivan with a similar appearance.

After I'd put on my gloves and placed my gun case in the back seat, I slid in and drove the speed limit all the way to Waukegan. The suburb was far enough away that the Chicago PD wouldn't track me—which was unlikely anyway, since this wasn't my first hit and I knew not to leave any evidence behind.

I drove to the edge of a park in a residential neighborhood and pulled over by a row of dense shrubbery. I scanned the area, making sure no one was around. Once I knew the park was clear, I grabbed my gun case and ditched the vehicle. Then I hoofed it several blocks, tossed the gloves in someone's garbage can and continued on until I arrived to where I'd parked my truck.

Finally in the driver's seat, I sat there in the dark for a moment as the adrenalin settled in my blood stream. Craving nicotine, I retrieved an open pack of cigarettes from the glove box, pulled one out and lit the tip. I sucked in a deep drag and released both the smoke and the energy bouncing throughout my body.

With an exhale, I started the engine and took a roundabout route, driving through several town to make sure I wasn't being followed, before heading to a motel several towns away.

Once in the room, I dropped my duffle on the bed and fished out my old personal cellphone—the one I've had since high school, and its charger. Despite using burner phones, I've paid to keep my old number active, and carried the phone around like a sad sack, because it had old messages from Krew and Regina.

It was duct taped and the screen had a spiderweb of cracks, though it still worked. Although, I rarely charge it. I should have replaced it years ago, but then I would have lost the old voice messages from Krew and Regina.

No sooner had I plugged in the old phone into the charger, my burner cell vibrated in my pocket with a text. I pulled it out and stared down at the message, smiling.

Unknown: *Money deposited.*

It was followed by an email notification from one of my accounts alerted me that two hundred and fifty grand had been deposited. Elation raced through me at seeing those numbers. I loved payday, especially when I rid the earth of scumbags like Kane Maxwell.

This payday had come at a steep cost, though. The price had been putting fear on Krew's face.

I never imagined I'd point a gun at my best friend—along with all the bullshit lies—I hated myself for it. Every word was probably festering in my boy's brain. He would, no doubt, be replaying everything I had said over and over until he couldn't ponder on it any more. But it was necessary, even if it created distrust between us.

However, I couldn't worry about what Krew thought of me. Our friendship had been dust from the second my old man used his connections to have me thrown into the military.

Franklin Moss had promised me that one day I'd serve our country, and I'd given him his wish the moment I slid into the back seat of that goddamn car Teke had stolen.

Still feeling on edge, I decided to shower. I needed to rid my body of the filth of the job.

I stepped inside the stall and let the hot water wash away all the present bullshit and the past memories that were clogging my brain. Some refused to leave, and I got lost in those memories, my mind replaying those last perfect days before everything in my life went to hell.

"So how does it feel to be an adult?" Regina's beautiful smile lit up the entire lunch room.

"No different from yesterday," I admitted, shoving fries into my mouth.

"But you can stay out late—"

"I could do that even before I turned eighteen." I winked at her, then took a bite of my burger.

"I know." She scrunched up her nose, then chuckled. "But now you won't get in trouble with the cops or with your father."

"What are you two talking about?" Krew sat down next to her and scooched close. For the briefest of seconds, my jealousy bubbled up, until I truly looked at my two best friends, and all the possessiveness evaporated.

"I asked Deck how he felt about turning eighteen today."

Krew smiled as he practically echoed my answer. "No different than yesterday."

"Yup, that's what he said," Regina laughed, as she covered her beautiful full lips with her hand. Her tinkling laughter did something to my insides, but I quickly tamped down my yearning, because I needed to be good for her. For all of us.

"It's true," I added with a shrug.

Without a thought as to who was around us, Krew used his thumb to wipe ketchup from the corner of my lips before popping his finger into his mouth. He then leaned in; his face close to Regina's and whispered, "Are we still on for tonight?"

"All set," she whispered back with a mischievous grin.

"What are you two up to?" I swung a glare from Regina to Krew. "I'm not going to like this, am I?"

Regina lifted her stubborn chin and pointed a finger at me. "Decker Joseph Moss, you will and are going to like it. Do you hear me?" Determination was fixed in her light brown eyes.

I quickly raised my hands in surrender. "Fine. I'll like it. Now tell me what am I going to like?" I had a feeling what Regina had planned. I hoped it was like the intimate party she organized for Krew's birthday last year. But I wasn't going to spoil her fun by demanding answers.

"Nope," Krew and Regina said in unison.

"You've done too much already. Three days in a row?"

Regina reached out her hand and clasped mine. "Because you are worth it."

"You are," Krew echoed as he placed a hand on top of ours.

"Whatever," I mumbled and refocused on my food. "You know I hate surprises."

"You'll like this one." Krew winked with a mouthful of fries. His eyes conveyed the same sentiment Regina held in hers. Pure excitement.

A blast of frigid water shocked me back into reality. After shutting the shower off, I got out, stepped onto the mat and wrapped a thin towel around my waist.

I stood there, eyes closed, water dripping from my hair onto my chest, remembering the kisses I had received later that day—innocent ones from Regina and not-so-innocent, hungry kisses from Krew. That was the last birthday I celebrated with my best friends. Nothing in my life had compared to those moments of bliss.

Then the image of her at the underground fight slipped into my mind. She was still so beautiful—more so now, if I was being honest. Her hair was no longer blonde, or long. It leaned toward darker brown, with a hint of red under the industrial lights that hung high in the building.

She had also filled out, and just thinking about *that* brought my dick to life.

Imagining what was under her slinky, black dress had my dick at full mast. There was no chance of the thin cotton towel around my waist being able to hold down my rigid shaft. I dropped it, spread my legs slightly apart, and ran my palm along my length.

Then Krew—my best friend—my ex-lover, swirled into my thoughts and I swallowed the lust that man always brought out in me. Even to this day.

He was still insanely gorgeous, with an ass—*Fuck*. I wrapped my fingers around my girth, squeezed and a moan escaped past my lips. Between the real, heady sensation of my hand around my cock and the memory of the night I took Krew's virginity—how he let me claim him as mine, this was going to be quick.

But I didn't want to be a two-pump chump, I squeezed my dick at the base, held it tight, and then repeatedly thrust my hips, gliding the shaft through my fisted hand. I groaned out in pleasure as I drove myself higher. As predicted, it didn't take long for me to spill my seed. With a low grunt, I came quick and hard.

The euphoria lasted about five seconds until I caught my reflection in the mirror and— "Jesus Christ." I scrubbed my clean hand over my face. What the hell was I doing? I couldn't afford to think about the past. Or what could have been. I wasn't that Decker anymore. He died long ago with the first bullet I shot that had killed someone.

My shoulders slumped with the realization that I wasn't good for anyone, especially for Regina or Krew. And the evil things I'd done—no way I could bring that baggage into their lives. I didn't want to linger on my festering emotions, so I washed my hands, wiped my dick, and cleaned up the jizz on the floor.

I stepped out of the bathroom and stilled when I recognized the sound. My old cell phone was pinging.

A slow smile crept across my face as I stepped closer to the bed. I glanced down at the screen as eagerness tore through my gut. Only one person would be blowing up my phone with text messages.

"Son of a bitch," I chuckled.

I unlocked the phone. The texts were all from the same number.

I shook my head as a smile split wide across my face. He couldn't listen to save his life—not back then, and apparently not now. My eyes began to sting, knowing that we might have been apart all this time, but he still remembered my old number.

Krew: *It's me... Krew.*

Krew: *I know you told me not to follow you, but you never said I couldn't call. I chanced it and tried your old number, and it worked. Well... I hope this is you. Call me.*

I chuckled. "Christ. He hasn't changed." Elation thrummed through me. "Krew." His name fell from my lips like a wish.

Krew: *Damn it, Deck. Call me. Text me. I don't give a fuck how you do it. I'm pacing my ass off worrying about you. CALL ME!!*

I wasn't going to answer, but as I pictured him marching back and forth, frantically talking to himself, ready to do something stupid, I changed my mind.

Me: *I'm good.*

It was all I was willing to give him. Then I shut off the phone, dropped it onto the bed, and let my mind wander to the past again. The day I'd had with Regina and Krew in our private spot at the Honey Pot. Then that night, when I had been with Krew, and how we had explored with our mouths, our bodies, and our dicks.

There was only one way to cure the lust churning in my groin again. I grabbed a lube packet from my wallet, and slicked up my cock.

I stroked myself until there was nothing left in my balls. My body was physically satisfied. But my heart? My soul? They still wanted Krew and Regina.

I'd reconciled to the idea that the wish I had made long ago, that Regina, Krew and I would live together in bliss somewhere outside the narrow-minded town of Elida, was just that, a wish that would never come true.

But maybe... Maybe my luck was changing.

Regina's Diary

June 10th, 2011

Dear Diary,

I know it's been a while since I wrote to you, but I have a secret.

A great big one. Not even Maya knows about it. And I can't tell anyone other than you, Diary. I got to kiss both Krew and Decker today on the cheek. It felt sweet and naughty at the same time. I want more, but I have to be good because it's Decker's birthday.

Krew and I want to surprise him with a birthday treat of his favorite foods. And Mom's famous chocolate cake. I had to lie to her so she would make it for me. I should feel bad, but I don't. I know Mom and Dad don't like Krew and Decker. They think they're too old for me. Diary, they're going to be juniors and I'm going to be a freshman—it's not a big deal.

My parents think they're up to no good and rotten (my mom's words). She keeps telling me good girls don't hang out with boys like that. I told her that's too bad, because they are my best friends, and I won't give them up.

But Diary, I'm confused. When I kissed each of them on the cheek, I wished they were kissing me at the same time, on my mouth. And what's even more confusing is that I liked watching Krew kiss Decker. It gave me tingles in parts I can't write about.

I don't know, Diary. Am I sick or evil to think like that? Did I do a bad thing? Me kissing two boys? Watching my friends kiss each other? Am I a sinner like my mom says? Am I as wicked as the people that do wicked things? I'll write more later. I have to get ready for the last day of school.

Love, Regina

Chapter Seven
Krew

I was a glutton for punishment. Even though Decker had pointed the gun in my face, I knew instinctively that my best friend would never shoot me. His words stung, yet they weren't enough to make me stay away—or keep me from texting him. I needed to make sure he was also safe.

I pulled up my contacts, hoping that I still had Decker's old phone number. Luck was on my side. Though, it had been years since I last called and texted him. It was a long shot that the number was good, but I had to try.

Once I sent the first message, I waited all of five minutes. I wasn't willing to give up just yet, since the text hadn't bounced back as undeliverable. So, I messaged him once more.

Now, I glared down at my phone, willing Decker to answer my texts. He didn't.

"Bastard," I hissed, shoving the cell into my jeans pocket as I resumed pacing in the Motel 6 parking lot.

Then the damn thing vibrated, and I anxiously pulled it back out. I quickly typed in my password and then tapped the messages icon.

Two words blared up at me like a taunt. *I'm good.*

What the hell did that mean? I waited for more, but nothing else popped up.

I rubbed the back of my neck in frustration as the radio silence continued. Though I was somewhat relieved Decker was safe, I wasn't happy about his two-word, fuck off salute back to me.

I returned to the motel room, closed the door, and leaned against it for support. After I took a couple of deep breaths, the tension left my body.

I stripped and went into the tiny bathroom. Not sure when—or even if Teke would return to the room, I locked the door and climbed into the shower. With how tall I was, I had to bend slightly to wash away the sweat that coated my skin. As I slid my soapy hands over my body, an image of Decker and Regina—together, touching me, flitted across my mind.

Jesus, it had been years since I'd last thought of them together. Kissing each other—them kissing me. The memory of their touches had always soothed my soul—especially when the warden put me in solitary confinement. Those memories had kept my sanity in place, until I got the hell out of there.

I closed my eyes and slid my hand down to my semi-rigid cock. I stroked it until I was rock hard and the urge to come had my balls drawing up—until a crash jolted me out of my lust-induced stupor.

The slam of a door had me looking at my dick. "Sorry," I sighed and dropped my hand.

Assuming it was my brother, I took my time rinsing off the body wash and got out of the shower. As I grabbed for the towel, Teke pounded on the locked bathroom door.

"Where're you, motherfucker?" I was pretty sure that was what he'd said. But Teke's slurred words sounded more like 'were you, moth-furker'. A drunk and coked up Teke was a nasty thing to encounter.

The lock was so flimsy even my asshole brother could have

easily broken in with one kick. Since he didn't have a brain cell working at that moment, so it was safe enough for me to dry off.

"Be out in a second," I called out casually while towel drying my bald head.

"Ya fur-king leff me," he hiccuped. "I adda to walk. Git out…" The rest of his words were muffled.

I stayed silent, listening to his bullshit on the other side of the door. He hadn't walked. I saw him get in that BMW.

Another crash, like glass shattering, had me clenching my teeth. I didn't have enough cash to cover whatever he was breaking. I opened the door, a towel wrapped around my waist, and stormed out to see what havoc my idiot brother had created.

On the floor, by the bed, Teke was face down and not moving. Guess he'd had too much booze with the drugs he snorted up his nose. I used my foot to roll him over—and goddamnit, there was a gun in his limp hand.

Fucking A. Now where the hell did he get that nine mil?

It wasn't a surprise that my brother had somehow gotten a gun. But why was it in his—wait. Was he going to shoot me?

I wasn't planning on finding out. Not sure if the damn thing was hot, I kicked the gun out of his hand as I stripped off the towel. Then I picked the weapon up with the towel, checked that the safety was on, and placed it next to my bag.

The broken lamp hanging off the nightstand caught my eyes. That was coming out of his pocket, not mine. The stupid asshole deserved to pay for it, especially after he dragged me here to fight.

The next time he wanted cash, maybe *he* should be the one in the ring. Or he should get a damn job—right, that would never happen. From now on, Teke was going to have to find his own way to earn money. I was done being used as his mule.

I didn't bother waking Teke up, just left him lying in the shattered glass. I quickly got dressed, threw on a hoodie, and packed my shit in the duffle—including the gun, and dropped the keys for

Teke's piece of shit car onto his chest. The last thing I wanted was for my brother to accuse me of stealing his ride.

As I turned to leave, my brother surprised me, and clocked me in the back of the head. I stumbled forward—the momentum had my body crashing against the door. I quickly righted myself, spun around and blocked Teke's next swing before it landed on my face. Guess he wasn't completely out of it after all.

"I told you to never hit me again. You just don't listen," I growled.

Teke grunted, then started swinging like a madman. He got in a few lucky hits to my ribs and one to my face. This time, though, I wasn't going to be a willing target for his rage.

I threw my blows, harder and faster, aiming for his face and kidneys. My fists were a brutal force but Teke wasn't going down. He was a tenacious son of a bitch.

"Wer the furck ya're goin', pussy? Runnin' back home?" Spittle sprayed from his mouth; saliva dripped down his dirty, scruffy chin.

Now how could I have forgotten that Teke was meaner when he was hopped on drugs and booze? Alcohol, especially, made him feel invincible. Then add the drugs, and my only choice was to knock his ass out. Or he'd keep coming at me.

"I'm done with this. I won't fight for you anymore, Teke," I hissed, then dodged his right hook and came back with an upper hook, catching him on the jaw.

He swung again and missed. "If ya quit, how're we gonna eat? What about Dad?"

"That won't work on me anymore. I'm through."

"Where're ya gonna getta job? No one wants an ex-con." More spittle flew past his lips as he raged on. This was Teke's way of keeping me under his thumb. I was finally done doing his dirty work.

"Don't worry about me. You should be thinking about yourself." *Like you always do.*

Teke kept bouncing around, taking wild swings at me, while I dodged them and countered. "Ya musta got too many hits to yar thick skull? Noo-body wants a jailbird?"

He knew how to hit below the belt. That last verbal shot hit like a real punch to my nutsack.

"If it wasn't for you stealing that car, I wouldn't have gone to jail." I jabbed.

"Don't furcking blame me. No-one said to be a he-hero." Teke barked out a laugh before he spat at my feet, adding to the insult.

"Well. I learned. I'll let you hang next time."

"I say—" hiccup, "when you're done, motherfucker." He kicked out and nailed my outer thigh.

He tried to tackle me, but I kept the upper hand. Teke might be older and meaner, but I was bigger, faster, and stronger.

I twisted away, got behind him, and put all my hundred and ninety-seven pounds of muscle and bone into the gravity of the punch. The blow landed on the side of his head. The second my fist made contact, my brother twisted, and dropped like a rock onto the carpet. He was out cold.

I stood there for a short moment, breathing heavily, and watched blood trickle from his nose and his chest go still. I bent down and touched two fingers to his neck and found a strong pulse. His rhythmic heartbeat was steady.

I didn't want to kill my brother, only incapacitate him. Though, I felt no remorse or doubt that Teke had deserved this ass kicking.

Since he wasn't dead, I picked up my duffle and hoofed it out of there.

When I'd gone about a mile down Jackson, I finally slowed my stride into a steady walking pace, trying to not look suspicious. I didn't trust the police—not after what they did to me.

However, this area was just as sketchy. I stopped, grabbed the gun from the duffle and tucked it into my hoodie pouch. At least I could defend myself in case some fucker tried to jump me. Again.

As I neared the corner of Oak and Jackson, I noticed a pickup truck was rolling up beside me and kept pace. I held my eyes forward, not wanting to provoke the driver or anyone else inside the vehicle.

Jesus, when it rained, it poured. I wasn't surprised that more chaos was piling up onto my already shitty night.

Out of the corner of my eye, I saw the front passenger window slide down.

"Get in."

I came to an abrupt halt as I recognized Decker's raspy voice, and the truck also stopped moving. I slowly turned and stared at him for a long minute, not sure if I was truly seeing him or if my imagination was playing tricks on me.

"Get in the truck, Krew, or do I have to pull out my gun again? There's no room for arguing in this neighborhood at three in the morning," he ordered as he looked around the area. He was pissed. Why?

"I'm good." I pulled out the gun. Decker's nostrils flared, and his blue eyes turned icy.

"Put that fucking thing away, and get in the damn truck, K." His clipped tone brooked no argument and I slid the gun back into my pouch. He sat in the truck, glared at me and waited.

I was too damned tired to argue—or to fight. Teke had drained most of it out of me. Besides, I wasn't in the right head space to debate with this man. Not knowing where I was, or how safe the streets around here actually were, I got in. As soon as my door shut, Decker put the vehicle into drive and took off.

"What are you doing here? How did you find me?" I asked, while shoving the duffle down by my feet.

"My handler tracked your phone," he growled, as though he was angry with me. "And give me that gun before you go shooting your dick off."

"Your *who*? And no. I feel better keeping the gun." I had a tight grip on the gun, which was still in my hoodie pouch.

"Never mind who." He tilted his head slightly, until I was only able to see the part of his face lit up by the street lights we passed. The rest was hidden in the shadows of the dark cab. "Christ," he muttered.

"Why did you track me down? Especially when you made it clear that you don't want to see me again." I tried to remain calm, but my fury built with every petulant word out of my mouth.

Decker turned his face fully away, adjusting his body before he blew out a heavy breath. "I never said that. I told you to leave, because I didn't want to see you in jail."

"That still doesn't answer my question about why you tracked me down."

"You're the one who texted me. You're the one who won't leave it alone."

"That's right. Blame it on me. Such a typical Decker Moss move," I snarled, like a hungry Rottweiler wanting the bone being dangled in my face. I wanted the real answers. "Stop playing games, Deck. Tell me the truth. Why did you track me down?"

Decker grazed his thumb across his lower lip, and my eyes tracked the movement. I swallowed deep, trying to tamp down the sudden overwhelming lust brought on by a vivid memory of those lips wrapped around my cock.

He met my eyes. "I missed you and wanted to talk," Decker finally said in a low timbre. The tip of his tongue peeked out between his lips, and I shivered slightly. It seemed he was aching for me as much as I ached for him. But I wasn't going to give in to my desire—no matter how desperate I desired his touch, until we got some things straightened out.

"You missed me and you wanted to talk." I leaned closer to him and coldly said, "Okay. I'm here. Talk."

"Fuck off. I said I missed you. That's the truth. So don't act like you haven't missed me too," he hissed, and pushed me away from him.

"Yeah?" I couldn't hold onto my frown.

"Yeah."

"Then where have you been all this time?" I asked, easing back to my side of the truck. "Why didn't you reach out to me? How in the hell did you get into killing people?" I couldn't stop—it was as if the dam holding back all of my questions had burst.

"Jesus fucking Christ, K," Decker said with fierce intensity. "I need a drink."

A chuckle slid out of me. "I need food. And since we have years to catch up on, let's find a place to eat."

Decker grumbled something under his breath before saying, "I saw an all-night diner a few miles back."

"Let's go."

"All right." He turned the truck around, and headed in the opposite direction.

I leaned my head against the headrest and the window, watching the night and the few other cars on the road zipped by in a blur. My eyelids began droop, being lulled into sleep by the moving truck and the silence.

Although, I could feel Decker's eyes on me. Maybe it was the fear of being separated from each other, after all this time—I didn't know.

Nevertheless, I wasn't losing Decker again.

Chapter Eight
Decker

Krew was quiet; a quick glance at him again and I was mesmerized. He was sleeping. His eyes were shut and he was breathing evenly. Even in the darkness of the cab, I could see the circles under his eyes, and the bruises on his jawline—fresh ones. Ones I hadn't seen a few hours earlier on that street corner in Chicago. Still, he was beautiful.

Yet... those bruises.

He hadn't fought tonight—my bullet through Kane's forehead had seen to that. Instinctively I knew who put those bruises on Krew.

Teke. *That motherfucker.*

Now that I had Krew with me, I'd make sure that bastard kept his hands to himself. Or he'd see what I was capable of.

I wanted to reach out and touch Krew's face, but I held back. I didn't want to wake him.

Studying his profile, I recalled Krew's questions—lots of them. However, I couldn't conjure up a single word.

Where have I been? What have I been doing? Why didn't I reach out to him? They were all legit questions, but I had no idea *how* to respond. How to give him the answers he deserved to hear—or how much of my past, which was no picnic, I should reveal.

At the next red light, I pulled out the burner phone from my pocket, brought up the message app and sent a text to my handler.

Me: *Need a week off.*

I didn't get an immediate reply, yet I wasn't concerned. Sabrina would eventually respond. And as the light turned green, she texted back.

Sabrina: *Should I be worried—scratch that. Okay, bossman.*

I quietly chuckled and placed the phone in one of the cup holders in the middle console and drove in silence.

I drove until I found a parking spot about half a block down from the diner. It was a precautionary tactic I'd learned from a retired hitman.

I had befriended Merrick Gentry while we served together in the military. After all the bullshit I got caught up in, I barely managed to get out with an honorable discharge. Merrick approached me soon after with a *career opportunity*—as a hitman. Thinking about his job proposal still made me chuckle.

Now Merrick was retired, and I haven't looked back on my decision once.

"Wake up. We're here," I said softly, shaking Krew's arm. He slowly came to, his intriguing eyes glazed with sleep but no less beautiful.

"Okay," he said with a yawn, stretching his arms out, as he looked through the windshield.

I got out, tucked my Ruger inside a pocket of my hoodie, and walked around to the passenger door and opened it. "Why don't you put the gun in your duffle?"

Krew's eyebrows drew into a vee and he studied me for a long minute, then did as I suggested before he slid out and closed the door. I locked the truck and headed toward the diner. Krew fell into step beside me.

I pulled open the diner door and motioned him to walk through first. He glanced at me with a strange expression before entering the place.

Christ, I needed to stop treating him like he was mine. Krew wasn't. Not anymore. We were here to talk, catch up, and then go our separate ways. Leave him for good.

As I crossed the threshold, I automatically scanned the interior. The diner was nearly deserted at this time of night—or morning. There was only one other patron, and he sat in the booth closest to the door.

The smell... it had hit me as I entered. Greasy fried foods, strong black coffee, and the too-sweet doughnuts and desserts— the aromas mingled and I took a good inhale. My stomach growled.

When was the last time I ate?

Krew gave me another strange glance over his shoulder before he turned his attention to the short, rail-thin, fifty-something waitress heading our way. In cropped jeans, a tight t-shirt with the diner's logo stretched across her ample chest, and heavily lined eyes, her attempt to look younger was a sad failure.

She approached us both with a huge smile, her breasts jutted out, but her eyes were only on Krew.

"Sit wherever you like, handsome," she greeted, her husky voice filled with appreciation as her eyes roved over Krew's body like she had every right to.

I wanted to pull out my knife and dig her eyes out for staring at my—

Jesus. Fucking get a grip.

"Right here is fine. Thanks," Krew said as he pointed to the nearest booth and slid onto the bench facing the back of the diner.

I sat across from him, my eyes pinned the waitress like she was a bug. She ignored me, and passed the two menus to Krew.

"What would you like to drink, sweetie?" the waitress asked as she purposefully stepped closer to Krew's side of the booth as if I wasn't even there.

A low growl seeped pass my lips, like I was some damn protective animal. She finally glanced at me, but her mouth stayed shut.

Then Krew's warm hand covered mine, shifting my attention to him. He turned my palm up and entwined our fingers, blatantly displaying where he stood with me, and to the waitress.

A small smile slid across his face, and there was desire in his eyes. I wanted to reach over, clasp my hand around the back of his neck and pull him in for a kiss. Show him what he'd been missing all these years.

"How about two coffees, and we need a minute to decide on the food," Krew said to the waitress.

"Oh—sure," she chirped in surprise. I smirked as her wide, black-ringed eyes glared down at our joined hands. A frown creased her face before she spun around and strode off.

"Still the same old Decker," Krew said, pulling his hand away. I wanted to snatch it back, but I tucked my hand under the table instead. I didn't trust myself around Krew.

"What does that mean?"

"Still very possessive," he uttered with a soft chuckle.

I skewered him with a sneer before glancing down at the menu Krew slid over to me. I opened it, trying to wrangle in my annoyance.

A full minute passed before Krew said, "I thought about you and Regi all the time, especially when I was in... jail."

I wasn't sure what to say, other than "I'm sorry," but that didn't seem appropriate. I settled for, "Yeah. It was hard for all of us... for me... Krew—"

I wasn't able to finish my confession, because the damn waitress was back with two cups of coffee, a bowl of creamers, and another bowl of sugar options. She dropped the items onto the middle of the table before she stomped away. The woman didn't give a crap that the hot liquid splashed onto the Formica top.

Without a word, Krew snagged some napkins from the dispenser and wiped up the mess. I would have left that shit for the bitch to clean up.

"There goes her tip," Krew muttered under his breath, which made me smile.

"So what are you ordering?" I asked, chickening out on my declaration of how much I had missed him and Regina. Or how my chest hollowed out every time I thought about them being together.

"Not sure yet," he said.

I lifted the coffee to my lips, took a sip, and glanced up—Christ, those damn dimples. Krew stared at the menu, smirking without realizing it.

I dropped my eyes to the menu in front of me—and immediately regretted it. A grotesque photo of a meatloaf dinner stared back at me, gray and lumpy. I grimaced.

Except, the real distraction was across the table. I'd struggled to control myself around this man, and clearly, not much had changed.

Krew was smirking again—that infuriating, cocky little curve at the corner of his mouth. I wanted to wipe it off with a kiss he'd never forget. Instead, I glued myself to the chair and forced my eyes back to the menu, pretending to care about the list of entrees.

I slapped the menu down on the table. "I know what I want."

"You do?" He briefly met my eyes before dropping his back down to his menu. "Everything looks good," he said. "What are you going to get?"

"Meatloaf dinner," I quickly replied. The shock on my friend's face had me frowning. "What?"

Krew glanced at the menu and then back at me. "Really? Meatloaf?"

"Yeah." I shrugged. "Why not?"

"Because you hate meatloaf," he said incredulously.

"That was then," I gruffly retorted and looked away.

Krew leaned back against the booth. "I don't think so..." Something was percolating in his head and I wasn't liking it. "Are you going to answer any of the questions I asked earlier tonight?"

"Call the waitress. I'm hungry," I grumbled, hoping the distraction worked.

He shook his head. "Stop changing the subject, Deck."

"I'm not." I leaned back, matching his frown. Before I got a chance to open my mouth, the damn waitress walked over.

"What'll you have, *boys*?" I couldn't ignore the condemnation in her tone.

"I'll have a burger, medium, loaded. Fries, and a Coke," Krew rumbled out.

"Same," I added, my gaze fixed on Krew's widening grin.

"Sure thing," our irritable waitress griped, before striding toward the partially open doorway to the kitchen.

Krew waited a beat before he leaned forward, a glint of humor in his eyes. "I..." he trailed off as the chimes that were hung on the diner's door rang.

I leaned slightly to the left, and caught sight of two men—and stiffened, because I recognized one of them. A hitman named Jay. The other one, I didn't know. However, from the way he scanned the diner and then narrowed his gaze on us, he too, was a killer.

Every warning bell in my head sounded. The guy who was sitting by the door must have felt a shift in the air too, because he scooted out of the booth and fled, leaving only me and Krew and the two new customers.

I wanted to grab Krew and run, except Jay and his buddy had strategically blocked our exit. Hell, they weren't here for a social visit.

With their eyes trained on our booth, I realized they were here for me. Why? I had no clue, but I'd find out soon enough.

The problem was that Krew was here, too, and in danger. Whatever was about to go down with these hitmen, I had to make sure their sights were solely on me, not on my friend.

I leaned in, checking the pocket where I stashed my nine mil, and whispered to Krew, "Don't move. Keep your eyes forward and I'll be right back."

"What's going on, Decker?" A flash of fear widened Krew's eyes.

"Like I said, don't move unless I call your name, and if I do, drop under the table. No hesitation. Understand, K?"

He went rigid, then gave me a barely perceptible nod of understanding. I slid out of the booth, stood, and took three steps toward the hitmen, blocking their sight of Krew.

I stared down the two men for a good thirty seconds before shifting my eyes to an empty table near the door. They understood immediately what I wanted. They each took a seat. Jay planted his skinny ass in the booth that faced the back of the diner—kiddy-corner from me. The other sat in a chair that partially faced the entrance.

The only other people I wondered about were the waitress and the cook. They had to have heard the door chimes. So why didn't the waitress come out from the back? Was that Jay's doing? I decided not to worry about it.

I grabbed a chair from the adjacent table, turned it around, and sat in full view of both men, all the while keeping an ear on Krew. With my Ruger still in my hoodie pocket, I rolled my shoulders and peered at Jay and his friend.

"What are you doing here?" I asked Jay. I did a job with him three years ago that involved the Columbian cartel. I saved his ass when they tried to separate his head from his body with a machete. Saving his life had created a bit of a bond between us—or what passed as one.

"The word is out that someone took the prize for Kane

Maxwell," he said before sliding a glance over to the guy I didn't know.

"Who's that?" I also looked over to the other hitman, who appeared to be an anxious mess, or just hopped up on something. I assumed the latter. His right leg bounced like a jack hammer and the pointer finger and thumb on his right hand kept flicking together.

Is that his trigger finger?

He blew a piece of his greasy, blue-black hair away from his cold, lifeless, dark eyes. They reminded me of obsidian. Fathomless. Deadly. And they were centered on me.

From the way he kept shifting his rangy build in the seat, he was a tweaker, and even more unpredictable and dangerous.

Then the asshole honed in on Krew, and I wasn't having it. "Keep your eyes on me," I growled before turning back to Jay. "What are you doing here and who the hell is this guy?" I tipped my head toward the fucker.

"Don't worry about me." The cunt chuckled like he had made a funny. But all I saw was a dangerous clown with a twitchy itchy finger.

His unblinking scrutiny would have been unnerving to the average person. To me? I took him in, and glared right back like I was impenetrable.

"This is Frankie," Jay said, his thumb jerking toward his friend —if one could call him that. In our world, there was only a thin, fractured line between an enemy and a friend.

Ignoring the tweaker, I refocused on Jay. "I'm not going to ask you again."

"The word is that you killed Kane." Jay smiled.

"Why does it matter?" Not wanting to fully commit to the deed, I deflected. "For all I know, it could have been you."

"No, man. I'm a good shot, but that was way out of my league, especially with that many eyes on the target." Jay shook his head. "I know only two men who have the balls and the talent. And one of them is vapor."

He meant Merrick, but I didn't react or say his name.

My eyes slid to Frankie, who slowly pulled a pack of cigarettes out of his front shirt pocket, smacked the bottom of the pack with the palm of his other hand and then ripped the top open.

Christ, I could use a smoke right about now.

After Frankie took a cigarette out, he placed it between his yellowed teeth, lit it and took a long drag. He then pointed to my crotch. "Big brass balls you have there," Frankie taunted, his gravelly voice full of vinegar. Tendrils of smoke filtered out of his nostrils and mouth.

"Man, I don't have time for a social visit." I didn't want to waste my breath on these fuckers. The way Frankie kept looking toward Krew... Suddenly everything clicked into place. This was a hit. I knew deep in my gut. But who was the target?

Shit.

I was so caught up on hanging with Krew, that I let these pieces of shit infiltrate the space. No matter, Krew was walking out of here alive. Me? I'd take my chances. Only I'd kill these assholes first before I bit the dust.

"Jay?" I asked as casually as I could muster while shifting my feet slightly apart, so I didn't rouse suspicions that I was ready to reach for my nine.

"Sorry, Moss," Jay said evenly, also shifting in his seat. It was a small tell—enough to cause my trigger finger to twitch. In our line of work, reading body language could mean the difference between life and death.

"For what?" I asked, as my eyes bounced between Frankie and Jay.

"We shouldn't have come in here." Jay kept his palms up—he was here to talk. But Frankie was way too fidgety for my liking.

"Then leave."

"No, man. We came here for the food," Frankie said with a fake, wide smile, his hands were palms down. He was ready to strike.

Two can play at this game, motherfucker.

"Then why ask about Kane?" I casually moved my right hand to the table, adjusting my position again, so I could also reach for my gun.

"Just curious." Jay shrugged. Another tell. Something big was happening, but he wasn't saying. Yet.

"You know what they say, curiosity killed the cat," I replied, my eyes staying on Frankie.

"Who's your friend?" Frankie pointed the cigarette at Krew.

"He's none of your business." Then I said to Jay, "I suggest you find another place to eat."

"Oh, come on." Frankie stood nonchalantly, lit cigarette back in his mouth, and I went on high alert. He took one last drag before squashing it on the Formica tabletop. With a wild gleam in his eyes, his smile—all teeth like the Cheshire cat, and held his arms out wide. "We can all be friends."

In the split second before Frankie took a step toward me, I knew how this was going down. "Krew," I shouted.

Frankie yanked a Desert Eagle from behind him and aimed it at me. I simultaneously moved, my nine pointed at him.

"Wait a second," Jay quickly said. I wasn't sure who he was talking to, until he looked straight at me. "I didn't come to start any shit."

"That asshole pointing the gun at me says otherwise," I hissed.

"*I'm* here to start some shit," Frankie laughed as he waved the gun in his hand until the semi-automatic pistol was now trained in Krew's direction. Either Krew hadn't obeyed my instructions and was still sitting there, or Frankie was bluffing to distract me.

"Shut the fuck up, Frankie," Jay hissed over his shoulder before turning back to me. "I swear on my dead mother's grave I didn't come in here to rumble you."

My eyes bounced between Jay and that greasy turd with him. "I don't believe you, Jay," I said in warning.

I pulled the trigger the same time as Frankie did. My shot went wide; his bullet hit something outside my periphery—that something better not have been my best friend.

I didn't get a chance to look before I launch myself at Frankie. My sole purpose was to take this bastard down with prejudice.

The asshole was fast, and kicked my Ruger out of my hand, but so was I. With a counter kicked, I knocked the gun out of his grip, before we exchanged blows.

For a moment, he had me pinned. As he cocked back his fist, I punched my arm upward, and my fist landed a solid jab to his throat. He fell backward, choking. I twisted and rolled, shoving him off my legs.

I scrambled to my feet, and saw his Eagle was in reach. I grabbed it, took aim and shot twice—one to Frankie's chest and the other to his head. I pivoted and trained the gun at Jay. He was pointing his Sig at Frankie, who was face up, his blood was pooling around him on the linoleum.

Fear cut through my focus that Krew had been shot by Jay while Frankie and I brawled. But I didn't dare look away from Jay, who now trained his gun on me.

"Don't move," Jay demanded.

"Do you have a death wish?" I narrowed my eyes on the man.

"No. I came here to warn you, man."

"*This* is your warning?" I growled out my fury.

"No. This asshole liked to play Russian roulette with his life. But not me." Jay kicked at Frankie's lifeless body and spat, "Good riddance."

"Tell me what you want to say and then get gone." I made no move to lower the gun.

"Your friend over there is marked." He pointed a finger toward Krew. "A hundred grand in the next twenty-four hours. You saved my ass back in Columbia, so I'm calling us even. I'm going to back out of here and leave. And don't worry, your boy is alive. I won't go after what's yours."

"How do I know you're telling the truth?"

"There's no reason for me to lie. I owed you a marker, and now we're done, Moss. He's safe—Oh, and by the way, there's one other mark—not sure if you know the bitch," Jay said without lowering his gun.

"Who's the other target?" I asked, slowly standing to my full height, keeping Frankie's Desert Eagle still aimed at Jay's head.

"Some woman named Regina—I don't fucking know. I'm sure your handler can find out."

Behind me, Krew gasped at Regina's name. I didn't even blink. "Who called in the hits?" I asked, easing back from Jay.

"Don't know and don't give a shit." Jay pointed the gun at Frankie's lifeless body for two beats before it was trained back on me. "That's on you to figure out. Now I'm out of here." Jay backed his way out of the door, keeping his eyes on me until he was outside.

I inwardly counted to ten, so absorbed on Jay and what he said, I didn't register Krew standing beside me.

"He was talking about our Regi," he said unsteadily.

"Yeah," I admitted without looking at Krew. I continued to watch Jay's figure melt into the dark, remaining vigilant in case the hitman changed his mind and came after me and mine.

Even though Jay had given me his oath that he wouldn't go after mine, I didn't trust the man as far as I could throw him.

Two minutes passed before I turned away from the door. I searched around, retrieved my gun from under a table, and jammed it in the pocket of my hoodie. I then snagged a couple of napkins, wiped my fingerprints from the Eagle and placed it in Frankie's lifeless hand.

There were going to be repercussions if his body was left here. But first, I had to get Krew away from this place.

"You need to leave," I said over my shoulder and scanned the diner for cameras... And there they were. *Fuck.*

"We need to get to Regi," Krew demanded.

"First, I need you safe." I fished out the truck keys out of my jean pocket. "Take the keys, and I'll meet up with you at the Holiday Inn in Waukegan on Milwaukee." I grabbed his wrist and put the keys in his hand.

"I'm not leaving you." He shoved them back into my hand. "We go together or I stay and help."

"Don't be a stubborn ass. Take the keys and get the fuck out. I have a feeling if the waitress called the police—"

"Forget it," Krew growled out. "I'm not leaving you here to face this bullshit. Besides, we didn't do anything wrong."

A low hiss left my lips, and a moment later, sirens tore through the night air.

"Shit," Krew muttered.

"Too late." I grabbed him by the shirt and hauled ass around the counter. We headed toward the back of the diner, where the kitchen was located, and the greasy smell was the strongest.

The space was empty. I bet the waitress and the cook were far from here. Though, I couldn't worry about them. My only concern was to get Krew out of the diner.

I pushed him out the back door, and we rounded the corner into the back alley just as red and blue lights reflected off the side of the building. "Jesus-fuck."

We dropped down next to the green metal dumpsters as the cop cars zipped by.

"That was close," Krew whispered.

"Too fucking close. But we're not out of danger yet," I said, taking off down the alley.

Krew matched my quick pace. As I turned left, so did he, and we were back on the same street as the diner, about a block from my truck and a block and a half from the restaurant.

From this distance, the street in front of the diner was lit up like a parade of flashing lights. Fortunately, it wasn't quite dawn yet, so we moved under the cover of darkness toward the truck.

There was a slim chance we could go unnoticed. If we got caught, then we had to pretend ignorance to what had happened inside the diner.

"How good are your acting skills?" I turned to Krew, taking his hand and drawing him close.

"W-what?" His eyes were riveted to our clasped hands.

I'd caught him off guard. Good.

"Pretend we're lovers. Put your arm around me, sweetheart." I smiled, and he swallowed hard.

"Deck..." There was a heavy meaning behind my name. An unspoken desire we'd both been harboring. I saw it in his eyes when we reconnect in the alley. And again, in the diner, when he took my hand.

This close, I could see his blown-out pupils and hear the heavy breaths he was pulling in and out of his lungs. After a slight stumble in his steps, Krew wrapped his arm around me like I had demanded.

As we neared the back end of my vehicle, I saw two cops striding toward us. I didn't think, just whirled Krew around, pushing his back against the driver's side of the truck. Then I kissed him hard, like we were about to fuck right there out in the open. I was sure Krew could feel the gun in my pocket, but he didn't say anything.

Instead, Krew opened for me immediately, and the welcoming

taste of his mouth was instantly intoxicating. Just like I remembered.

I tried to maintain some awareness of the police activity nearby, but that proved impossible with Krew's luscious lips on mine. The world faded away until there was only Krew. Only him, and my sudden desperation to strip this man naked and fuck him until neither of us could walk.

As I ground my groin against his, I couldn't miss that both our dicks were rock-hard.

Krew moaned and clamped his hand on my ass and pressed our cocks even tighter together. "Deck, I need this—need you," he whispered in my mouth.

Jesus—the fucking rush. I wanted more too—demanded it from his mouth, from his body.

Krew pushed his left knee between my legs, and deepened the kiss. I groaned in response to his salacious assault on my senses, my body was ready to combust from my overpowering desire for him.

"For Christ sakes." A voice behind me yanked me out of my lust-induced haze. Krew stiffened and pulled back slightly.

I moved my lips to his ear and whispered, "Keep kissing me."

"Tell them to do that somewhere else," another person growled.

"Why me?" the first person whined.

"Because you're closer. Now do it—we don't have time for this bullshit. I have to go talk to the detective."

"Jesus. Fine."

A moment later, a strong tap on my shoulder had me releasing Krew. I reluctantly turned my head, purposefully keeping my body—and the gun in my pocket, pressed into Krew, and looked at a uniformed cop, who was far from comfortable.

The man was pissed off, and disgust was written all over his ugly mug at our very public display of affection. I hoped it was enough to sidetrack him from asking us questions about the diner.

"Unless you want to be in jail for public indecency, take your queer asses out of here," the cop commanded.

"Yes, sir," I uttered, and got into my vehicle. Krew went around to the passenger side, and did the same. Before the cop changed his mind, I started the truck and swung it around, heading in the opposite direction of the chaos at the diner.

I'd driven several blocks before I realized Krew was still breathing hard. I glanced his way, and he was so still, I wondered if he was going to be sick.

From kissing me?

"Krew?" I turned onto a side street, pulled over and shut off the engine. "What's wrong?"

I could barely see his face. Without any street lights nearby, we were sitting in the dark.

"Krew," I uttered again.

He turned and leaned toward me. His breathing was still heavy, but now I could see his eyes—and they were filled with the same desperate desire I was feeling. As I was about to reach for him, his mouth slammed against mine as his fingers dug through my hair. The pain on my scalp was a welcome pleasure, as was the press of his lips, his tongue invading my mouth.

I took what Krew was giving, and I gave it right back. Between our frenzied hands, we frantically undid our jeans, and untucked our cocks. My hand on his. His on mine. And never once did our mouths lose connection.

"Fuck," I growled against his lips. The friction of his grip had me rocking my hips upward to meet his downward strokes. "So good."

"Deck," he groaned as he pulled away slightly and stared into my eyes. "I missed you so damn much."

I tightened my grip on his cock. "Don't stop stroking my dick." My command was sharp, and I regretted my domineering tone until I looked into Krew's eyes—the glazed lust in them conveyed he'd liked it.

Krew crashed our mouths together again, the kiss hard and drugging. He then pulled back, and focused on stroking my dick in earnest.

As his hand jacked me faster, the familiar pleasurable surge of electricity was building up in my balls and I was about to come. But I didn't want to come alone.

"Deck, I need to taste you."

My nuts instantly tightened and my gut constricted at his words. "Too late," I hissed and came all over Krew's hand. Not two seconds later, Krew grunted out my name, shuddered, and spilled his seed onto my hand.

As Krew's eyes met mine, he lifted his hand to his mouth and ran his tongue over the milky fluid. Another shiver ran through my body as I watched him lap up every drop of my essence—and the need to taste my cum on his lips had my softening dick quickly getting hard again.

I lifted my hand and greedily licked up every drop of Krew's spend before I leaned in and kissed him. The taste of our combined jizz when our tongues met only heightened my need to turn Krew around and fuck him until we couldn't move.

He chuckled, which pulled me out of my lustful thoughts. Neither of us said a word as we sat there, in the dark, in the hushed quiet of the truck cab. The only sounds were our breathing, and the smell of sex in the air.

I absorbed the serenity of the moment, knowing words would only complicate things. I then realized that Krew and I had always... flowed, like the quiet water of a stream. The same went for Regina, Krew, and I, when we used to be together. As strange as that seemed, even back then, as kids, we worked. Until we didn't.

In this moment was like the quiet before the storm. That was what I knew to be true. And I'd take every second in silence with Krew then the solitary life I'd been living.

In the peaceful interlude, so mesmerized by Krew, I savored the taste of us on my tongue. Then reality crashed down around me and the levity of what we just did sideswiped my brain.

"We can't do that again, K," I uttered, cutting off the near morsel of sadness that crept into my heart.

The blissfulness on his face disappeared in a blink. Krew's eyes pinched, before he straightened in his seat and tucked his beautiful dick back into his jeans.

What I said was for his own good. I wasn't worthy for anyone, and the sooner Krew got that through his thick head, the better. Furthermore, we had bigger issues to worry about, like the contracts on his and Regina's heads.

Krew cleared his throat. "What that Jay guy said, how bad is our situation?"

I was surprised he didn't respond to my comment about messing around again, and more than a little disappointed that Krew didn't argue with me about it.

Move on. That is what you want.

I shook off that thought and any lingering desires, and answered him. "Pretty fucking bad. But I'm going to fix this, K. I promise you. And Regi..."

Krew rubbed the back of his neck. "How in the hell is Regi messed up in this?"

"Or you, for that matter. We need to find her and figure out why someone wants you two dead. Regi has to have the answers I need to fix this shit," I say, tucking my limp dick back into my jeans. "Do you know where she might be? Where she lives?"

"No. Tonight was the first time I'd seen her—since the day I was arrested. Hell, Deck. What is going on?" Panic rose in his voice. Fear shadowed Krew's eyes, for the girl we both were once in love with. "There has to be a mistake."

"I don't get it either, but I sure as hell am going to find out." I grabbed my phone from the holder. Jay was right about one thing. Calling my handler was the only way to track down where Regina lived.

"Who are you calling?" Krew's voice went an octave higher.

"Calm down. I know a person who can get the answers we need." I said nothing else, as I tapped Sabrina's number.

"Can you trust them?"

"Yeah. She's my handler."

"Your handler?" Krew's brows rose high on his forehead. "Like she's your babysitter or something?"

"No—and you can fuck off," I growled. "Sabrina's kind of a hitman PA." I didn't go into her back ground or detailed out what she did for me.

Out of all the black hackers out there, she was the best in the business. Sabrina could track down Regina for me in a hot second. And then I'd make sure Krew and Regina were safe before I went after the fuckers who put hits out on my friends.

Chapter Nine
Regi

I turned onto my side and forced my eyelids open a slit to glare at the old clock radio on the night stand. The illuminated red numbers showed it was nearly six a.m. I wasn't going back to sleep, and even if I wanted to, my walnut-sized bladder insisted it was time to go to the bathroom.

The problem was, I didn't want to get up. I was too exhausted from that nightmarish dream—it clung to me like sticky sweat on my skin.

After another twinge of my bladder, I got up and padded down the hall to the shared bathroom. Surprisingly, Maya wasn't awake. She was the early riser between the two of us and usually monopolized the bathroom at this time of the morning. Luckily, she was still sleeping.

I sat there, peeing, but my eyes studied the bandage on my thigh. That was a reckless thing to do. I needed to keep myself in check, because I wasn't going down that dark rabbit hole again.

Since Maya still wasn't up, I took the advantage and brushed my teeth and washed my face. I'd shower later—after I worked out. I made a mental checklist of things I needed to do today. Since I had the day off, I'd do my errands this morning and then do the laundry this afternoon.

As I stepped out of the bathroom, I decided to check in on Maya since she had to be at work at ten. Her shift was only for a few hours, so maybe—when she was done, we could do laundry and mani-pedis.

I tapped on her door, and it opened a crack. To my surprise, the room was empty and her bed was made, like she'd never slept in it.

That's strange. Maya never makes her bed.

I stepped away from her door and took a sniff. If she'd already left, I'd smell the lingering aromas of toast and coffee. Two pieces of buttered toast and a cup of coffee was her usual morning breakfast. *Hmm. I don't smell anything.*

I entered the living room and froze. The apartment door was wide open, and Maya was gone. "What the hell?" I panicked, and quickly closed and locked the door.

My breaths sawed in and out of my lungs as I scanned the area, including the small kitchen, and found nothing out of place. I checked for a note on the fridge—our usual place to leave things for each other, but there wasn't one.

I pivoted back to Maya's room and checked her night stand for a clue about why she left without closing the door. She knew safety was the number one priority if she was going to live with me. I could only guess that Maya had left the apartment abruptly. But it wasn't like her to leave the apartment door open.

Baffled and slightly worried, I closed her bedroom door, went back to the living room and dropped onto the sofa.

Should I call the cops? —no. Maybe she forgot to leave me a note before she left. She could, at times, be clueless, but not about our safety—never our safety. Not after what had happened to me.

Lately though, Maya hadn't been herself, not since she started dating Jess. She'd been more distant, and we hadn't hung out for a while—other than last night.

We'd been close once, as two friends who grew up together in a small town often were. She knew my secrets and I knew hers... or so I'd thought.

"Where did you go, Maya?" I uttered to no one. I let out a breath, surrendering to the notion that this was just a fluke mishap. I'd talk to her later about it.

I got up from the sofa and made coffee. Then I whipped up some scrambled eggs, cut up an avocado, and made toast.

I'd taken a sip of my coffee and a bite of my breakfast, when a jiggling sound came from the apartment door. I paused, glanced at the clock on the wall, and assumed it was Maya.

What the... I thought Maya forgot her key. I took two steps toward the door, ready to give her hell, when it slowly opened and a meaty arm—holding a gun—extended past the threshold.

I froze for a moment, before my survival instincts kicked in and I silently flattened myself against a wall that would hide me from the intruder. I frantically looked around for a weapon, but I wasn't fast enough. The owner of that arm crept inside the apartment. The guy was massive.

Jesus. It would take a bulldozer to knock him out.

Instead of trying to find a weapon, I dropped to the floor, crawled to the pantry and crammed myself inside. Thankfully, I'd left the bifold doors open after getting out the loaf of bread. Maya had pulled apart the lower metal shelving the other day and hadn't put it back together yet. Her laziness had inadvertently created a good hiding place.

I crammed myself into the tight space. With luck on my side, the trespasser wouldn't see me.

The meathead left the front door open and I heard him stalk off toward the bedrooms. Now was my chance to close the door to the pantry. At the last second, I decided to leave it open a crack in case I could get a better look at the intruder's face, and tell the cops.

Damn it. I just realized that my phone was charging in the bedroom.

There was a quiet curse, before heavy footsteps pounded toward the kitchen. I braced myself, as I watched through the crack at the intruder closing the apartment door. He then entered the kitchen and loomed near the pantry. I held my breath and silently prayed that he wouldn't open the door and look inside. From this vantage point, I could see his ugly mug and the scar that ran across his right cheek.

He pulled a cell phone from his pants pocket and called someone.

"She's gone..." Pause. "Yeah, the roommate's gone too..." Then a longer pause. "Will do..." Pause. "Okay. We'll keep a look out." He shoved the phone back in his pocket.

Panic and fear mixed with my confusion, but I remained as still as possible and waited to see what the lug nut was going to do. I didn't wait long. He looked around the kitchen, stopped and stared at my half-eaten breakfast, and I lost the ability to breathe. I closed my eyes, trying to wash away the dizziness, when I heard the soft click of the front door.

I popped my eyes open and listened intently for more sounds. After a good five agonizing minutes, I peered through the opening and didn't see the guy. I was so sure that he'd left that I climbed out of the pantry and took a shuddering breath. While the panic in my gut settled, I shook my hands out to ease the sting from wringing them so tightly and then wiped my sweaty palms down my pajama pants.

Who was that asshole? And what does he want with me and Maya?

Something inside told me that he'd be back, and I had to get out of there. I raced to my room, exchanged my pajamas for yoga pants and a long sleeve shirt, and jammed my feet into my black Hey Dudes. Then I grabbed my backpack out of the closet and began shoving clothes and other necessities into it. I threw in my cellphone and charger, and remembered my toothbrush and toothpaste. One foot out of my bedroom and I froze midstride. The same enormous guy was standing in the hallway.

"I knew you were here, bitch," he said gruffly, an evil grin sliding across his face. He pointed the gun at me and closed the gap between us. "I told Grater this was going to be easy money."

I stumbled backward into the bedroom, tripped over the backpack I had dropped in my fright, and landed hard on my butt. The back of my head hit the floor with a thud as I crumpled. My brain rattled and stars floated across my vision.

As my eyes cleared, I saw the bastard coming at me. The meathead was so huge, he reached me in three long strides. With the gun pointed my way, he hovered close like a death wraith, ready to extinguish my life.

My heart jackhammered, and the air in my lungs all but evaporated. I was suffocating in utter terror.

"You're dead, bitch," he said with a smile.

Right as he aimed the gun at my forehead, there was a crash behind him. The meathead spun around, grunted, and took off back toward the living room.

I wasn't waiting around for that asshole to come back to kill me. I got up, grabbed my backpack, and headed to the window and the fire escape.

Grunts, curses and another crash of something drew my attention. I knew I shouldn't, but I couldn't help myself. I dropped my backpack, tiptoed down the hall and peeked around the corner. The floor lamp by the sofa was toppled over and its glass shade was broken. The only light was coming through the curtains.

A battle was going on my living room. The original meathead and another huge guy. I couldn't see this new guy's face, but he landed an exceptionally hard punch to the side of the meathead's temple.

Meathead crumpled forward and fell onto his hands and knees, but there was a gun his hand.

"Gun," I shouted. I had to warn my would-be savoir from being shot. However, the meathead turned his head and saw me in the hallway.

He grinned and aimed the gun at me. "You're dead, bitch."

I sucked in a breath, for certain I was going to die. An instant later, the meathead went face down on the floor with a bullet in the back of his head.

A scream tore from my throat as I spun around and raced to the bedroom. I slammed the door and locked it, but stumbled as I moved backward—tripping over my own feet.

When I reached the window, I tried frantically to open it. *Too late.* The bedroom door crashed open and there were two—*two!*— men looming in the doorway.

"Regi."

At first, it didn't register that they were calling my name. Then arms wrapped around my middle and I started to fight with every- thing I had.

"Damn it, Regi—it's me!"

The deep, raspy voice finally pierced my brain and I paused to look up at the face I saw last night. "Krew?"

"Yeah, it's me." His voice gentled. Krew released me, and he cupped my cheeks. "Come on, we need to get out of here."

I was so stunned and confused that I didn't realize that I was shaking my head no. "Wh-what are you doing here?" I gasped. "Are you the meathead's partner? Are you Grater... Him..." I stabbed the air repeatedly in the direction of the hallway.

"I have no idea who that was, or anybody named Grater. We're here to rescue you," Krew said with urgency. "We'll explain later."

"What? What do you mean *we?*" I shook off Krew's hand and took a step back. "That doesn't make any sense. What do you mean *rescue me?"* I squeezed myself into a corner of the room—*Brilliant move, Regi. Now you're trapped.*

I stood there, shaking and refusing to look at the man I once cared about.

"Exactly what it means." The sharp, penetrating voice had my eyes darting to the door, and every molecule of air in my lungs evaporated. The last person I expected to see was standing there.

Decker Moss. "Hello, Regina."

Then I saw black.

Regina's Diary

August 24th, 2013

Dear Diary,

This is bad, Diary. I can't explain how horrible I feel. My insides feel like they are being ripped out through my crotch and butt. My face hurts from the bruises and so does my ribs.

I can't even go to the bathroom without it hurting, without crying in pain. The bleeding finally stopped, but the agony I'm going through hasn't. I can't tell anybody what happened. Maya is the only one I can trust. She is sworn to secrecy.

This was supposed to be the best summer before my senior year—now everything has gone wrong—Dear God, I swear I can still feel him inside me. Make the misery go away.

I can still smell his sweat on me, and his nasty breath in my face. I jump at every little noise I hear, for fear he's coming after me. I cry, knowing I can't ever look Krew in the face again and not see his brother. I can't ever tell Decker, or he'd go to jail for murder.

I can't even tell my parents. It would crush them to know their only daughter wasn't clean anymore.

My father would track him down, and Dad would go to jail too.

I have to run, Diary. I can't let that jerk find me. I'd rather die before he touches me again. Maya told me I have to leave, and I agree. To stay safe, I have to run. I don't know where I'm going, but it's better than being here—near him, where he can easily find me.

Regina

Chapter Ten
Krew

"What's wrong with her? Why isn't she waking up?" Concern laced Decker's voice. He paced, keeping his distance from the bed I laid Regina on.

"I don't know, man. Maybe shock at seeing us?"

"Not possible. Maybe she hit her head." Decker stopped pacing, grabbed his bag and rifled through it until he pulled out a small box. He ripped the top open and retrieved a white tube. "It's an ammonia stick." He cracked it in half with his fingers and waved it under Regina's nose.

Regina finally stirred with a slight jerk of her head. Her eyes fluttered opened, and she looked dreamily at me. "Hmm." She smiled, closed her eyes, and snuggled against the flat pillow. "I'm still dreaming." Her words were muffled by the pillow.

"Regi." I gently stroked her cheek. "Open your eyes, sweetheart."

She scrunched her nose before her eyes popped open wide, and panic immediately took root in them. She scrambled away from me. "No—No way. This can't be."

"It's us, Regi. Deck and Krew." I raised my hands and slowly backed away from her, hoping the space eased her alarm.

"What the hell is wrong with you?" Decker's censure didn't help. He turned to me and frowned. "Maybe she did hit her head, and that's why she doesn't recognize us."

"Regi, you're safe with us." I infused calm into my voice, but she kept shaking her head.

"You killed that guy," Regina said accusingly, glaring at Decker. She turned her gaze from him and looked around the room. "And why did you bring me to this disgusting place?"

"Regi—" I began to say before she cut me off with a gasp.

"I'm not doing anything with you two—I have to leave—I have work tomorrow." Her frenzied words and what she implied was like a hard slap to the face.

Decker snorted, as an angry sneer sliced his lips downward. "Get over yourself, princess. We brought you here because you and Krew are in trouble. There are killers after you both." His verbal hit was a bullseye.

Regina stilled, her eyes going unbelievably wide while her parted lips slammed shut. She began to tremble. "I have to get out of here," she murmured as tears trailed down her cheeks.

She stared at the motel room door, and then rolled off the bed and ran for it.

"I don't think so." Decker stepped in her path, blocking the door. "You can't leave."

"Get out of my way," she screeched in his face as she reached around him for the doorknob. But Decker caught Regina around her middle and hauled her up off her feet. "Calm down, hellcat."

"Don't fucking call me that." Regina scratched and tried to bite his arm.

"Jesus Christ." Decker shook her roughly. "I'm going to knock you out if you don't stop scratching and biting me."

Regina went slack in his hold. She dropped her head forward, and went silent.

Decker sat her down on the bed, and the moment he stepped back, Regina scooted toward the headboard. She shook uncontrollably and I knew we wouldn't be able to reason with her until she calmed down. It wasn't like her to react to us in this manner. Then again, it had been years since she had seen us and someone tried to kill her this morning.

"Regina, please—"

That's not my name anymore," she screeched.

"Not your name?" Decker countered with equal ferocity. "Then what the fuck is it?"

"It's Regi—Regi Martin," she said, but she still wasn't looking at us.

"Okay, Regi... There's things Decker needs to explain," I pleaded, trying to coax her to look at me.

"Regi," Decker scoffed and shook his head. "She's not going to listen."

"Try," I demanded, glaring back at Decker.

Decker clenched his teeth and turned his focus on Regina. "Someone put out kill contracts on you and Krew. That asshole back at your apartment—he was a killer trying to collect on the contract out on you."

"That's fucked up, you know that?" I spat, before turning back to Regina. "Regi."

She dipped her chin down to her chest, her shoulders folded in and her arms wrapped tightly around herself. "I have a life—a good job. You're going to get me fired," she whimpered before she tipped over onto her side and curled up into a fetal position.

"That's what I'm trying to tell you. You can't go home," Decker railed.

"I *want* to go home." She sounded illogical, completely ignoring his warning.

Didn't she understand the enormity of the situation? Losing her job was the least of her problems, not when there were hired killers out there searching for us.

In the past, whenever she was upset, ice cream would do the trick. I doubted a sweet treat was going to work this time. I had never seen her this distraught before.

Decker bent, bringing himself eye level with Regina's partially covered face. "Look at me, Regi," he gruffly ordered.

I didn't like his terse tone, but it worked. She lifted her head and stared at Decker with watery, red-rimmed eyes.

I lowered myself until I was also eye level with Regina's face. Pain carved through my heart at the abject fear blooming in her brown depths. What made her so fearful of us—of me? I had to know.

"Reg..." Her name died on Decker's lips as she quickly scuttled back against the headboard again like we were lepers.

"Don't touch me," she hissed.

"Why are you being this way?" Decker demanded in outrage. Frustration creased his brows. He climbed onto the bed, his face inches from hers. "What the fuck's wrong with you?"

Regina jumped off the mattress and raced into the bathroom, slamming the door. The click of the lock was like the cock of a gun.

"What the hell, Deck. Can't you see she's scared?"

"Scared? Of us? We never gave her any reason to be scared." The truth of those words hit me as soon as Decker had spoken them.

"I know." I dropped onto the bed, feeling lost. Out of all people in this world, I wanted to reconnect with Decker and Regina. Even if it was only for friendship. I had trusted them back then and my gut told me I still could—even if Decker was a hitman.

God, I had missed Regina so damn much with every part of my being. Even though she never contacted me—not once—not while I was in prison, I had plans for us when I got out. But when I was released, I learned that she disappeared soon after I was arrested. Not even Maya knew where she was.

At first, I wanted to track her down, hold her, and tell her that my love had never died. However, something in my gut told me that expressing the truth about my feelings wouldn't help, and I was right. Even though I still didn't know why she ran all those years ago, I realized there were deep wounds inside Regina—wounds I couldn't see.

"We haven't seen her in all these years and suddenly she's acting like we physically hurt her," Decker growled.

"I don't fucking know," I snarled back. "Maybe she needs time."

"You might not want to push, but I *need* to. We don't have time to waste, and I'm going to find out why she's acting so strange toward us."

"Christ, Deck, someone—I think the guy named Grater, is who tried to kill her this morning."

"I know Grater. The guy I put a bullet in wasn't him," Decker said with a frown. He stalked to the bathroom and pounded on the door. "If you don't get your ass out here, Regi, then I'm coming in after you."

"Jesus, cut her some slack," I rumbled out, reaching his side. "Let me talk to her, Deck. You're too hotheaded right now. Take a walk."

"Fuck. We don't have time for this shit." Decker glared at the bathroom door, turned and tore out of the motel room, slamming the door.

Now it was up to me to soothe a whimpering Regina, hiding in the bathroom.

I swallowed the pain bubbling up in my chest, took a calming breath, and carefully turned the knob. The door opened easily. What a surprise, the lock didn't work. Slowly, I widened the door, until I saw Regina in the tub, curled up, her eyes filled with wariness.

"Can I come in?" I asked, standing at the threshold. I didn't step into the small space because I didn't want to add to her anxiety.

Regina was trembling, smashed against the farthest side of the tub, her arms wound tight around her legs. She dropped her gaze to her knees and a soft, barely audible *no* came through. That one word cut me even deeper than any before. She was afraid of me.

I dropped my ass down in the doorway, my attention never leaving her face.

She didn't move, or say anything else. Neither did I. We just sat there in the quiet.

I sat there in silence, unmoving for so long that a dull ache settled into my tailbone. When I got up, I caught her flinch. Her negative reaction to me only added to the pain ripping at my heart.

Did someone hurt her? If so, I want to know who.

Nevertheless, I refrained from asking.

I walked away, leaving the bathroom door open. I glanced out the grimy window, trying to spot Decker, but he was nowhere in sight. I figured he either went down to his truck or took a walk to clear his anger. Either way, I hoped he could get his rage in check, because we needed him to get us out of this insane mess we'd been thrust into.

A gut-wrenching sob echoed from the bathroom and had me rushing to Regina. She trembled violently. I didn't care if she hated me; I still loved her. Without hesitation, I reached into the tub and scooped her up. I climbed in, managed to contort my big, bulky frame until I sank back down, and cradled her in my arms.

Rocking back and forth, I murmured to her all the wonderful things we used to talk about when we were kids. I refused to let her go—even when she struggled to get out of my arms. It was a futile effort on her part—I was much stronger and more determined. She eventually quieted down, even though her tears didn't stop flowing.

Decker appeared in the doorway. "Is everything alright?" All of his bravado and anger were gone. Or tucked away.

"For now." I stared up at my best friend, my own eyes filled with unshed tears. I had never seen our girl so broken before. She'd always had a sweet disposition and loads of self-confidence, and it killed me to see her folded in on herself.

I was ready to take on the world, just to make her smile.

"Give her to me," Decker said.

"Don't yell at her," I quietly demanded.

"I won't," he replied softly, with his arms out.

I reluctantly passed Regina to him. She didn't protest. He left the bathroom and headed to the bed. He laid her down in the center of the full-size mattress and spooned himself against her back. Decker pointed to the other side of her, silently telling me to lay down.

At first, I wasn't sure if I should. Deciding, I climbed onto the bed and we sandwiched Regina between us like we used to when we were kids, whenever she had been upset, especially pertaining to her mother. That last summer at the Honey Pot was the worst.

Her breaths fanned my neck, which, in an odd way, eased my worries. I kept my left arm at my side, and watched her.

Decker gently stroked her short dark brown hair. "I miss the blond," he whispered, and Regina stiffened like a board between us.

"It doesn't matter what color hair she has, our Regi is still beautiful," I countered, hoping she'd relax, but she neither moved nor spoke.

Regina's eyes closed, her breathing evened out, and her clenched fists eventually relaxed.

How ironic, we were right back to where we were, before all hell had broken into our lives more than a decade ago.

I lifted my head and glanced across the bed, and met Decker's eyes. With unspoken understanding, I slowly slid off the mattress and so did he.

Once I covered Regina with the blanket from the other bed, I followed Decker outside and quietly closed the door.

"Something happened to her, I know it," Decker grated out. "And we need to find out what."

I glanced at Decker as he stared at the early morning sky. The profile of his handsome face hadn't changed much since he was young. Although the fine lines etched in the corners of his eyes made him look dangerous, I supposed that came from life as a hitman.

I trusted no one else but Decker Moss with my life—with Regina's too.

He turned to me, the harsh slant of his sexy mouth softened. "You agree?"

"Yeah," I said easily, but I dreaded what we were about to uncover. From the way Regina had rejected us, it had to be bad.

Chapter Eleven
Decker

"I need to make some calls—one to my handler. And since you're still living back at home, why not call your dad? He might know what's happened to Regi since that fucked up day with Teke," I suggested.

Krew shook his head. "Dad's useless. Trust me. After I got out of prison, I looked for her. All he told me was that she ran away, and her parents didn't bother lifting a finger to find her."

"You keep saying jail—you mean juvie," I corrected, watching as Krew's face shut down.

"No. I mean prison. Specifically, Chillicothe Correctional Institute," he bit out through clenched teeth.

"That's not right—"

"What's not right is you telling me what happened when you weren't even there." Krew turned his back to me. His shoulders slumped, as though a two-ton weight had dropped on them.

Slack jawed, my mind fought to understand what had happened to Krew. When he mentioned jail earlier, too much shit was happening around us at the time for it to sink into in my skull. I'd just assumed he meant juvie. But Chillicothe?

It might be a medium security prison, yet something had happened inside there for Krew to be tight-lipped about his time.

My heart revolted against this knowledge. Those demoralizing pricks had put Krew in with convicted felons doing hard time. And for what? He'd only been trying to do the right thing and not rat out his brother. Instead, he'd marginalized his own innocence and gone down for the theft of that damn car.

I wanted to reach for Krew, pull him into my arms, but pity and remorse seemed to be the last things he needed right now from me. "Tell me what happened."

"Some other time. Right now, we need to stop the killers from coming after us." Krew dismissed me like I was a gnat. He went back into the motel room, and quietly shut the door.

I stood there for a long moment, mentally ticking off the minutes until I could put a bullet in Teke's brain and then bury his sorry ass in a shallow grave as payment for what he did to his own brother. I pulled out a cigarette, needing the nicotine, lit it and took out my cell phone.

"Yo, bossman," Sabrina chimed in.

"You're not funny," I grated out, then glanced at the closed door of the motel room. I took the metal stairs down to the parking lot. "What do you have for me?"

"Word's out that you're in the game, and you're not gonna be happy about the players involved," she said, as rapid tapping echoed from her end. There was no doubt Sabrina was digging deep into the search for whoever put out the contracts on Krew and Regina.

"Who are the players and who threw my people under the bus —I want to know specifics. Those are the three things I need to know," I demanded, climbing into my truck and leave the door open. I glanced up at our room and saw an edge of the closed curtains move.

"Hold on. I text you the list of who the heavy hitters are, but…" More frantic tapping on reached my ears. "Shit, this doesn't make sense," Sabrina muttered.

"What doesn't?" I dragged in a deep inhale from the cigarette and let the smoke fill my lungs before I released it into the chilly air.

"From the information you gave me on your friends, I don't understand why these two are targeted. They grew up together—you already know that. What I'm not seeing is any connection between them for at least ten years. There's nothing on the radar that's bad. There's no connection to any criminal organizations. They aren't friends with any scumbags who need their faces rearranged."

"That doesn't give me much, Sabrina," I huffed out, and climbed into my truck.

"Hold on bossman—"

"Will you stop calling me that?" I slammed my fist down on the dash, as frustration fueled the need to do some damage.

"Chill. Ever think about alternatives to nicotine or coffee? Caf—"

"Sabrina," I hissed in warning.

"Sor-ry. Okay, I… wait." More vigorous tapping met my ears. "This doesn't make sense."

"You already said that." I barely refrained from yelling at the infuriating woman.

"You're not understanding me. I just pulled up the original contracts again, making sure I got all the details correct, and there are new images attached, replacing the ones from before. I'm sending you those photos now."

My phone pinged and I tapped on the screen. "Is someone messing with us?" I slid my fingers up and opened the images Sabrina sent me.

"It looks like it. The original photos and names attached to the contracts matched the images of your friends that you sent me earlier. These new photos are now attached to *those* contracts, but the names remain the same. The men look nothing alike. But the female... she looks almost exact to your Regina."

I blew out an irritated breath. "The photos are grainy. I can't decipher the images," I admitted, trying to enlarge the pictures, but the faces blurred even more. "Who am I looking at?"

"Give me a second. I'm going to try to clear the images up."

"I'm racking my brain over this. How can anyone change a contract kill that's been out for over twelve hours? And why would anyone change the headshots—no pun attended—on a contract, but not the names?" I took another deep inhale, wishing for answers.

"Whoever took out the original contracts fucked up royally and tried to correct it, or someone is fucking with us. It looks like—what the hell—wait a second." Fast clicks over on Sabrina's end had me grinding my teeth while I impatiently waited for her explanation.

"I don't have all damn day," I grated out.

"Two more contracts just came out, and you won't believe who they are for."

"Tell me," I demanded and closed the door. More cars entered the parking lot and parked around my truck. The last one was a white work van, but I paid them no mind. My eyes trailed back to what Sabrina was saying.

"Same exact details, but different names. Same images as the grainy ones I just sent you. And these marks do have connections to Kane Maxwell."

"Who are they?" I was so pissed that it hadn't dawned on me until now that there were four contracts on the table.

"The female's name on the second set of contracts is Maya Darvy—"

"Fuck me," I barked. I Hers was the last name I expected to hear.

"Damn it, I'm losing my frickin' touch," Sabrina rumbled in frustration. "The new mark has the same address as your girl—shit. And, wait for it... the bitch is dating Jess Duncan. He's the other new mark. This Jess Duncan is—well, *was* connected to Kane, and his not-so clean associates. Frickin' A, I need to fire myself."

I wanted to throw my phone through the windshield. Instead, I gripped it tight and took another drag on my cigarette to calm my temper. "Where's Maya and Jess now?" I clipped, as rage tipped into my bloodstream. Never would I have guessed that Regina's best friend from school was a part of all this. I hadn't trusted her back then because she was jealous of Regina, but our girl had never seen Maya in the same light as Krew and I had.

Whenever Regina wasn't around, Maya had offered herself up to me and Krew—especially to Krew. Her desperation to get into my guy's pant was nearing stalkerish. And every one of Maya's advances had been rejected with prejudice.

"I'm sending you those new contracts," Sabrina said, drawing me out of the past. I opened the jpeg, and immediately recognized the guy's face. He had been standing next to Kane at the fight. And Sabrina was correct when she said that Jess bore no similarity to Krew.

With Maya's short hair, her height and build, it was uncanny how much she resembled Regina. Right down to the color of her brown hair.

"Give me today and I'll track her and that Jess guy down, along with who's after yours," Sabrina promised before all I heard was dead air. Merrick complained once that she never said goodbye, Sabrina just hung up on him—and I was beginning to see his point of irritation.

I dropped the phone in my lap and took the last drag of the cigarette and tossed it out the window.

I couldn't wrap my mind around the idea that Maya—Regina's

best friend, was involved. The way she and Regina looked alike... "Shit." *Was that done on purpose?*

Then I remembered Regina at the fight. The woman next to her...

"Fucking hell." I threw my head back, banging it on the headrest, pissed at my own lack of focus.

My sole attention had been on my girl, that Maya wasn't even in the periphery. I had blinders on before I shifted my sights on killing Kane.

Frustration cut through me and my concentration had been off from the moment I'd caught sight of Krew and Regina at the fight. Though, not enough to separate myself from them.

The guy... Jess—he was standing next to Kane in the ring. They must have been partners—and if that was true, then why hadn't there been a a contract on Jess's head at the same time as Kane's? I could have done a two for one.

Where did Maya fit into all of this? And now there were four kill contracts out—one for Maya, one for Jess, one for Regina with Maya's grainy picture, and one for Krew with a crappy image of Jess.

What. A. Clusterfuck.

It seemed that the contracts on Regina and Krew might have been a case of mistaken identity, or someone had been purposefully messing with the contracts, like Sabrina suggested. Nothing mattered at this point. Because as long as the contracts were out there, some hitman would chase the pot. And I was going to make damn sure not one bullet harmed either Krew or Regina.

With a last drag from the cigarette, I lowered the window and flicked it out. As I was raising up the glass, I caught sight of the white van. It was parked two spaces down from me. The more I stared at the vehicle; there were similar scratch marks and dents on the driver's side of the van.

It looked like the *exactly* like one that sat in front of Regina's apartment building this morning.

From my vantage point, I could see that the engine was running, and the guy in the driver's seat was fixed on the second floor.

I snagged my phone and texted Krew to stay away from the window. Then I slowly reached for my glove box and retrieved my Ruger and silencer. This was a shitty area, and the sounds of gunshots would not be uncommon, but I didn't want to attract anyone's attention. Especially unwanted witnesses. Or the cops.

When the driver looked down, I carefully slipped out of the truck, left the door ajar, and dropped to a crouch position. I got to my truck's taillight and glanced around, making sure nobody was nearby.

Cleared to go, I dashed to the back of the van. Surprising the fucker was my goal, since he was on the driver's side and in case he had a gun ready. I had no room for error.

If it was me, I'd have the doors locked—not every hitter thought like I did, though. If I had to, I'd shoot through the glass.

After I took a slow even inhale, screwed on the silencer, and slinked to the passenger side. I didn't hesitate—I reached for the handle and yanked the door open.

Luck was on my side because the idiot hadn't locked the doors. The driver snapped his head in my direction and audibly gasped.

"Surprise, dumbass." I aimed my gun at his head. "Oh, no, you don't. Keep your hands where I can see them, unless you want to find out just how fast I can splatter your brain all over the window."

The hitman's gun was on his lap. And from the fury boiling in his pale blue eyes, the hitman wasn't about to listen.

"Final warning," I said evenly, giving no clue to how trigger happy I was feeling in that moment.

He must have seen that I wouldn't give two shits about putting a bullet in his brain. He slowly raised his hands and sneered, "What do you want?"

"Just warning you that you're going after the wrong people. Those two up there aren't the ones you're looking for. I just confirmed it with my handler. So if you want to stay alive, I suggest you leave."

One side of his lip curled up and the coldness in his eyes revealed everything I needed to know. He didn't believe me. In a flash, he reached for the gun in his lap. He was fast, but not faster than me.

I pulled the trigger, nailing him in the right eye. On impact, the back of his head bounced against the driver's side window and he slumped over. Blood oozed from the now-hollowed-out orifice, and his brain matter dripped down the cracked glass.

I waited a moment, listening intently for the sounds of any commotion around us. There was nothing except for normal parking lot noise.

I climbed into the van—keeping the gun pointed at his head, I checked his pockets for identification. I pulled his wallet from his coat pocket—a sure sign of his inexperience, and glanced at the driver's license. "Thomas J. Malone," I uttered in a snort before shoving the wallet back in my pocket.

I then manipulated the dead man's hand to turn off the van and I climbed out. Using my shirt, I manually engaged all the door locks and wiped my prints off the door handle.

This place wasn't safe anymore. Eventually someone would discover the dead body in the van and they'd call the cops and report it.

I had to get Regina and Krew out of here before another killer showed up. Though, that was the simple part. Telling them about Maya's involvement, and the screwed-up contracts wasn't going to be easily explained.

There was no clear-cut way to break the news to them gently. I was pretty sure Krew would take it well. But Regina? Based on her reactions so far, she wouldn't handle it well.

I returned my gun to the glove box, locked the truck, and rushed back up to the room with only one purpose, to get my friends out of there. Instead, I ended up walking into chaos, with Regina and Krew screaming at each other.

Chapter Twelve
Regi

I slowly opened my eyes, and took in the warmth and quiet that surrounded me. Then memories snapped into place, destroying the peace and throwing everything off-kilter. I sat up straight and looked around as panic lodged in my chest.

Through the semi-darkness of the room, my eyes sliced to the window's closed curtains, then to the chair adjacent to the bed. I rubbed my eyes to clear away the remaining fuzziness and froze. Someone sat there. It was too dark to see their face, and the silhouette was so still, I swore it was a ghost. Except, I didn't believe in apparitions.

A spike of fear laced with panic sliced through me, as I swallowed the hard lump that lodged in my throat.

Then I noted the shaved head. "Krew?" I unsteadily whispered his name, almost afraid that the shadow would answer back *no*.

"It's me, Krew." He turned in the chair and moved the curtains a bit to let in a little light.

The brightness from the window temporarily blinded me.

He shifted in the seat, and I got a glimpse of his right eye. He had said he was Krew, but the amber... It reminded me of *him*.

Krew's brother. And I quickly looked away and my entire body froze as shame slid into my belly like a poisonous snake.

"Regi." He reached out a hand. "Don't be afraid."

I flinched away, not ready for his touch. "Don't come any closer," I choked out, trying to reclaim the oxygen that escaped from my lungs.

"What can I do?" Panic coated Krew's tone.

"I'm... okay." *Liar.* I kept repeating to myself that this was Krew. *He* would never hurt me. And yet, I couldn't move as tears blurred my vision.

Breathe, damn it.

I finally sucked in a stuttered breath, and gathered my courage to glance at Krew once more. Hurt and dejection marred his sculpted face, and that cut me to my soul. As much as I wanted to reach for him, to soothe the wound I had caused—for him to soothe me, I couldn't move.

Krew shifted, and I flinched again. "Oh, Regi—why are you afraid of me?" He got off the chair, dropped to one knee and leaned on the edge of the bed. "I won't hurt you."

I didn't want to feel this way about Krew—really, I didn't. Yet, my brain couldn't separate him from Teke, even though the brothers didn't look anything alike.

"I'm not." I assured him. But the longer I sat there, the more horrific memories from that terrible day rushed back, contaminating the present. The boy I knew—who was a man now, didn't know what had happened after I ran from the vehicle Teke had stolen.

Even though it had been years, the trauma of that night wasn't something I wanted to relive again. Ever.

In my head, I wanted to keep that moment locked up tight. I couldn't imagine how Krew would react if he found out what his brother had done to me. How Teke had destroyed me. He had ripped my soul apart at the same time as my body.

Since then, my life had been nothing except loose, tattered threads, which I had slowly woven back together. One thread at a time.

I had no doubt that Teke kept what he did to me to himself. If Krew had found out, I wouldn't have seen him at the fight, standing next to his brother.

But this was Krew—my Krew. *He* had never done anything wrong. I shouldn't be afraid of him touching me.

"I missed you, Regi. So damn much," he choked out, and bent his head down like he was avoiding my eyes. That hurt. Yet, my fear and reluctance were hurting him, too.

Gathering what courage I could muster, I tentatively reached out and touched his shaved head. "I missed you, too—I swear I did," I admitted earnestly. My heart ached from my admission. I'd held those words close to my chest for so long, never uttering them to another living soul.

"Did?" he questioned. He raised his head and I saw the wetness that filled his handsome eyes. "I don't understand."

"I can't do this, Krew. I can't—" I dropped my hand to my side and shook my head, avoiding his intense gaze. Those eyes haunted me in my dreams. "It's been years, Krew. We," I gestured between us, "are the past, and I need to keep it that way."

Krew winced as though I had struck him. He stood and stepped back as he wiped a runaway tear. "I don't understand. It has been years since I saw you—but my feelings never changed. After I... Why did you leave Elida? Ghost me? Us?"

"I can't explain why." My throat strained at the admission. I needed space to breathe—to think clearly, so I climbed off the bed. The desire to touch him again was only scrambling my brain. Especially after I'd hardwired myself to accept that I'd never see him or Decker again.

He looked me straight in the eyes. "I need more than that, Regi.

You owe me an explanation about why you never contacted me. Why you never answered my calls. Or any of my letters."

Agony ripped through me. Krew wanted answers I couldn't give him. I couldn't wipe my tears away fast enough. "I left town right after... I couldn't stay in that town any longer. I'm sorry that I didn't contact you."

"Me too," he uttered and turned away.

"I'm a different person now, Krew. I'm not that naive little girl you knew back then. I moved on with my life." The lie slipped past my tongue so easily, that *I* even believed what I was saying.

"I don't believe you," Krew raised his voice, which matched his rigid form.

"You have no choice, Krew" I shouted. "You have no choice."

The door abruptly swung open, and Decker strode inside. "What the hell is going on in here? I could hear you two outside."

"Decker," I breathed in a gasp.

"What's going on, Regi?" Decker asked with a frown, as his eyes bounced between Krew and me.

"Regi doesn't want nothing to do with us," Krew said, his voice lacking the conviction it had moments before.

"I didn't say that." My emotions were spinning out of control, especially around these two men. "I want to leave—that's all. I have a life. A job," I grated out, folding my arms across my chest like some petulant child, then I realized I didn't have a bra on. I glanced at the end of the bed and saw my backpack.

I reached for it, but Decker nabbed it first. "You can't leave, Regi. Not without us."

"What the hell—you can't keep me here against my will." I cursed. The bottle I'd long ago poured my anger into uncorked, and everything erupted out of me like a geyser. "I hate you both. For leaving me. For everything afterward. You have no right holding me here against my will. I have my own life and don't want you two in it. Do you understand that?"

Every hateful word that spilled out of my mouth had Krew flinching back, and there was rage in Decker's eyes. I didn't care. I needed to get away from them. They were a constant reminder of what had happened to me. The rape had stolen these men—and the life I could have had with them, from me.

"I can't *do* this anymore." My anger spent; I began to bawl. Great, heaving, ugly sobs. I stood there, chin to my chest, and cried to the point where I could hardly breathe. Fat tears dripped down my chin onto the nasty gray carpet.

I was a mess. I never cried so much—so hard, in my life. Well, not in a long while anyway. The walls I had constructed to protect myself had all but crumbled to dust the moment they reentered my life.

I felt so out of control that I didn't know what to do. These two men had ripped giant holes in all of my safety nets. I began to mentally curl in on myself and reach for that dark space in my head again.

Then Krew was there, his beefy arms wrapped around me. With one of his massive hands, he cupped the back of my head and held my snotty face nestled against his muscular chest. His familiar scent—musk and sweat, comforted me in ways I wasn't expecting. Even though I didn't want to accept his comfort, I still nuzzled in against him.

I didn't deserve it—not after the shit I had just spewed at him— at both of them. But I was drowning in so much desperation that I didn't see the full scope of what I was doing and fiercely grasped onto Krew like he was a lifeline, until it was too late and I was a goner.

There was heat at my back. *Decker.*

Decker crowded my back. His solid presence, along with Krew's, created a sense of safety I hadn't felt in such a long time. The surge of emotions I'd buried so deep burst from my chest, and made my throat hurt.

Decker's face nestled into the crook of my neck. Silent, and waiting. A memory I had forgotten surfaced. He'd told me once, years ago, that being nestled next to both me and Krew was one of his favorite places to be.

With their arms around me, it was just us, in the quiet solitude of the dingy motel room. The three of us, together again. I wanted to capture the moment, jar it up tight and put it away for those days in the future that I knew were going to be lonely and dark. Then I'd pull it back out and bask in the memory of this time.

The bubble popped when a pinprick of humiliation reminded me that I wasn't whole. That the damage done to me, the defeat I kept battling in my head—all of it was a giant, mangled-up mess. I wasn't the good girl they remembered me to be. Not anymore.

No matter how hard I tried to move forward in my life, the damage to my psyche—my soul, never fully healed. My heart had been permanently shredded into pieces, and no amount of stitching was going to mend it. The scars were too deep.

As I drowned in the quicksand of self-pity, I reminded myself that Krew and Decker deserved someone whole—and that wasn't me. I could never give myself fully to them.

"Let it out," Krew whispered to me in his comforting way. How could he be so nice to me when I've been such a bitch to him?

"I'm a mess," I croaked, wanting to push them away. Instead, I clung to them both like some limpet, desperate for their touch. They were the air I needed to breathe into my lungs to survive.

Giving false hope wasn't fair to them or to me. Maybe this *was* the time to come clean. To tell them what Teke had done to me.

"We're here," Decker affirmed with a tone that was slightly harsher—yet, somehow just as soothing as Krew's soft, loving words. "We're not going anywhere without you."

Decker had no clue how his honesty affected me. Unfortunately, his unconditional support made me cry even more.

The guys let me have my moment, again. And I appreciated that.

I finally calmed down and raised my head, swiping the wetness from my cheeks.

Krew walked away, and then came back with a large wad of toilet paper in his hand. "Here." He handed it to me.

"Thanks," I uttered, half chuckling and half still crying. Krew's sweetness continued to unravel my resolve to keep quiet about Teke.

The moment I locked eyes on Krew, I knew there was no way of hiding the past. Those eyes were always going to haunt me. The truth had to come out. One way or another, these men had to know what happened. At least to clear my conscience.

"Better?" Krew asked, and my heart lightened at seeing a glimpse of his smile.

"I'm sorry for being a raging shrew. It's just that..." I blew out a breath, and tried to ease the thrashing in my chest.

You can do this, Regi. You can tell them.

"Don't say sorry. I know it's a lot to take in," Krew said sweetly—so sweetly that I had to look away from his attention.

God, he thought I was talking about our current situation. If only that was *all* of it.

I dropped my head. "There are some things..." I couldn't finish. The truth was a giant burr stuck in my throat. I pulled away from both men, hoping the distance would give me clarity and the strength to confess.

"What?" Krew stood there, didn't move an inch while his voice was coated with concern.

Even though Decker's scrutiny was slightly unnerving, I swallowed down the hesitation, ready to tell them everything. I opened my mouth, but nothing came out.

Krew was suddenly in my space and kissed my forehead.

"Whatever it is, we're here to listen." Then his lips touched my temple.

I clutched the wad of toilet paper to my chest as the swell of emotion swept through my body. *I* used to kiss their foreheads when they were hurt or upset. It was an innocent action back then. Now...

The tentative touches of his lips on my skin made a bloom of desire spread like wildfire throughout my body, and a fluttery pulse started between my legs. I couldn't explain why his kiss affected me, but I wasn't going to ponder on it.

"Thank you," I said with a hitch in my breath.

"Whenever you want to talk about it, we're here," Decker added, as he stood next to Krew.

With utmost gentleness, Decker brushed my bangs out of my eyes. But his predatory gaze made my breath hitch in reaction. Krew had a similar look, just less wolfish. And that was my undoing.

The connection I was feeling with these men temporarily exorcised the demons out of me. Every reason to run disintegrated to dust. The yearning I thought I had lost years ago glowed bright, becoming a pyre of need and desperation the likes of which I had never experienced in my life.

Instead of telling them the truth about Teke, I stepped into them, cupped the back of Krew's neck, and looked into Decker's azure eyes. I pulled Decker down for a kiss, but he stiffened at my touch. I wasn't going to be deterred, though. I needed this from him and from Krew. Even if it was only for a short while.

I pressed my mouth gently against his until Decker opened for me. He tasted of cigarettes, which startled me, since I didn't remember him smoking when we were young. It was a potent reminder that, although he was still Decker, he was a man now, not a boy. And this man's tongue was dueling with mine in a frantic dance for dominance.

Then I felt another set of lips on my cheek. *Krew.*

I closed my eyes as Decker pulled away and Krew took over. His lips were warm, gentler than Decker's, and his tongue wasn't as demanding.

The last time I'd kissed each of them was when I turned sixteen —a light peck on their lips. Krew and Decker had shared open-mouth kisses, but they hadn't been comfortable with the idea of me joining in on their kisses.

I was too young, they had said, and we three had agreed to wait. So, we made a pact that I had to be of legal age. And I was okay with that at the time.

Now?

My intentions weren't innocent. Our kisses had awakened a torrent of longing within me that spun my desire into a demand of want. A greedy need that turned carnal. They were the only ones who could cast away the darkness that had been plaguing me for years.

Krew, now even taller, tatted up, and bulky with muscles, was my gentle giant. Decker, on the other hand, was all angles and hard lines, especially his toned, sinewy body. The contrast between these men, and their kisses, had me ravenous for more of their mouths—their touches.

I craved them in ways that didn't make sense to me, but they felt right. It was like I'd been empty for so long that my fear of intimacy didn't matter. My ravenous need to be with Krew and Decker outweighed the rising panic coursing through my body.

What was that saying? When in Rome? Okay, maybe that didn't fit this scenario. Still, I refused to give up because I was scared shitless. I shouldn't—couldn't turn away because it had been my dream to be with these men since I learned what sex was. I'd take what they were offering and then I'd run. At least I would have their taste, their touch, and the feel of their bodies imprinted on my memory.

Decker's overwhelming presence was intense. As his mouth deepened the kiss and his hands roamed my body as though he owned it, I still needed more.

I shivered, knowing Krew had stepped back and was watching us like some voyeur. The idea of Krew touching himself as he observed Decker devouring me shot another bolt of lust straight through my veins and down to my pulsating clit.

A pleasured pain exploded from my breasts as Decker pinched my already tight buds through the fabric of my t-shirt, bringing me into the present.

The part of my brain still capable of thought wondered why I wasn't afraid of what he was doing to me. Maybe I was just over-whelmed by lust—drowning in Decker's desire, determined to ride this wave of pleasure all the way to the end.

Soon Decker's touch wasn't enough. I hungered for both men's hands on me, like I'd dreamt about for years.

If my mother could see me now, she'd call me a deviant—a whore, for wanting two men. But in this moment, I didn't care.

I reached out for Krew, and he came back to us. He anchored himself behind me while Decker ran his fingers through my hair, gripped it tight and angled my head so that my lips were close to Krew's.

"Kiss her," Decker ordered.

Krew didn't give me a moment to breathe. He obeyed immediately, engulfing my mouth with so much passion, I almost suffocated in his longing. And I kissed him right back with equal fervor.

He then pulled back, his eyes on Decker now, equally hungry and desperate. I knew that look all too well. I remembered how Krew had looked at him. The intensity of their stares was nuclear.

Decker's pupils were blown as he leaned into Krew and captured his mouth. Their kiss was frantic and wanton, all tongues and teeth, like they were about to take a bite out of each other.

Sandwiched between Krew and Decker, I couldn't imagine

being anywhere else in this moment. Their connection ramped up my desire. And seeing these two men loving on each other, picturing them loving on me, filled me up with so much joy that I almost wept.

"I need to taste you," Decker demanded before I felt his hand sliding down the front of my yoga pants. His fingers maneuvered behind the tight waist band until he was inside my underwear.

Decker didn't hesitate and dragged his digits across my throbbing clit until he drove two of them inside me.

I gasped from the intrusion, and waited a second for the familiar panic to resurface… But it didn't and the pleasured pain grew into an inferno of desire I had never experienced in my life. Not even my vibrator on the highest setting got me to this level of want.

"Krew, you have to feel her. She so soft and wet for us." Decker dipped his fingers deeper into me and then pulled them out. He brought his hand to his nose and sniffed. "Fuck, Princess you smell good. Now how do you taste?"

He stuck his fingers into his mouth and groaned, while Krew stood still behind me like he was waiting for his turn.

"You want to taste her—don't you?" Decker asked Krew as he delved back into my pants, drove his fingers inside me and pumped in and out several times. I was about to come.

"Decker," I panted out.

"Don't come," he commanded before he pulled out and raised his hand to Krew. "Taste her—suck all her juices off my fingers."

Krew lowered his mouth onto Decker's fingers until his lips swallowed them down to the third knuckles before pulling back. "So sweet," he whispered in my ear.

"Give me your mouth." Decker clasped the back of Krew's neck and he lowered his head until their lips collided.

I couldn't do anything but watch these two men hungrily devour each other.

Then Decker pulled back and looked down at me. "Say yes to *us*, Regi."

The window shattered, and Decker swiftly wrenched Krew and me down to the floor. "Get to the bathroom," he growled, and scuttled us backwards.

"What the hell was that?" I whispered-screeched in outrage as I climbed into the tub, shaking badly.

"Don't fucking move from here." Decker completely ignored my question, then took off, slammed the bathroom door, and left me in there with Krew.

"Christ," Krew spat as he turned to me. "Are you okay? Do you have any glass on you?"

"A few scratches on my feet, I think. Otherwise, I'm not hurt." I admitted. "Are you alright?"

"I'm fine."

"What *was* that, Krew?" I tucked my legs tighter to my chest.

"I think that was bullets." He rubbed the back of his neck. "I hope Decker..."

My eyes widened. "Then why in the hell did Decker run out there? Is he fucking crazy?" My voice rose, until I looked into Krew's hardened gaze, and I quickly shut up.

"Because out of the three of us, he's the only one that can find out who's trying to kill us—Jesus, Regi—we tried to tell you," he said with irritation.

Bile rose quickly in the back of my throat, but I swallowed it down. "So, what you guys were saying earlier is true? There are people out there who are after us?"

"Not people, Regi—killers. Someone put a hit out on us both. Who did you think was in your apartment? Decker told you the truth. That guy was a hitman."

"You aren't lying."

"No," Krew said with a slow shake of his head.

"Why? Who would do that to us—to me? I'm a nobody," I

shakily insisted, not wanting to believe what Krew was telling me. All the wonderful feelings from moments ago—poof. Incinerated until only ashes remained, leaving behind fear and outrage in its place.

Krew stretched out a hand and took hold of mine. My eyes dropped to the tattoos running up his arm, to where his t-shirt sleeve hid the rest of the ink. "I don't know," he said quietly. "But Decker knows people. He said he'd take care of it, and I believe him."

I pulled my hand out of his hold, attempting to separate myself from Krew. This all started when I saw him at the fight. I should have listened to my gut and declined Maya's invite to go. I felt panic rising back up, so I clung to the tub wall, my eyes still glued to him. "Krew—"

Before I could say anymore, the bathroom door flung open and Decker stood in the threshold, his eyes glowing with rage. "Whoever was shooting at us is gone. We need to get the hell out of here, fast, before they come back."

"Alright," Krew said as he tried to help me out of the tub.

"I can walk out by myself." I resisted taking his hand, and avoid Krew and Decker's stares. The more distance I put between these men and me, the better.

"Your foot is bleeding," Decker growled, as he bent down.

"Don't," I barked. I walked around him and grabbed my bag, skirting the glass on the floor the best I could. I didn't mean to snap at Decker, but I felt too vulnerable to apologize.

Maybe Krew was wrong, and they weren't after me—that meathead had mentioned Maya—could it be that—damn it, I couldn't think straight.

Once I'd slipped into my shoes, I was ready to get the hell out of there. Away from them.

Decker had other ideas. He gripped my arm and spun me around. "I don't know what happened between where we were earlier to now, but I want your full attention, Regi." Decker released his hold and got in my face. "Your, full, attention."

I refused to look at him. Because if I did, I'd break down again. The way I felt safe in their arms was only an illusion. It was a mistake touching them. I had to run—it was the only way to be free. I had done it before, and I could run again.

"Damnit, get out of your head and give me your eyes, Regi." The force in Decker's demand caught me off guard, and I had no choice but to listen.

I raised my eyes to his and saw raw anger, mixed with hurt, in those azure pools.

"What?" I hissed back, knowing my anger was the only way to combat his fiery temper and the panic that was coursing through my veins.

Decker bent slightly, bringing his face close to mine. He raised his hand and I flinched, in case he was going to hit me. It was an involuntary reaction. Deep down, I knew he would never hurt me. Well... the Decker I once knew wouldn't. Did I really know who Decker was now?

Decker paused a second before he dropped his hand. "If you think I'm going to let you go without us, you're crazy. Until I get this shit sorted, you're not going anywhere alone. Krew and I finally got you back, there's no way we're ever going to let you go. You are ours. You know it and we know it." His voice wasn't laced with anger, but it was no less harsh. Then Decker turned to Krew. "Gather our things, we're out of here in three."

I stood there frozen by Decker's icy words. What he said about me belonging to them might have been true once upon a time. Not today, though. Not ever again. I didn't belong to anybody, only to myself. And the sooner they knew the truth about Teke, the sooner I'd be free of them for the rest of my life.

Regina's Diary

December 15th, 2014

Dear Diary,

Sorry I haven't written in a long while. I had a lot going on before I got settled somewhere safe. It took me almost six months, but I'm living in Phoenix now. Met some wonderful people, who I lied to about my name and where I came from. I said I ran away from one of those polygamist cults, and they believed me. I know lying is bad, but I can't be Regina Karen Morton anymore. With their help, I am now Regi Martin. They helped me to get a new social security number and a job at a grocery store, and a cheap room to rent.

I changed my hair, too. I dyed it black and cut it to shoulder length. It's cute. It's the new me. I think I have a knack for doing hair. Maybe beauty school is in my future, after I get my GED, and I'm working on that now. I'm safe for now, Diary. My body has healed, yet I'm still always looking over my shoulder.

God, I miss my parents. I wonder if they ever looked for me, Diary. But I tell myself that it doesn't matter anymore. Did Krew and Decker ever look for me? Did they really care about me? I hope they are happy together. I know from what Maya told me the last time I talked to her, that they were caught by the cops, but they are okay now. That was all she said before my cheap, pay-by-the-minute cellphone cut out and stopped working. I managed to save enough money to get another phone. I called Maya to give her my new number, and ask about my parents, and Krew and Decker. She never answered my calls and messages. I know she's busy with school. It's ~~our~~ her senior year. And I know there's a lot of things happening, but she hasn't returned any of my calls or texts in almost six months. I don't know why she's ignoring me.

I couldn't call Krew and Decker, even though I wanted to. Truth is, I was too scared to tell them—Krew especially. They would blame and hate me, just like ~~Teke~~ he said. God! Why did I even write his ugly name in here? It doesn't matter anymore. I'm on my own and free. Anyway, I have to go to work. I'll try to write more. But I can't make any promises.

Regi

Chapter Thirteen
Decker

The silence in the truck's cab was deafening. Krew was in the front passenger seat, and Regina was in the backseat, a scowl on her face as though it was a permanent fixture.

"Did anyone ever tell you that if you keep frowning like that your face will stay that way?"

"Did anyone ever tell you that you have a big, fat nose?" she countered with a middle finger to me. "Stop sticking it in my business."

For a second, I was stunned at her retort, until Krew burst out laughing. "Good one."

"Christ." I had to hand it to her, she developed a quick wit, something she never had before. "You know where I'd like to stick it."

Her cheeks flushed red as she turned away. "Where are you taking us?" Regina asked, completely ignoring my comment, her attention fixed out the window.

"I don't know," I admitted, briefly glancing at her through the rearview mirror.

"What do you mean you don't know?" Krew frowned. "You said you had this handled."

"Apparently not," Regina muttered with a light snort.

That brought a small smile to my face. It had been forever since I last heard her make that sound. Out of my periphery, Krew's lips tipped up and he began to chuckle. The tight knot in my gut loosened and the ease that was once a part of our friendship, the ease her snort just revived, settled over us—and then vanished immediately when my phone rang.

The display read, *Handler*. I didn't want the truck's Bluetooth to pick it up since I wasn't sure what type of news Sabrina had. I reached for my phone, but Krew laid a hand on my arm. Without having to say a word, I knew what he wanted me to do. Or not to do.

At this point, disagreeing with him would be moot, since this also involved him and Regina. And yet, I hadn't told either of them that Maya and her boy toy were also marks.

I reluctantly tapped the phone screen and answered, "What do you have?" I glanced at Krew, then at Regina in the rearview mirror as she straightened in the seat.

"Do you want the bad news or worse news first?" Sabrina asked.

Fuck.

"Who is that?" Regina whispered over my shoulder. I shook my head, silently telling her to be quiet. She dropped back onto her seat in a huff.

"Who's that?" Sabrina echoed, as the clicking sounds paused on the other end of the call.

"Who do you think?" I chided her. "Now what do you have?"

"Fine. First off, I looked into the other woman, and boy—that girl gets around town like STD at a retirement community. She had her hand on so many dicks at one point that I—"

"Sabrina." I growled, cutting her off. I caught sight of Regina's crestfallen face. Thank fuck, she remained quiet.

"Fine," Sabrina drawled. "Both marks are in the wind."

"That's the bad news?" Krew chimed in, but there was confusion lacing his voice.

"Hmm. Who's that?" Sabrina purred.

"Sabrina," I grated out. "Stick to the details."

"Chill, bossman."

"What did I say?"

"Alright," she huffed. "I did some digging and laid out the timeline for the five contracts that were put out. Maxwell's was first. And once that was completed, the other two popped up within an hour of the hit. Then in the last twenty-four hours the other two came through."

"So the worst news is that you still don't know who ordered the hits," I said, glancing again at Regina in the rearview mirror.

"As of right now, no. From what I could tell, the three contracts —Maxwell's and the two most recent ones are from the same source. I'm still digging into the original orders that have your friends' names on them."

"Just a FYI, we were blasted at the motel. Do me a favor and erase us from their surveillance and registration," I explained as my eyes darted to Krew, whose jaw muscles clenched.

"Will do, and I'll make sure to keep track of Jess and Maya."

"What?" Regina declared in a soft cry. "Why do you need to track Jess and Maya?"

"She's dirty," Sabrina explained. "And more."

"That's enough," I responded crossly. Frustration and regret grew in my gut because I should have explained to Regina and Krew that Maya was tangled up in this entire mess. I moved over to the side of the road, and parked.

"What haven't you been telling us, Deck?" Krew questioned; his eyebrows furrowed deep.

"Give me a second and I'll explain everything I know. Sabrina, what else do you have for me?"

"Your girl isn't going to like this. But the day before the fight, Maya emptied and closed out all of her accounts around the Chicagoland area."

"What do you mean *all* of her accounts?" Regina blurted angrily. "She could barely pay her portion of the rent each month."

"Your so-called friend was lying to you, sweetie. She has been since she moved into your place. Maya had five accounts, four of them with at least fifty thousand in each. The most recent account she opened held one hundred and fifty grand. It's hard to say if that was all *her* money," Sabrina explained.

"I don't believe it. Maya and I have been friends since grade school. Besides, she's always complained that she was broke," Regina admitted, anger radiating from her eyes. "She's a hair stylist like me, and there's no way she banked that much money—even on a good day."

"Believe it," Sabrina said sharply, then continued. "I got shots of Jess Duncan too, the morning after Kane's hit. He had shaved his head and was carrying several bags in hand, walking out of—get this —out of Kane's condo. The SUV he got into wasn't his either. The license plates are registered to one Waldo Hemmings Senior. He died the day before from heart failure."

"Jesus Christ," Krew pinched the bridge of his nose. "That guy is trying to look like me, isn't he?"

"You got it." Sabrina said, as taps echoed through the Bluetooth.

"This whole time, these killers were supposed to be going after Maya and Jess, but they got me and Regina mixed up with them instead? Wait... you said there are four contracts—five including Kane's. What am I missing here?" Krew asked. The answer to his question was what drove my fierce need to hide them until all this shit got fixed.

"You're missing the fact that there's another party out there that really wants you and Regina dead," Sabrina bluntly explained.

"Do you think Maya knew about these contracts?" Regina asked.

I met her eyes in the rearview mirror, and they reflected back betrayal and hurt.

"She had to have known something because she cut and died her hair short like yours, the day before the fight," Sabrina clarified.

"She did," Regina added. "Crap. But I never said anything about why she copied me until the day of the fight—Why? If she was in trouble, she could have told me—I could have helped her."

"Maya wouldn't tell you, Regi. Maya always thought of Maya, and nobody else. Even back then," Krew admitted. "She never cared about you or your feelings."

Regina flinched at his words, but Krew was telling the truth.

There was no doubt in my mind that Maya had thrown Regina to the wolves. "I agree."

Even back in the day, when we were kids, Maya wore her mask of friendship when she was with Regina, all her fake smiles hiding her jealousy. I saw it, and so did Krew, but Regina had blinders on when it came to her best friend.

Those times in high school—and there were many, Maya tried to hook up with one or both of us. However, Krew and I swiftly shut that shit down each time with malice. Yet, neither Krew nor I had ever had the heart to tell our girl what her best friend had tried to do. And that was on us.

"There's more," Sabrina chimed in, yanking me out of my thoughts.

"What is it?" I glanced at Krew, who had his chin to his chest, and then at Regina, who had fat tears running down her face.

"The two original contracts on Krew and Regina were for fifty K each, but as of this morning, they doubled."

I was speechless. That was the last thing I had expected her to say. "Are you serious?"

"Maya's in really bad trouble," Regina murmured.

"No, Regi. Those two contracts are for us," Krew declared.

"I want to know who is behind this and I want it yesterday," I demanded.

"Got it. And while I'm digging, you need to find a place to lay low," Sabrina said as the tapping on the other end got louder and faster, and then nothing. She hung up without another word.

I turned to Krew and Regina, who was wiping tears from her cheeks. "I promise you both, I'll fix this—even if I have to eliminate every asshole that gets in our way."

Krew's anger-fueled eyes met mine and he nodded, but Regina curled in on herself, her legs folded up to her chest and her face to her knees.

"I want to go home," she whispered, her voice hollow.

"To Elida?" Krew asked, his eyes wide with surprise.

"No. I'll never go back there." Her words sounded like a promise. "I want to go back to Chicago."

"No," I said, shaking my head. "It's not safe there—not anymore."

Regina popped her head up, glaring at me. "Then drop me off somewhere—I don't care. I don't want to be here."

What Regina wasn't saying was that she didn't want to be with us, and that cut me far deeper than it should. I glanced at Krew, who winced from her sharp verbal barb. And in that moment, we were back to being strangers. The stolen interlude we'd had in the motel room—the connection we'd begun to forge, meant nothing to her. And the silence in the truck made that truth more painful.

Maybe this was for the best. I was a killer, after all. I was no good for anyone—not anymore. Regina had changed into a person I didn't recognize. But Krew? He was the same man I remembered—

almost. I was sure he had secrets... Though, I guess we all had secrets we weren't willing to share.

"Where are we going?" Krew finally asked, his attention diverted to the window.

That was a million-dollar question. Where could we go? Where could I keep Krew and Regina safe until this fucked up situation was sorted out?

Then it hit me. It was a slim chance, but there *was* one person who could help—who I trusted. I unhooked my phone, climbed out of the truck and closed the door. I dialed Sabrina.

"Miss me already?" she snarked.

"I need you to call Merrick Gentry."

Silence.

I glanced down at the screen, thinking we'd gotten cut off.

"Are you still there?"

"Do you think it's a good idea to contact Merrick?" Sabrina finally asked, her trepidation clear in her voice.

For my handler to hesitate to call the retired hitman, I knew right then it was going to be a risky move. Yet there was no other place safe enough for Krew and Regina.

Two years ago, Merrick Gentry retired from the hitman business, for the love of his life. And if I was honest to him about what these two people meant to me, Merrick might help. If he didn't, then I'd find another place to hide Krew and Regina.

"Connect me," I demanded, before I could rethink my decision.

"It's your balls, but alright."

It took three tries before the man answered the phone. "What now, Sabrina?" the hitman's low growl sifted through the phone like a sand storm.

"It's me."

Silence buzzed in my ear, but I refused to let Merrick intimidate me. I waited until he spoke.

"What do you want, Moss?" Warning coated Merrick's words.

"I need your help. I wouldn't normally reach out, you know that. But this is important—a life and death important." I swallowed the lump forming in the back of my throat. "I have two loves in my life, and they are being wrongly hunted."

"Explain."

I did, followed by, "Now the two real marks are in the wind, which has made the people I care about the sole targets. I need a safe place for them, so I have a clear head and track those fuckers down. I can't be bogged down or distracted by having my people strapped to my hip. Can you..." I swallowed harder this time. Desperation clogged my throat. "Please, I'll owe you several markers."

Markers were a rare gift to be bestowed. For Regina and Krew, I'd gladly be indebted to Merrick if it kept them safe.

A heavy exhale came across the phone. I wasn't sure if that was a good thing or not. Though, I didn't have to wait long to find out.

"Me and Mrs. aren't home right now. We're on an extended holiday for a month. So, the place up north is empty. All you need is provisions. You have a month. But Decker?"

"Yeah?" Relief washed through me.

"You *will* owe me big time for this, and I *will* call it in."

The pressure in my chest eased and I was able to suck in a lungful of air, enough to commit myself to that promise. "I know. You have no idea how much I appreciate this."

He grunted. "Sabrina will text you the address. And Moss, once this is done, forget that address." Then Merrick hung up.

I glanced at both people I had once loved with all my heart and knew I had made the right decision. I only hoped it wouldn't take the month Merrick gave me to track down Maya and Jess.

When the text from Sabrina pinged on my cell, I memorized Merrick's address, then deleted the information. I got back in the truck, put it into drive and headed straight to Vermont. Neither Krew nor Regina questioned where we were going.

Chapter Fourteen
Krew

Decker drove nearly straight through, almost sixteen hours, including stops for gas, on-the-go food and bathroom breaks. In all that time, he refused to let me take the wheel—hell, he wouldn't even tell us where we were heading. Only that it was the safest place he could think of. I believed him. Although, I doubted any place on this earth was completely safe, especially with killers who could probably obtain information as easily as Decker could.

Decker may not have told us where we were going, but I wasn't blind. I caught the highway signs and knew we were heading east. And I saw the *Welcome to Vermont* sign on the side of the road.

I could understand it if Regina had demanded to drive, since she had done nothing but bitch for more than half the trip. But me? I'd given Decker no reason to not trust that I'd get us where we needed to go. He expected us to trust him, yet didn't return the favor. Even so, I truly *did* trust this man with my life—and with Regina's, so I didn't fight him on driving.

On the first leg of the drive, Regina argued with and baited Decker. She went as far as to try to climb into the front seat to face-off with him. Without being rough with her, I urged her back, but she wasn't having it. I told her if she didn't stop arguing, I'd kiss her until she did.

She clammed up immediately and stayed in the back seat. I wanted to laugh, but my chest felt as though she'd thrust a knife in my heart. It hurt to see her reaction—her lack of comment—it cut deep.

If Regina didn't want me to touch or kiss her, why did she let me hold her in the motel room? Her mixed signals only deepened my confusion. Still, it was that question—the *why*—that kept my hope for us alive.

At least I had gotten to feel her, and taste her.

Since then, the glower she'd worn like armor proved she wanted nothing more to do with us. Especially me. She refused to look at me whenever I turned in my seat and glanced at her beautiful face. Each time, she quickly averted her eyes, like it hurt her every time our gazes met.

Eventually, Regina fell asleep—and we needed her quiet. However, even in sleep she was restless, like she was fighting off something or someone in her dreams.

As Decker drove up a steep hill, the truck's headlights cut through the dark and lit up a little white house. He parked on the dirt drive a few yards from the door, but he didn't turn off the engine right away. My stomach cinched up, looking out the window before peering back at Decker.

"What's wrong?" I didn't like the frown on his face.

He turned off the engine, opened the driver's side door, and the overhead cab light turned on. "Nothing." Decker's left eye twitch. It was a tell. He was lying.

I covered the light with my hand and leaned toward him and whispered, "No. It's something. Spill, Deck." I glanced back at Regina, who was still sleeping, then at the house and finally back to him. "Do you think it's not safe here?"

He closed his door, which shut the light off. "It's just that..." He rubbed the back of his neck. "It's kind of surprising to see the normalcy of this place. Merrick was like me. A loner. He didn't mix well with others. That's why this job—this life, comes easy for people like us."

People like us? I couldn't believe that. I knew Decker—well, the old Decker. And that guy wasn't evil like he made himself out to be now.

"Merrick walked away from this life clean, all for a woman and for a *normal* life. I don't know if I could do that." *No twitch.*

Truth. I didn't know what to say. With Decker's confession, a bit of my heart died from the realization that he might never give up his life as a paid assassin. Maybe he found that he enjoyed killing people. Maybe Decker was right, and I didn't know him anymore.

Saddened by that thought, I let the matter drop and asked, "Should we wake Regi?" Without meeting Decker's eyes, I glanced over the seat to Regina, who was curled up with a blanket we'd bought at one of the warehouse stores we'd stopped at a few hours prior.

Decker wasn't sure what to expect from this place, but he'd been told to bring his own provisions. We bought blankets, pillows, a shit ton of food, and a few other necessities for off-grid living.

"No. Let me do a quick perimeter check first, then we can carry her up to a bed. And afterward, we can bring in the groceries and the other stuff. If you see or hear anything, take the truck and get the fuck out of here, okay?" Decker slid out of his seat and then looked at me for confirmation.

"Okay," I agreed, but this time *I* lied, because that was the last thing I'd do. I wasn't going to leave him behind.

Decker quietly closed the door and made his way toward the other end of the house, where he disappeared from my sight. The dark swallowed him up.

While I waited, it felt all wrong to stay in the truck. I was a grown-ass man—I could handle any bad shit that came my way. I'd done it for years. Except, the idea of disappointing my best friend was stronger than my need to get out of the truck and look around. Therefore, I clamped down the uselessness I was feeling and waited.

Not five minutes later, I could just make out Decker coming around the corner of the house. At his thumbs up, I climbed out of the truck, and quietly closed the door.

Decker bent, and I assumed he retrieved the key to the house. He opened the door and let himself inside. I opened the back door of the cab and carefully scooped a sleeping Regina into my arms. As I reached the front stoop, he walked out—his face had lost some of the intensity that had lined the corners of his eyes.

"All clear and safe," he whispered, his attention dropping to the beautiful woman nestled in my hold. I followed Decker inside and up to the second floor. "There are three bedrooms and a bathroom up here."

"Okay," I replied.

Decker pushed open the first door, and Regina slowly roused. She dazedly looked at the two of us for a moment before she smiled and then passed back out.

"Well," he chuckled, a rare, radiant smile lit across his face. "Some things haven't changed."

"It's kind of nice knowing she still loves to sleep a lot," I admitted, staring at Decker's lips as a swarm of need buzzed through me.

His simple grin brought back the boy I remembered. The boy I was still in love with. And just as fast, his smile disappeared as his stoic demeanor slid back in place.

I wasn't sure if it was Decker's reaction or my inability to confront the reality that my childhood friend had changed. Either way, I couldn't look him in the eyes any longer.

I glanced down at Regina, who for the longest time was the

light that I held on to. Especially in jail, when I thought that ending my life was better than fighting for it.

When we were young, she was what had brought the three of us together. She made us fit. Not in the sexual way—we were way too young for that. But emotionally? Regina taught us that love didn't have to hurt. The physical blows that were a daily part of my upbringing, and Decker's own emotional scars, were slowly healed by her gentleness and goodness. Until our lives had been upended by one person. By one terrible event.

Not wanting to think about my bastard of a brother, I refocused on the girl—no, the woman in my arms. The Regina I once knew had also changed. She had secrets of her own—a tortured past that was preventing her from trusting us.

"You can't stand here all night, holding her," Decker uttered.

"What?" I blinked up at him, not sure if I'd caught all he'd said. He was frowning at me like I'd done something wrong.

"I said to put her in bed, K." Decker pointed to the queen size bed.

"I will. But..." Whatever else I was going to say fled from my mind. I didn't know why I was suddenly feeling so out of control, like I was coming out of my skin.

"But?" Decker questioned as he opened the closet door and took out an extra blanket. He turned to me and concern wrinkled the corners of his eyes. "What's going on in that brain of yours, K?"

"Deck..." I whispered into the quiet of the room. But I couldn't hide the small amount of desperation rising into my voice. My heart started beating wildly against my ribs, and I was losing control of the air coming in and out of my lungs.

From the moment I reconnected with Decker in the shadowy underbelly of Chicago to saving Regina from the hulking assassin, from our kisses in the motel room to being shot at and the drive here—everything was finally crashing down on me.

The contracts on our lives, being on the run—all of it, I simply couldn't sort my feelings into categories my mind could manage. And with Regina in my arms, I couldn't fathom the idea of letting her go, ever.

Decker's face went in and out of my vision until his gaze bore into me like a sharp blade, cutting through my delirium.

"Hand her over." His harsh demand snapped me out of my panic. Decker didn't wait for me to move. He took Regina from my arms and placed her on the bed. I robotically removed her shoes while Decker covered her up with the extra blanket, since the house was chilly.

Without another word, I followed Decker out of the room, and he quietly closed the door behind him. "You empty the truck, while I get a fire started and heat up this damn house," he said. Without another word he headed downstairs.

I stood there, momentarily stunned, trying to gather my composure. I expected Decker to say something about my near breakdown, but he didn't, which caused another round of emotions to ripple through me.

What did I expect from him? A hug of reassurance? No. And I needed to remind myself that this Decker wasn't my person. Wasn't the boy who had professed to be mine all those years ago. No. This Decker had a heart of steel and the sooner I got that through my head, the better I'd be.

I took several deep breaths to calm my still-racing heart and left to grab the rest of the supplies in the truck.

I made several trips between the truck and the small home, carrying in most of what we bought—as well as the chill from outside. But Decker was quick and started a fire in the fireplace. When I commented on it, he gave Merrick credit for having left it already set up.

"Your friend—" I stopped beside him and watched the flames grow.

"He's not... actually a friend," Decker corrected with a bite to his words, then quickly fell short on his bravado. "Merrick's more like a colleague."

"Well, I appreciate that he's allowing us to use his place."

Decker didn't say a word as he stoked the fire, using the poker to shift the logs before he added more.

I guess he's done talking.

I couldn't stand the dead silence any longer, so I went back out to the truck and grabbed the rest of the stuff. The chilliness of the wind gave me clarity, which I sorely needed.

As I brought the last bag into the house, Decker was coming down the stairs. "I started the two heating units upstairs. Just give it some time for the rooms to warm up."

"Okay," I said, placing the final box of food on the counter. "Your... colleague should consider investing in a heating system down here."

"I'll get right on researching that for him." Decker cracked a small smile, then it disappeared like a ghost. "If I told Merrick what he should be doing with his own house, he'd have my balls."

Smart ass. I shook my head. "Anyways, the two coolers that are filled with drinks are in the corner over there." I thumbed toward the kitchen.

He yawned and stretched his arms above his head, which made his shirt rise and exposed his taut, six-pack abs. My mouth watered, and I couldn't look away.

Decker chuckled. "It's been a long day and you look like you're ready to drop. Let's go to bed and we'll talk tomorrow," he said hoarsely. His eyes shifted to the fireplace, then he nodded, and turned to the stairs.

For a second, I assumed he meant that *we* were sleeping in the same room, in the same bed. My insides lit up and so did my cock. "Sounds good."

Then he added the verbal hit. "The last bedroom down the hall is mine. It's small, and it only has a twin bed, but there's a table to clean and set up my rifle. Take the room across from where we put Regi. It has a king size bed."

I quelled the sudden disappointment that coiled tight in my chest like a constricting python. I learned a long time ago from my father and brother, to brush off the hurt and keep moving. But this? From Decker? The ache was beginning to fester as he continually drew the proverbial line across our friendship.

"Okay, if that's what you want." I tried not to sound dejected, but I couldn't hide the defeat in my voice.

I wasn't expecting sex, just something... anything to reconnect with Decker. What we did in the truck—in the motel...

"For Christ sakes, K." His hands were balled into fists at his sides. "Don't look so disappointed. I made no promises to you. And here you are, pissed that I won't fuck you."

"I'm not pissed—and I don't want you to fuck me," I hissed, but I didn't sound convincing.

"Liar." Decker's eyes blazed with fiery anger as he took a step toward me. "Do you want to be fucked that bad? Do you want me to just whip my dick out and bend you over? Or would you rather get on your knees and suck my cock until it's nice and slick and then I'd bend you over and fuck your ass until you can't sit down for a week."

He had no idea what his words were doing to my body—what imagery he set off in my head. And if I was in a right head space, I'd let him fuck me, and more.

Nonetheless, Decker was right. I was pissed—pissed off that he was callously disregarding my feelings. Or that he thought all I wanted from him was his cock. He knew me better than that—well, he used to anyway.

Instead of punching the asshole, I moved back. "Get over yourself, Moss. I wasn't looking for your dick," I hissed.

With his hot and cold attitude, I was regretting the dicking around we had done in the truck. Except, when we were getting each other off in the truck, and then in the motel room, I would have sworn I saw affection like he'd once had for me burning in his eyes. I guessed wrong.

"Fuck." He kicked the sofa before turning back to me. "What do you want from me, K?"

"I don't want shit from you," I growled between clenched teeth. "I'm going to bed."

Before I could take a step, Decker got between the stairs and me. "Can't you see that all this—keeping the two of you safe, is hard enough without piling on all of this emotional crap?"

"I know," I said sadly, without looking at him.

"You don't get it."

"What don't I not get, Decker? That you're sacrificing your life to protect ours? I got it."

"If only it was that easy." I finally looked at Decker, and saw a storm of guilt filtering through his eyes and for the first time, I saw my old friend—that boy I grew up with, hidden in those depths. "If I had only known early enough about the damn contracts on you and Regina, the two of you wouldn't be in this mess."

I cupped his face with both hands. "Hey. Don't go putting all this on yourself." The need to be close to Decker was overwhelming and I drew him in for a hug. At first, he resisted, but I didn't let him go. Just held him tighter to me until he relented and wrapped his arms around my waist.

"You're a pain in my ass," he said against my shoulder, before he quickly pulled away.

"Decker," I whispered, but he shook his head like he knew what I was going to say.

"I can't, Krew. I'm..." Decker straightened to his full height, before he averted his eyes from mine. Even though he was standing right in front of me, Decker felt miles away. "Go to bed."

I winced at his gruff tone. "Yeah." I cleared my throat, unable to hide the defeat coursing through me. "Good night." I turned and made it to the first step.

"Wait." Decker approached me cautiously, his eyes finally meeting mine. His arms hung stiffly at his sides. "Listen to me, K. I'm sorry if I hurt you, but you need to understand something about me. I'm not that guy you once knew—not anymore, and I told you that. I have to stay sharp. Because if I don't, one or more of us could end up dead, and then the rest of us will fall. Unless the three of us live through this, we all fall down. Do you get that?"

Decker didn't mince words. He was telling the truth, and no matter how painful his repeated rejection was—or how badly I wanted to curl into this man, he was trying to keep us alive. While me? I just wanted him, since it was my heart that needed tending. Not my dick.

"I do," I finally conceded, but his explanation still didn't dilute the bitterness of his rebuke.

To my surprise, Decker leaned in and brought our foreheads together. I tried not to be distracted by how close his lips were to mine. Or how his intoxicating smell—earth and musk, like a pheromone, was driving me crazy.

"Okay." He hesitated, then pulled back slightly.

I held my breath, my eyes lasered in on his mouth.

He stood there—inches from me, and did nothing. Decker studied my face. I was about to combust and I nearly did when he leaned in, and our lips met for a brief kiss. It was barely there, almost nothing to the touch, while at the same time, it was everything to me.

I should have accepted that one tiny morsel of affection and walked away. But that subtle touch wasn't enough for me. Like a greedy, starving man, I took the advantage I had and shoved my fingers into his messy hair, anchored his head and pushed my tongue between his delectable lips.

I ravaged his mouth, like it was the last kiss I was ever going to get. And he wasn't fighting me either. I took all he was allowing.

Alas, he finally pushed me away. "I have shit to do." He grabbed his gun case and duffel, and without a look my way he headed upstairs.

With a low growl of frustration, I lowered my head, feeling like a kicked puppy. I promised myself, going forward, I wouldn't take what wasn't offered. Yet as I savored his taste on my tongue, I knew that promise was an empty one.

There was no way I could sleep now. My mind was too caught up on how Decker's mouth had felt, how his tongue had danced with mine. How he made my body hum.

Memories of the past—when we first touched, tasted, and took from each other, slid into my head. All of it flooded back in a cyclone of want. All of the desire I had stored up for years was about to erupt in a plume of desperate need. And if I didn't get my emotions under control, I was going to combust.

I suspected Decker would come back down to do a safety check, I locked the front door and checked the back and made sure the *multiple* deadbolts were engaged. After I checked in on Regina, I went into the bedroom that was adjacent to Decker's and closed the door.

The space wasn't big by any means. There was a king size bed against the far wall, a nightstand next to it with an old-fashioned table clock. A tall, skinny dresser was on the wall next to the door, leaving barely enough room to walk around. that was fine, since sleep was the only thing I'd be doing in here.

There was still a chill in the room—it was at least ten degrees cooler than the lower part of the house. But the cold was a bonus because my skin felt too hot.

I stripped out of my clothes. They stank of sweat, dirt, and whatever else had gotten embedded in my t-shirt, jeans and jock during this long ass day.

I sniffed my pits and—Christ, I needed a shower. The last time I showered was the night of the almost-fight. After everything that happened in the past thirty hours, I was too tired to clean up. Shaking my head, I switched off the lamp on the nightstand and climbed into bed.

As I scissored my legs to warm the bed, I dragged the blanket over my body, causing friction along my dick, and that made my balls ache. I spat in my hand, slowly stroked my hardening shaft and let my mind wander right back to the kisses Decker, Regina and I had shared yesterday in the motel room.

While I was in jail, I had clung to the belief that the three of us would see each other again and pick up where we'd left off all those years ago. Now it seemed there was no chance for an *us* anymore. Then it dawned on me that for the first time in three days, since before Teke had dragged me to Chicago, I was alone, with my own thoughts. And I didn't like it.

I pushed those thoughts out of my head, closed my eyes and refocused on my hand stroking my length. Of course, I'd rather have Decker or Regina—or both, touching me instead of my own hand. For right now though, I concentrated on how good Decker's hand had felt back in the truck, and how Regina had tasted on my tongue.

I concentrated on each rough glide of my hand. After I spat into my palm again, I kicked off the covers, gripped my thick shaft tighter and stroked. With each slide down to the base and back up, I squeezed the tip. With my other hand, I cupped my balls, tugging on them to draw out the pleasure. My body shuddered at the anticipation of coming.

As I stroked faster, precum began to pearl on my cockhead. Dragging the pad of my thumb along the tip, I then slipped the digit into my mouth and sucked the salty bitterness.

A familiar surge of electricity shot to my balls, and I shivered. But I needed more. Needed that hard edge before I let myself go.

I closed my eyes, parted my legs wider, and tugged at my drawn-up nutsack—just beyond the ache, which brought me closer to the brink of coming.

Then a memory of when Decker first touched me slid into my mind. I groaned as that night—so long ago—played out like a movie.

It had been just the two of us, in his father's Cadillac Seville. He was almost eighteen and I had just turned seventeen. Decker had told me it was his birthday gift to me. At the time, I had been so desperate for his touch that I would have done anything—would have let him do anything to me. Even risk getting caught in his asshole father's prized possession.

Decker had edged me mercilessly until the yearning to blow had engulfed my senses, and I came within three minutes of him sucking me while he had a finger in my ass. What had been even more fantastical about that night was that he swallowed every bit of my cum, then he kissed me.

I sucked in a deep breath and released all the pent-up anxiety gnarled in my gut. My grip tightened around my steely shaft, as a low groan slipped past my lips. My hips moved in rhythm with each firm stroke, and the bed began to creak.

Fuck—I was so damn close and I bucked faster, chasing my orgasm.

Then the bedroom door banged open, catching me off guard.

Decker stood in the threshold, breathing heavy, his eyes blazing with fury. He'd caught me stroking myself and I didn't give a shit if he watched.

Chapter Fifteen
Decker

"What the fuck?" I charged into the bedroom and slammed the door. My attention dropped to Krew's steely pole, still fixed in his grip, before my eyes slid up his chest, past his parted lips, and stopped at his lust filled eyes.

He held my gaze, the desire in them taunting me as his lips curved into a wicked smile. He was testing my patience, but he'd soon find out that there were repercussions to his teasing.

"Are you purposefully fucking with me?" I growled low, as my focus returned to his engorged cock and the now-slow slide of his hand.

"Hmm," Krew groaned.

"I need to teach you a lesson about keeping quiet." I stepped to the bed, my legs pressed against the mattress. *So close.* I gave no warning to Krew before I climbed on top of him and slapped his hand away from his cast-iron length. "I didn't give you permission to touch yourself either."

He opened his mouth to tell me what—to fuck off? I narrowed my eyes and slowly shook my head *no*, daring him to talk.

Krew's throat worked, but he kept his mouth shut. *Good.*

As I studied his tatted body, I ground my covered shaft against his rod. "If you want this prize..." It took everything in me not to come right there. "You have to show me you can be quiet."

"It would be a better incentive if you were naked," he breathed, as his hands slid up my jean-covered thighs.

I snagged his hands and shoved them over his head, wishing I had a set of handcuffs to bind him to the wrought iron headboard. "Leave them right there," I commanded, then leaned down—torso to torso and pressed my nose in his armpit and inhaled deep. "I missed your smell."

"There's a better place to put your mouth," Krew whispered, as he undulated his hips.

"I still need to teach you to shut up." I bit his right pec. Hard. Leaving teeth marks and a reddening bruise.

He hissed, arching his hips upward against me and silently mouthed, "Please."

I wanted to bite him again, and again. Leave my marks on his skin, own him like I had when we were young. Then lick those bruised spots until he purred out my name with desperate want.

Biting Krew wouldn't be to punish him for talking, moaning— or even touching what was offered to me. No. It would be for the way Krew was making me feel. Possessive. Hungry. And downright surly. I wanted to be balls deep in this man. I wanted the heat of his touch on my skin. His lips bruising my mouth. His cum down my throat. And most of all, I wanted to be surrounded by his love—

No.

The thunderous echoes of that single word as it ricocheted through my mind shifted my perception to what was right in front of me. Krew, lying there, exposed and vulnerable. The repercussion of being so exposed would only lead into heartbreak. For him.

I refused to let this be emotional. I had no room for it—not with all the fucked-up monsters in my head.

But if Krew would let me have him until we parted ways, then I'd give him what he wanted—what we both wanted—physically.

I lowered my face until it was inches from his. "Tell me this is all we're going to do, Krew. This will be nothing more than sex."

He stilled below me, silent, as he contemplated what I was offering him—almost demanding of him. We weren't rekindling our past relationship. This was purely for release.

I didn't dare move, or breathe. A battle was being waged inside me. For uttering those shallow words. For ignoring the history we had together as friends and lovers. Most of all, for looking at him as nothing more than a hole to fuck.

No, he was better than that. I couldn't fuck him—not just yet. Still, I was willing to prime his cock until he couldn't stand it any longer, and then let him come down my throat.

"Yes," Krew whispered so low that I almost missed it.

Relief and remorse clashed inside me, but I wasn't going to deny Krew's or my own needs.

I angled my face, nuzzling my nose against his cheek, before kissing him briefly on the mouth. "Good," I answered, and sat up. "Now that I have you where I want you, scoot down—and hold onto the headboard."

A gorgeous smile slid across Krew's face as I got off the bed and stripped out of my clothes. His eyes tracked my every move like I was prey. Though, he was mistaken. I was the predator.

I climbed back onto his chest and adjusted myself, and my balls drew up the instant we were skin-to-skin. A pearl of precum formed on my tip, and Krew zeroed in on it.

He licked his lower lip and I had a sudden urge to shove my dick down his throat and make him gag. The greediness in his eyes as he homed in on my cock sent tingles along my spine. "Focus on my face, K," I ordered in a whisper.

He met my eyes as I readjusted my position and straddled his chest, putting weight on my knees. Not once had Krew moved his hands from the headboard. *Good boy.*

I rubbed the head of my cock against Krew's closed lips. "Open up—and don't make a sound."

He didn't hesitate and sucked my tip into his welcoming mouth. I pushed forward, until he had my entire length down his throat. Krew gagged, and I pulled out, giving him a moment to breathe before I surged back in.

"If this is the only way to keep you quiet, then we'll keep doing this until you learn, or until I'm satisfied. Nod if you understand." I pulled out again, waiting for his response. His eyes were still riveted on my face, and he nodded.

Krew's lips thinned—like he was fighting the urge to talk, but complied with a nod.

I told him to be quiet, and he listened, yet it wasn't enough for me. I needed to hear his voice. Needed that verbal consent on what we were doing was good. "Now tell me," I demanded.

Like me, he remembered how to play this game, and I didn't have to wait long for the answer.

"Yes. I want it all." It wasn't only carnal lust talking, his spoke the truth. I could see it in his eyes.

Right then, I pushed forward and my dick was surrounded by his wet heat again. "I so missed your mouth on my dick." As good as that felt, I wanted to do more—edge him to the point he couldn't take it.

The drive to be inside of Krew was riding me high. I forgot about doing another perimeter check. About making sure every door and window was closed and locked. My only focus was Krew's talented mouth and his thick length still in my hand.

As I pumped my hips, a faint squeak caught my attention. I turned my head slightly and saw the door I'd slammed closed was now partially ajar. Movement flickered in the narrow sliver of space —a thrill shot through me and my cock became harder.

It was Regina. *She* was watching us.

Maybe she wanted to be a part of this—a part of us after all.

I shifted off of Krew, and he groaned in displeasure. "Shhh," I warned as I positioned myself next to his head, and to give Regina a better angle to watch us. Krew turned his head, started sucking on my cock again while I leaned slightly and stroked his engorged dick. "Yes—that's it, baby. Suck it down. Fuck—how I missed your mouth."

A low moan—so quiet, it came from the hallway. Through the crack of the open door, I could see her hand working between her legs. I let out a groan of my own. Damn, Regina was touching herself—as she was watching us. My balls drew up tight, and the need to release my seed down Krew throat became paramount.

"I want to come, Deck," Krew pleaded, his words garbled between my thrusts.

I stroked his dick faster. "Don't come until I tell you to," I demanded loudly, talking to both of them.

Krew moaned, as he went back to sucking down my length.

A wry smile stretched across my face, as I decided right then to torment him—and her, a fair bit more. I could tell Krew that Regina was watching us, but decided not to—just in case he became cock-shy. "Not yet," I ordered. "You still haven't learned to be quiet."

As I ran a hand down his body, I noticed a few scars on his defined torso, and one deep wound near his hip. Four all together. I wanted to ask where he'd gotten them, but I didn't want to break our link.

Then sixty-nine came to mind, and I pulled out of Krew's warm mouth and straddled his face. I grazed my teeth over his scarred hip bone. "Do you see me?" I asked, more for Regina than Krew.

Krew answered. "Yes." His dick—engorged and deep red, with a bead of precum at the slit. "My cock missed you."

I wrapped my fingers around his girth and squeezed, which

drew another moan out of him. "I see that." His quads bunched—Krew wanted to touch me. But he didn't and listened, keeping his hands above his head.

"Do you remember when, a long time ago, in the back of my father's car, I took your virginity?" I licked up his shaft and sucked the tip into my mouth. Salty and slightly bitter. All Krew.

"Yes," Krew moaned. "I remember... Do you want a repeat of that night?"

Jesus Christ. "I want to defile you right here—fuck you until neither of us can move." It had been too damn long since I'd got off with another person... Not since—I quickly shook off that thought and refocused my attention on Krew. "Would you let me?" This question was for both Krew and Regina.

"Deck..." My name trailed off and desperation laced in his plea.

I sucked his tip into my mouth and pulled away. I turned my head toward the doorway and licked my lips. "So fucking good. You're missing out."

Regina shifted, her body moving closer to the door. Was she tempted to join us? I had no doubt that Krew would come right then if he saw our girl had come to play. And yet, the door didn't move.

So be it. I shoved my face into the short dark curls surrounding Krew's dick and inhaled deep. "You smell so fucking good." I licked up his shaft, and sucked down the engorged mushroom head until I popped off.

"Decker," Krew growled, his right hand gripped my ass cheek and squeezed hard. "Stop teasing me."

It had been a while since I last had a guy's dick way down deep my throat, but I'd gladly choke on this man. I took every inch of his hard flesh until my gag reflex triggered.

I repeated again and again as Krew pumped his hips upward, thrusting his cock into my mouth faster. All the while, he was choking me down.

I forgot all about my order to keep his hands above his head. Or how Regina was getting off while watching us.

Pleasure rode me high. A charge of electricity at the base of my spine surged forth, and the need to come was pure desperation.

This had to go one way. All three of us coming at the same time. I added more pressure on Krew's cock while I eyed the crack in the doorway. Immediately, I captured Regina's brown depths. She widened the door a bit more, and leaned against the jam, her hand never stopped moving inside her pants.

Brave, princess.

"Fuuck... Yes. More," Krew crooned.

He sucked my cock back into his mouth and choked me down. I released Krew's dick, but kept jacking him, wanting to see the show. I then growled, "Come."

Krew shouted, I sucked his tip into my mouth and he spilled down my throat. Regina moaned, her eyes closed and her head tipped back. I grunted, emptying my balls at the same time.

It wasn't long before my vision cleared and I saw the bedroom door was shut again. Disappointment cut into my euphoria.

I fell onto my back, Krew's feet by my head, and we lay there until our hearts slowed to an easy pace.

"I could lay here all day," Krew uttered in a lazy drawl.

"That would be nice," I replied with a smile as I spun myself around and we lay shoulder to shoulder, our faces turned toward each other. "Hey. Where did you get those scars on your body?" Some of them looked as if they'd been deep enough for stitches. I ran a finger down a long, jagged mark on his right side. It had to have been a knife of some sort, but the blade... Then it hit me. "You got this when you were in jail."

Krew stilled. His eyes went blank before he turned away from me.

"K." I pushed on Krew's shoulder and rolled him onto his back again. "Tell me."

He said nothing for a long moment, while he avoided my stare. "Krew—"

"Yes," he grated out, bowing his body forward, both hands covering his face. "I don't want to talk about it, Decker. Just leave it alone."

"Jesus fucking Christ. First Regi, and now you. Is there a reason why you don't want to talk about it, or do you just not want to talk to me period?" I shot back, hurt radiating from my chest.

The entire time I was away, I thought he was safe. That Krew had made a life without me, and I hadn't wanted to intrude. Hell, I moved on too. Apparently, I was wrong.

How did our moment just now go from blissfully wonderful to a tragic instance of slap-me-in-the-fucking-face reality in one heart beat? But Krew's silence was telling, and I almost didn't want to know what had happened to him.

I blinked away the pain of Krew's stubborn silence, and got up from the bed. "I'm going to check the area."

He didn't respond, or moved from his side of the bed.

I dressed quickly, hurried out of the room and slammed the door, like some toddler having a tantrum, totally forgetting about Regina in the other room.

As I moved through the house, my rage became an inferno. I had to let the fires of rejection burn themselves out before there was nothing left of me.

Krew and I once had an unbreakable bond—or so I thought. The years apart severed it and the trust we had for each other was almost nonexistent now. Even so, I for one couldn't let our friendship lay limp like a flaccid cock.

I might have lied to myself all these years about planning to track Krew and Regina down and resurrect what we had lost. However, the truth was that I remained distant for a reason.

Now they were back in my life, I could see that Krew and I

were combustible. Add Regina into the mix and the result would be explosive. If I wasn't careful, I'd be the one who'd burn up and lose.

Regina's Diary

May 27th, 2015

Dear Diary,

I'm having a tough time—I should be graduating today with my friends.

God, I wish I could see Krew and Decker's faces. I miss them so damn much.

I need something to kill this pain, Diary.

I have to go.

Regina

Chapter Sixteen
Regi

The sound of a door slamming shut jolted me awake. At first, I was slightly disoriented, but as I looked around the dark room. My heart ratcheted up and I started my calming mantra. *I'm alive. I'm safe. I'm alive.*

I repeated those words several time, until I realized we had to be at the destination Decker was so hush-hush about.

As I slowly slipped out of bed, my foot snagged on my bag's strap and I stumbled. I caught myself just in time and sat hard on the edge of the mattress. My heart hammering again, I took a deep breath, and that was when I heard it. A moan.

I stilled, closed my eyes and listened. There it was again.

Nosy me needed to know where the sounds were coming from —and who was making them. I tracked the noises to the bedroom across the way from me.

As I stood before the door, more moans—quieter than the earlier moans, came from the room. Could it be Krew, or Decker— could it be both? The idea of those two gorgeous men getting each other off had my lower region curling tight and the sudden need to touch myself pulsed to life.

It had long been a dream of mine to watch them—to see how they loved each other. Touched each other. Sure, I'd browsed those kinds of porn sites once or twice, but *this* was Krew and Decker. *They* were my ultimate fantasy.

As I reached for the doorknob, I paused, questioning if my morals were on the wrong foot. Did I have the right to intrude into their private moment? Or did I have the right to watch them?

I marched back to my room, steadfast to block out the sounds they were making. But at the threshold, the yearning I had for these boys—these men, had my belly flipping about like a drunk gymnast and I turned right back around.

My hand on the doorknob, I oh-so-slowly turned it and opened the door enough to see what Krew and Decker were doing.

I sucked in a breath, then quickly clamped my hand over my mouth. The view of them touching, licking, sucking...

Oh, God.

Krew was on the bed, spread out, all gloriously naked. Every bit of his tatted flesh exposed. Jesus, he was big—so was his cock. Erect and hard. I swallowed hard, imagining what it would be like to take that badboy down my throat or... Elsewhere. Suddenly, my mouth watered for a taste.

My eyes shifted to Decker, who was sitting on Krew's chest—he was equally beautiful. and bare assed, while they were... What was Decker... Looking at me.

Was I loud? The door didn't make a sound. Yet, his eyes were trained on the door I opened. He then moved off of Krew and repositioned himself next to Krew's head. I sucked in a breath. His cock was equally impressive.

"Shhh," Decker hushed, his attention was back on Krew.

My heart went into a full gallop when Krew turned his head and took Decker's dick down his throat.

I couldn't breathe—too caught up on seeing Krew's mouth full of Decker's length, and Decker's hand wrapped around Krew's monster cock, stroking it.

Desire exploded like an atomic bomb in my core, and I was engulfed with fiery lust and need that I wanted to rush inside and join them. Instead, I stayed rooted in the hallway, slid my hand into my pants and rubbed my pulsating clit. I leaned against the door-frame for stability, peeking through the three-inch gap like it was my personal voyeuristic window—just watching them get each other off.

My pussy throbbed. I was so wet, but I needed more. I slipped two fingers easily inside me and tried to fuck myself. A groan slid past my lips, and I quickly clenched my teeth tight and rode the building frenzy.

"Don't come until I tell you to," Decker commanded. Who was he talking to? I could've sworn he was talking to me—demanding me to listen. Whether he spoke to Krew or me, I was not to come.

I listened, and I kept touching myself until I was near the breaking point. Yet, his verbal crooning nearly undid me.

I closed my eyes, and worked my fingers faster, pinching my swollen clit, before sliding them back inside me. I didn't care if I looked like some deprived slut, getting off to two guys.

"Do you see me?" Decker's words slammed into me, my eyes snapped open and our gazes met. I couldn't turn away. I was so caught up on what he was doing to Krew that I almost missed his next word. "Come."

Decker's final command sank in. I threw back my head, my eyes shut tight, and I came so hard that I saw stars behind my eyelids. Ecstasy turned me into a cloud—light and airy. I was floating—literally floating on my bliss.

I couldn't believe I had just climaxed while watching Krew and Decker give each other blowjobs. They were so damn hot, that thinking of the two of them again, I was ready to come a second time.

Jesus, I need help. Maybe my mother was right and I am wicked.

These men—who I'd never had sex with gave me the best damn orgasm of my life. What would happen if I let them touch me, fill me up—front to back—like I've seen in one of those pornos. Let them love on me like I wished for many times in those dark moments of loneliness and self-deprecating sorrow.

Gah! Get a grip. That will never happen. These men aren't yours anymore.

I got a hold of myself, straightened away from the doorway and quietly closed the door. I rushed back into my room and hoped neither Decker nor Krew heard me.

Even though my clit was still pulsing from the orgasm I'd given myself, my heart was pounding out of my chest from a different adrenalin high. I leaned against the door; a sigh escaped my lips in relief at not getting caught.

Too tired to think, I climbed back into bed, closed my eyes and let exhaustion drag me back to sleep.

Chapter Seventeen
Decker

I kept to myself for the next two days, leaving Krew alone, giving the space to think without me intruding. I even went as far as sleeping in the truck, for those few hours I *did* sleep, but it was too damn cold, so I ended up in that tiny room upstairs, sleeping on the twin bed.

When our paths had crossed, especially in the kitchen, I didn't bring up the subject of his jail time.

Still, my mind kept replaying the moment I asked about his scar—his rejection, the silence that followed—on an endless loop.

What tore me apart the most was that Krew wouldn't tell me *what* had happened to him while he was in jail. His lack of trust in me felt like a knife to the gut. Was he afraid that I would judge him?

Each tick of the old-fashion alarm clock on the nightstand in his room was like proverbial blade, slicing deeper and deeper until I couldn't take the pain. I could only hope he understood why I couldn't stay, couldn't lie beside him any longer. Not with that silence draped over every passing second like a heavy shroud.

So, I'd left.

It wasn't hard to stay busy. Though, I was getting antsy to get on the road and track down Jess Duncan, but I couldn't leave until I made sure Krew and Regina were safe here.

Then Merrick texted about the traps he had set throughout his land—which was a good thing, because I'd be down one leg otherwise. Once I'd confirmed the locations of his snares, I added a few of my own and texted him their placements. I constantly patrolled the area, following the invisible perimeter line I had mapped out in my head, and made sure my early warning signals were set so if anyone besides the three of us were on Merrick's property, I'd know about their presence immediately.

While I intentionally avoided Krew, Regina made it easy on me. She hadn't left the house since we had arrived. It appeared that she only came out of her bedroom when she was sure we weren't around.

The second night, I heard rustling downstairs. I crept down and saw her eating one of the sandwiches Krew prepared for each of us. Maybe this was the perfect time to question her about Maya. As I took the next step down, I changed my mind, and left her alone.

Mealtimes were... Different. Krew took over the kitchen and cooked. If Regina and I didn't join him, he left food for us in the fridge.

I'd finally reached my breaking point—the silence had gone on long enough. I needed to talk to both of them. I had questions that needed answers, and I intended to get them later today. Especially with Regina. Her responses would be the deciding factor on whether to leave and track down Jess and possibly Maya, or stay put.

It was nearing four in the morning, and the house was quiet per usual. I decided to do one more check on the west side of the property, where there was an acre of hilly terrain and an abandoned cabin that Merrick had bought four months ago.

I was so far in my head that I wasn't paying attention to how my booted feet gobbled up the ground. My arches began to ache from the climb, and I needed to slow down. As I reached the western boundary of Merrick's property, I caught sight of the rustic cabin he texted me about.

Judging the distance from Merrick's house to the cabin, this place was way too close for comfort—not even a click from where we were hiding.

What drew me up short were the white plumes of smoke from the stone chimney and the interior lights, which glowed like beacons through the curtain-covered windows.

I didn't see movement, although I had no doubt someone was inside. My gut cinched up, because my instincts said that whoever was in that dwelling was here for us—for Krew and Regina.

There was no immediate threat. So before I went half-cocked, I reevaluated what Merrick had texted me. Could he be wrong? Unlikely. Knowing Merrick, he would have told me he had neighbors.

Could I be wrong on the distance? Maybe. I may have been too caught up in my thoughts to realize just how far I'd walked, but at the same time I wasn't an idiot. The Rangers had taught me to keep my sense of direction, and it hadn't failed me yet.

I took out my phone, glanced at the screen, trusting I could get a signal out here.

Yes. Two bars.

I fired off a text to Merrick, hoping he'd answer immediately. I needed confirmation before I went on the hunt.

Me: *Did a perimeter check at the cabin. Lights on. Smoke from chimney. Do I need to worry?*

Merrick: *That cabin should be empty. No one should be in there.*

Shit. Why did I think coming here would be safe?

Me: *Could it be squatters?*

Merrick: *Get them gone.*

Me: *What if they're not squatters?*

Merrick: *You know what you need to do.*

Me: *Got it.*

Lucky for me, I had my nine and K-bar. I drew them both without a sound, crouched low and crept toward the cabin, my boots barely leaving a trail in the dirt. When I got close, I caught the sound—muffled voices inside—at least two.

Then I spotted an ATV behind a large bush, loosely covered by branches.

The voices got progressively louder. The yelling allowed me to continue creeping forward until I was under the window closest to the door. I listened to be sure they hadn't made me, and for any useful information before I stormed inside and killed them.

With every passing second, the conversation escalated.

"Their settling in, babe. I want to give them the illusion of safety. Give it an hour or two, and then we'll go, make the hits, and collect our prize," a coarse burly voice announced with a chuckle.

Icy tendrils chilled me to the bone at the implications of '*illusion of safety*'. The bastard thought himself cunning by waiting a few more hours before he took out Regina and Krew. No fucking way I'd let that happen.

Besides, how did they locate us? Did these assholes put a tracker on my truck? That thought added fuel under my ass to put a bullet in each of their heads. But I couldn't go in half-cocked, based on those words alone. I had to keep listening. Had to be sure.

"Not *we*, Jerome," a shaky voice countered. "You. And I don't feel right about this. I listened when I placed the tracker on his truck. I listened when we followed them all the way here to no man's land. Now you want me to hurry up and wait longer? For what?" After a pause, he continued. "You said it wouldn't take long. I don't have the right clothes with me—and are you sure we have the right vehicle? I mean, your handler sometimes misses the mark. He did mist—"

A loud growl echoed out of the cabin. "Babe! For one, Dan doesn't like it when you talk about him like he's a dumbass."

"He *is* a dumbass."

"And two. It's not like we're going to dig up buried treasure. We're here to kill the bad people," the other guy grated out.

Buried treasure? The right clothes? What the fuck?

I wanted to snort at the absurdity of what I was hearing, but I clamped my mouth shut and kept my ears tuned to what these assholes were saying. At least I now knew about the tracker.

"I'd rather dig for treasure than sit here and wait."

"Stop being a pussy, Josh. You do want that trip to Paris, don't you?" Jerome's voice was laced with annoyance.

"I don't want to kill for it," Josh growled. "I'm not like you, Jerome."

"Yes, you are, sweetheart. Just nicer doing it."

"Thank you, but that still doesn't change the fact that you lied to me. You dragged me here under false pretenses. How do you expect me to feel?"

"Jesus H. Christ, Josh. How in the fuck am I going to make the kind of coin I need to keep you happy? You're the one who wanted that trip in the first place. I'm doing this for you."

"Oh, no. Don't you be blaming this shit on me. You lied about coming here. Then once we got here, you told me you had contracts for two marks—and when I asked you if they were horrible people and if they deserved what was coming to them, so I wouldn't feel guilty about their deaths—you gave me nothing. So, I can't. I won't, Jero—"

A gunshot echoed from the cabin. I dropped, belly-to-the-ground, and stilled, listening for more.

"Fuck," Jerome bellowed. "You made me do this to you."

Shit. The guy just killed his partner.

"You asshole. Why couldn't you just keep your mouth shut for once." Another gun shot, and a grunt.

I waited and listened. Not a second later, the door to the cabin crashed open and a tall, large black man raced out. In his arms, was a much smaller white guy, cradled to his chest.

"I'm sorry," Jerome mumbled. "I didn't mean to shoot your leg."

Even in the dim light of early morning, I could see that Jerome's shirt was covered in blood. The amount was enough to tell me the other guy was dead, or near to it.

Jerome laid the small man on the ground and began frantically pulling the branches off the ATV.

Right as he turned around, Jerome abruptly stopped and trained his sights on me. He screamed and ran toward me, his gun aimed my way. His first shot missed me by a yard. The second? Too damn close to my left shoulder.

I didn't know what had given me away, but I had the advantage. Still on my stomach, I aimed my nine at the dead center of his chest, and pulled the trigger.

One shot, and the big bastard hit the ground hard.

I cautiously got up and carefully walked over to him. He was gasping, eyes wide and looking at me like *what-the-fuck.*

"You came for what is mine," I muttered, kicked his side and gave him the final send off. A bullet between the eyes.

A groan from the left caught my attention.

Shit. The other guy is still alive.

I contemplated for one second what I should do. Finish him off and bury the two? Or... I could hear Regina in the back of my head, telling me to help the man.

Jesus. Am I turning into a milquetoast?

I tucked my gun into the back of my jeans and stalked over to the smaller guy, who seemed barely alive. Surprisingly, he appeared to only have one gunshot wound. Had one of Jerome's shots missed?

The left leg of his jeans had a bloom of blood—the bullet must have hit his femoral artery. I checked his pulse. and it was weak, yet still strong enough for him to survive if I got him to a hospital in time.

"Can you... help me? My boyfriend tried... to kill me." He choked up, but his sharp eyes centered on my face.

"Hold on," I said, uncovering the rest of the ATV.

When I reluctantly picked him up, he started wiggling in my arms. Right as I was about to climb onto the four-wheeler, the twink pulled out a pistol and shoved it against my cheek.

"Don't move, motherfucker." His tone gruff and the gun steady. "You killed my man. An eye for an eye."

I could drop him where I stood, but at this close range, I'd be dead with a bullet in my brain.

"And here I thought being nice would get me into heaven. Guess not," I said to him, refusing to show any fear.

"You killed Jerome, fuckface." He moved the end of the barrel to my temple and pressed hard. "I loved him."

"I was doing you a favor," I said casually. "He's the one who shot you."

"Don't do me any favors. Now put me down. Slowly," he said acidly.

I put him on his unsteady feet as he demanded and backed up, carefully tagging my nine from my back. Without the end of his gun in my face, my pulse calmed. Still, he was too close.

"Show me your hands, motherfucker," he said, waving the gun back and forth. His steadiness gone now.

To throw him off, I asked a question, seizing the chance to gain an advantage. "You're a hitman?" I took another small step back.

He opened his mouth, then quickly shut it like he wasn't sure what to tell me. Then he fired his pistol. Thank Christ, I drew mine first and fired. The shot went through his neck. He sputtered and flailed, and in the end, Josh was dead at my feet.

A sting grazed the side of my head. I touched the area and my fingers came away wet. Blood. I dropped my hand, and ignored the pain. It wasn't life threatening.

Staring at the now lifeless body, I rolled my eyes upwards at the sky, where the dawn was creeping in. Before daylight spotlighted my good deeds, I needed to hide the bodies. It was going to be a long while before I headed back to the house. And when I finally got there, I had to search the truck for that tracker—and any other that was planted on my vehicle.

My decision to stay was made the second those killers found us. Who knew who else might crawl out of the woodwork to hunt Krew and Regina? Didn't matter. The second I clocked them in my crosshairs; they were already dead.

Chapter Eighteen
Regi

I bolted upright and sat in the dark for a long minute, trying to calm my racing heart and clear away the nightmare that plagued me again. It had been years since I'd dreamed of that horrible night, but in the past three days—the same damn one seemed to carve a piece out of me every time I closed my eyes.

Finally, I lay back down and glanced at the digital clock on the nightstand. It read ten after six. The sun barely peeked over the horizon, its soft glow seeping through the sheer curtains and the partially open bifold slats on the window.

I'm alive. I'm safe. I'm here. My body relaxed, yet my mind wouldn't follow—too restless, too afraid to drift back into the nightmare that woke me.

I stayed to my room, only coming out at night—after I knew the boys had gone to bed—or whatever they did after dark—

Don't think about them in bed, Regi.

Too late. My nether region did remember and it began to ache. I let out a silent groan of need and frustration. I couldn't get the picture of them sixty-nineing out of my head. That was the real reason I kept my distance—to avoid talking or looking at Krew and Decker—especially them together.

I still couldn't get over the fact that I saw them having sex. While I watched! And got off at the same time, too!

I had to think—clear my head. Between everything that happened and all I'd learned from the time the guys grabbed me from my apartment to now, I'd been bombarded with conflicting emotions and information.

Decker was a hitman. Someone who killed for money. I couldn't wrap my brain around the fact this Decker Moss worked in the underbelly of society. He wasn't the person I remembered.

And the idea of killers searching for Krew and me—that someone was willing to pay a lot of money to have us murdered... It sounded too bizarre to be true. I was a stylist, working in a high-end salon. I did hair for God's sake. I didn't hang with anyone other than Maya. I was a homebody. I didn't go out.

And Krew... Actually, I didn't know what Krew did for a job. Was fighting his thing? Or did he work elsewhere?

Then there was Decker's female friend, Sabrina. He called her his handler and she called him bossman, which he hated that title. She had said the real targets were Maya and Jess.

That last piece of detail actually explained some things, which happened a few days before the fight. Like how Maya had packed a much bigger bag than she usually did for her overnight stays with Jess. Or how she had mimicked my hair cut and color. And let's not forget how I found the front door to our apartment wide open at the crack of dawn the morning after the fight.

Could all this be coincidental? Was Maya innocent in all this?

I slowly got up, went to the door of my room and leaned in. Putting my ear to the wood, I listened for any voices, moans or footsteps. All I heard was the silence of the house.

Phew! I really needed to go. Having to time my trips to the

bathroom to avoid the guys was the hardest part of my self-imposed isolation.

I opened the door, and immediately stepped back, surprised to see Krew standing in the doorway of his room. He looked... tired, maybe dejected. His eyes were bloodshot and his shoulders slumped. I wanted to ask him what was wrong, but I stayed silent.

"I made breakfast," he eventually said before he turned away from me.

"Thanks," I said, finally discovering who was making food and leaving it in the fridge. As much as I wanted to reach for him, I refrained from moving. I couldn't. Even after what we shared in the motel room back in Chicago—which I saw now was wrong of me to initiate—I still couldn't look at Krew and not see his brother.

Just as his door was about to close, shutting him away from me, his name flew out of my mouth. "Krew?"

The wash of emotion in his tired eyes had my heart lurching. And yet, my feet remained firmly anchored to the floor boards, as conflict warred within me.

"I truly do appreciate that you took the time to cook for me... and Decker." Which was true. There were usually two plates in the fridge.

He rubbed at his eyes before looking tiredly at me. "It was my pleasure. And I don't mind." Krew's voice cracked.

He was about to close the door when I slipped into the hallway. "Can I do anything for you?" I narrowed the gap between us a little more and hoped he wouldn't close the door in my face. The dim bulb overhead cast a yellowish hue on Krew's skin. Dark circles framed his eyes—no doubt he hadn't slept in days, or at least not well.

He shook his head. "No, I'm good."

"Are you?" Why did I have the feeling Decker was the cause of Krew's wounded expression?

Between the two men, Decker had always been the hothead.

His mouth worked faster than his brain. He had a knack for shoving his big fat foot right into it—especially when things didn't go his way. A lot about Decker might've changed, but I doubted that had.

Krew, on the other hand, was the thinker—always processing before he reacted to a situation, even on the simplest matters.

If I had to sum them up, they were the yin and the yang. Or maybe they were at one time, and I was completely off. Granted, I hadn't exactly taken the time to figure out who they were now.

"Don't worry about it, Regi." His words snapped me out of my thoughts. Krew dropped his attention to the floor. "Remember, we aren't your problem."

Ouch. That hurt.

Krew's withdrawal unsettled me in ways I couldn't describe. While I was pissed at being put in this position, he was also a target. Furthermore, he didn't deserve my wrath for being biologically linked to my rapist. No matter how hard it was for me to look at him straight in the eyes.

His dejection was killing my insides and my internal struggle to remain distant cracked.

Krew turned his back to me, closing the door between us.

"Please," I whimpered, not sure what I wanted to say to him. Apologize? But not to his retreating back. When I placed my hand on his bicep, he stiffened like a board, as though my touch was poison. "Sorry." I pulled my hand away.

"No, I'm the one who's sorry. It's just that... I thought you hated us—hated me." He looked over his shoulder and the truth of his words slashed another protective layer from my heart.

"I don't hate you, Krew—never could hate you." Which was the truth. "It's just that..." How did I explain this to him without divulging what had happened to me?

Your brother did...

I quickly shook off the horrid memory edging into my mind. It wouldn't do anyone any good to bring up the past—not right now. Maybe not ever.

"Just what, Regi? You locked yourself in that bedroom—avoided me and Deck, like we're the fucking plague. And now you want to talk to me—hell you can't even look me in the eyes." He was so close, I could feel the heat from his body, his breath fanning across my face. Still, I couldn't look at him. "Talk to me," he rasped out in desperation.

I automatically stepped back from the ire lacing his words. I tried to ignore the sickening sensation rising in my stomach and the panic choking the breath out of me, but I was losing control of this situation.

He's not Teke. He's not Teke. I kept reminding myself of this fact over and over again.

"Regi." Krew's voice dropped to a low timbre, commanding, and I quickly dropped my eyes down to the floor. He didn't need to see the pain I used as a Teflon shield. "Look at me, damn it."

I couldn't deny him any longer. As my eyes traveled back to his handsome face, I silently appreciated his body. Even back then, Krew was tall and had muscles from the hard work his father made him do at the feed store after school. I used to love touching them whenever he flexed his arm. The way his body was now molded to utter perfection, and the power it held within scared me.

This is Krew—not that asshole.

When my eyes met his, I homed in first on the amber hue of his left eye, then on the hazel of his right, and finally on the tiny patch of brown in that same eye, like a fleck of earth in a storm. How had I forgotten about Krew's heterochromia? I'd been so focused on the amber—

"Why are you looking at me like that?" He cupped my face gently.

My body went liquid against him. This was one of the men who had my heart, and I shouldn't be afraid of him. Krew might be the one who deserved to be held right now, but it was me who needed his touch.

"Krew, kiss me," I whispered. I was desperate to drown in his warmth—fill myself up with only him.

Eager to erase the apprehension that was slicing into my conscious mind, I didn't give him time to debate, or myself a moment to get mired in the past. I leaned in and kissed his lips, taking the initiative before I chickened out.

Krew was a solid presence, like a brick wall. Sturdy, reliable, but also comforting. When I pulled back, a fleeting look of concern raced across his face, and I wanted to relieve him of it. "Krew."

"Are you sure?" he questioned, more insistent than before.

"Yes." I didn't falter. The verifiable truth was that I still loved him—even after all this time—even after my past trauma. I wanted Krew—I was hard up for his love, and his giving, gentle nature.

Krew didn't waver, he picked me up and slammed his mouth on mine with ravenous hunger. My legs instinctively wrapped around his waist and my arms around his neck.

"I missed you so much," I admitted against his kiss, not regretting my declaration.

He tightened his hold, as his talented tongue delved deeper into my mouth like he was claiming ownership.

The solid rod grinding against my pussy sent a jolt of need straight to my core. I was giddy—no, drunk on the idea that Krew was as desperate as I was.

I kept my eyes closed, moaned his name, and ground myself against his steely length. "I need you, Krew." Desperation filtered in as I rocked my pelvis, craving the friction.

"Regi." Krew's voice shook, and I snapped my eyes open. My brain spun out of control the second I saw his pupils—blown wide. It wasn't the black that held my focus. It was the speck of brown, almost swallowed whole, and my attention was forced back to the amber.

All the air left my lungs, Krew's face melted right in front of me like someone had cast a spell and poof, Teke was the one holding me. Giant. Abrasive. Assaulting. A monster.

I wanted to scream, but a boulder sized knot was lodged in my throat and my voice was blocked, and so was the oxygen I needed in my lungs.

I closed my eyes again, thrashed out of his arms, and wished Teke back to the pits of hell, where he and the memory belonged.

My feet landed on the cold floor, and I knew I had to escape, but firm hands gripped my arms before I had a chance to run away.

"Breathe, Regi—damn it, breathe for me," Krew's frantic words penetrated my sheer panic and I opened my eyes.

This is Krew. This is Krew, I repeated to myself as I looked for the hazel in that one eye, but Teke's face kept getting in the way and driving my burgeoning terror into an utter frenzy.

Krew cupped the back of my neck and drew me in to his chest like he was my safe harbor in this storm of emotions. I shivered at the solid reassurance his touch brought me.

"What the hell is going on?" Another voice boomed, startling me into stillness.

I slowly swiveled my head and saw Decker standing at the other end of the hallway. Then my eyes lasered in on the blood and dirt on his clothes, on his hands. Swiftly, the world spun around me and I was falling again.

My mind spiraled back to Teke dragging me by the hair into the denser part of the woods. I'd screamed from the pain and fear. He had punched me in the face a couple of times to shut me up but I had fought back. With my fists, my nails, and my teeth. Yet, nothing had stopped him from taking what he had wanted. From shredding that sacred part of me—that part I'd been saving for Decker and Krew.

Then Teke was gone and I was in the dark. Cold seeped into my body—bone chilling and wet. I was back in that ditch again.

My vision went black, and everything stopped.

"Breathe, baby." Krew's panicked voice forced its way into the black space in my head. Then a foul, sharp odor filled my nostrils and flung the heavy, dark fog from my mind.

"Thank fuck." That was Decker. "Why did she pass out this time?"

"I don't know," Krew barked. "Open your eyes, Regi. It's me, Krew—damn it—open them for me." The sheer terror in his voice pulled me further from the edge of my nightmarish abyss.

I wanted to soothe Krew, but the cold—

"Damn it, Regi. Don't do this to us," Krew roughly whispered.

What was he talking about—the foul odor hit my sinuses again, and I was finally dragged back into reality. I blinked, then coughed, then sluggishly opened my eyes. Hovering over me were two blurry faces.

"Decker? Krew?" I croaked, then blinked, trying to clear my vision.

"It's us." Decker met me with a frown. Seeing his handsome face distorted with worry sliced right through me. I was still befuddled from whatever had happened just moments ago and wobbled a little as I tried to sit up.

"Take it slow," Krew said as he helped me into a sitting position. I was in a bed—in a different room from the one I'd been sleeping in.

"Maybe she should stay lying down," Decker reasoned.

My head swam like it was filled with muck, even though Krew kept a steadying hand on my shoulder.

I stared at Decker's naked torso and all of the tattoos that covered his skin, and my clit suddenly thrummed to life. Disgusted by the lust pulsating between my legs, I looked away as

I asked, "Why are you shirtless—never mind, I don't want to know."

Then I remembered the blood on his shirt. I shut my eyes and swallowed down the bile threatening to rise up my throat.

"Maybe Decker is right and you need to lay down," Krew said, as he bent to look at my face.

I shook my head in response, and immediately became dizzy. My temples ached and as I dug my fingers against the pressure points, my stomach churned with distress.

I didn't want to see their faces—not when I felt so weak and I'd just barely managed to stitch back together what was left of my crumbling fortitude. I needed time to rebuild the fortress that protected my sanity.

However, there was no staunching the rush of heat in my cheeks, as I returned my gaze to Decker's muscled, fully tatted chest. I wondered if each of the tattoos that covered his skin had meaning. Probably, but it wasn't likely that he'd tell me.

What the hell is wrong with me? Who cares what his tattoos mean?

I squeezed my thighs tightly together to ward off the desire. I couldn't keep putting myself in the path of these men, fantasizing about how it would feel to be moving against their bodies—holy hell, I nearly had sex in the hallway with Krew. All because I wanted to forget for a little while that I wasn't whole. I had just wanted a little piece of him before I didn't have either of these men in my life.

"Where did... the blood..." I couldn't finish what I wanted to ask, I was about to throw up. I clamped my lips shut and swallowed down the vile taste in my mouth.

Krew's finger gently rubbed the back of my neck. It was sooth-ing, though, his touch didn't stop my heart from racing out of my chest or relax my breathing.

"You don't want to know," Decker said gruffly, "What is more important is what's going on with you, Regi. Before you fainted, you said, *The blood—all the blood.* Now what does that mean?"

"It means nothing," I lied, as the roiling in my gut started again and I couldn't talk about it.

"Again, you're lying—what are you hiding from us, Regi?"

There it went. I hauled myself over to the side of the bed and threw up. I hadn't eaten in the past twelve hours, so only yellow bile splashed across the wooden floor.

"Je-sus." Decker scrambled backwards while Krew took off out of the room. He rushed back moments later with a wet towel and a metal bucket. I stared blurry-eyed down at the pail, wondering where he had pulled that out from, and told him it was a bit too late.

"Just in case," Krew said as he handed me the towel.

I slowly straightened, took the cold, wet towel out of his hand and wiped my mouth. The foul taste at the back of my throat had me gagging again, but I choked down the acrid tang.

"Why did the blood trigger you, Regi?" Decker questioned, his eyes narrowed into pinpricks. "What happened to you?"

"I'm not hiding anything," I defended, lying—again. "It's only a bodily fluid, Deck." I said with a shrug, not wanting to use the B word, in case it incited another bout of vomiting.

"Regi, you fainted," Krew said. I was momentarily distracted by the sight of him folding his beefy arms across his broad chest. When my gaze returned to his sad eyes, his worry was still plain to see.

I shivered and diverted my attention to the mess on the floor. My insides were raw like a reopened sore, one that was being constantly picked at. My yearning for these men was an internal battle I was continuously waging with myself. And yet, I had enough fortitude to remain steadfast in my lies.

"It would trigger most people. Don't make a big deal out of it," I said with another shrug.

"Don't make a big deal out of it? Fucking A—is she for real?" Decker spat—literally spat in the vomit and I wanted to laugh at the absurdity. "Why are you lying to us?" Decker growled in frustration. "You never used to lie to us."

"I'm not that little girl anymore, Deck!" I shouted the first truth I'd said since we'd been back together. "I'm not that Regina you remember. The girl who was too naïve for her own good. She's dead and buried."

Everyone was clueless—these men were clueless, and I kind of liked it that way. Their lack of knowledge of who I was now made it easier to spin my web of lies like a spider.

"You made us promise, a long time ago, to never lie to each other. Do you remember that, Regi?" Krew's gravelly voice shook my focus, because I remembered that day clearly.

It was one of the days Krew and his brother fought, and Krew came away from the fight with a busted nose and a black eye. The same day, Decker went after Teke and kicked the crap out of him before Krew's father aimed the shotgun at Decker and warned him off his son and his property. As broken as these two had looked, they lied to me about where they'd gotten their bruises. Until I found out the truth from Maya. I made them swear that, from that point on, we would always tell each other the truth. What a childish promise to make.

"Those promises don't mean much now. We're adults—not kids, Krew," I defended.

"Adults or kids, we made a promise to each other. If you can't keep your promise, if truth between the three of us isn't important to you, then maybe I don't know you anymore."

Shit, that stung deep.

"Well, you don't." I clenched my teeth and looked away, for fear they would see behind my false bravado.

What could I say to them? Yes, I was the biggest liar of them all? When I was young, I couldn't lie—not to them. But I wasn't that girl anymore—and I told them that. Didn't they see I was no longer Regina K. Morton—the good girl who fell in love with two boys from school.

I may not have been a good liar back then, but I was a great liar now. Not even my ex-best friend, Maya, knew I lied to her about things in my life I didn't want her to know.

She knew firsthand about the rape—Maya was the one who found me in the ditch. But the dreams that haunted me for years... I tried to keep them to myself. Still, I'd woken her, and eventually, she made me talk about my nightmares.

How would I even explain the hell I went through back then? Or how I had never truly recovered from losing myself, the life I thought I'd have, and the love of my family and these men? Or how lonely I was now? I'd rather swallow a pound of rusty nails then tell them all the evil that had been done to me and the shit I had to crawl through to reach some level of sanity.

What would it achieve? Nothing but carnage. Krew would track down his brother and beat the hell out of him. Or worse. And Decker? He'd put the hurt to my rapist first before he finished him off with a bullet. I had no doubt what Decker was capable of, especially after watching him kill the hitman in my apartment and seeing the blood he had on his skin and clothes today—blood I knew wasn't his. Then they would be hauled off to jail, all because of me. So no, I wouldn't let them put their lives on the line for me. I couldn't have that on my conscience.

"You don't know me," I repeated stridently. "Neither of you know me. I keep telling you, I'm not the same person you knew back in Elida. The sooner you get that in your heads, the better." I refused to look away from Decker's eyes, even though I could feel them drilling through my armor.

"Maybe you need a good spanking to get you to tell us the truth," Decker warned.

I sucked in a shocked breath. "I swear if you touch me, Decker Joseph Moss, I will cut off your balls," I shouted.

"Since you want to be a hard ass," he pointed to the vomit, "you made the mess, you can clean it up. When I get back, it better be clean enough for me to eat off of."

"You can't tell me what to do," I screamed at him.

"Deck." Krew glared at Decker. "Maybe—"

"No, K. If she thinks it's no big deal to lie to us about what she's hiding, then we will treat her as such. As a liar." Then Decker turned to me. "We won't bother you any longer. You don't have to worry about us asking you anything. I'm done with you, Regi." He sneered at me and I almost flinched. "Out of respect for my friend, who owns this house, you're going to clean up this puke, or I'm going to spank your ass like you deserve." Decker stormed out of the room.

"You can go fuck right off, Decker," I shouted at his retreating back, turned and faced Krew. "Get out." I snarled, like it was his fault for what just happened.

Krew glanced at me with eyes filled with sadness, before he walked out of the bedroom without another word.

I didn't know what was crushing my heart more: Decker's words, the sneer I gave to Krew or the anger radiating from my soul.

I stomped to the door, slammed it out of pure frustration, and locked it. I covered my mouth, slid down the door, and silently cried. They would surely hate me now.

Regina's Diary

December 31st, 2015

Dear Diary,

It's been a whole year since I wrote to you, and so much has happened this year. So many good things, that I didn't have time to sit down and put my thoughts to paper. But New Year's Eve is a great time to catch up, right?

I finally managed to not cry when I lit a candle for Decker and Krew's birthdays and prayed that they doing well without me. I bought a small chocolate cupcake to celebrate, but it didn't taste as good as my mom's.

I finally got my GED, around the same time I would have graduated at school in Elida. Then through a friend from the shelter I volunteer at, I was able to get a hardship scholarship to go to beauty school. There were stipulations though. I had to move up to Chicago, volunteer four days a week at their affiliated shelter there, and get a part-time job. I was also told they already had a place for me to live— for free. For FREE, Diary. I couldn't say no to that, and I had always wanted to visit Chicago.

Even though I thought it sounded too good to be true, I decided since I already survived so much crap, I could handle anything for a chance at a better life. So, I took the offer. And it was the best damn decision I ever made.

Sorry Diary, I had to put you down for a bit, but... Surprise! I'm already here in the Windy City, and now I know why they call it 'the windy city'. Though, I didn't realize that I would also freeze my butt off, but that's okay. I got a warm winter coat and boots at a thrift store near the shelter.

I start beauty school in a month. In the meantime, I'm working in a salon, shampooing, cleaning, and sweeping up a lot of hair. Tips are great, so I can't complain. And since I don't have to worry about rent, all my money goes for food and anything else I need. I don't eat much, Diary, so I save. My bank account is growing.

It's been a couple of years, but I still miss Krew and Decker very much. I hope they are doing well without me. I miss my parents too. I called them last week on my nineteenth birthday, and my mother answered the phone. I was too chicken to talk to her, so I hung up. I guess I still wasn't ready and need more time to heal.

Well, it's nearing midnight and I have an early shift at the shelter tomorrow. I'll write soon.

Regi

Chapter Nineteen
Regi

Three more days went by—we'd been here practically a week, and I was still pissed at Decker for berating me like I didn't know my own mind. Although I regretted shouting at Krew.

As an apology of sorts to Krew, I made sure to clean up every speck of puke in the bedroom and sprayed air freshener I'd found in the bathroom. However, I'd made no other efforts to atone for my outburst toward him. I simply avoided both him and Decker.

Decker. I fisted my hands, wanting to—*Gaa!* I've never been an aggressive person, but he brought out the part of me that wanted to beat the hell out of his face. Just thinking about him now raised my hackles. I wanted to kick something of his—like maybe his balls, for treating me like I was a child.

And yet, my mind kept returning to his warning about spanking me.

Why did I think that was hella hot? At one point when I was cleaning up the puke, the idea of defying him had yearning and curiosity swirling in my stomach. Fortunately, I managed to cut off that notion immediately. Well, almost immediately.

Instead of the nightmares waking me the past two nights, it was wet dreams. In one, Decker had bent me over his lap and cracked my ass until I came. In another, Decker and Krew spit roasted me until I'd screamed out both their names. They'd made me come until I couldn't orgasm anymore. Then Decker and Krew took me both at the same time and claimed me as theirs.

Hmm. I shivered at the images those dreams left in my mind. The idea that my body could accept them both at the same time—like my heart did, raised another layer of yearning I had to squash.

I pondered on what I should do and decided there was only one way to handle these unwanted feelings. Stay away from both of them.

Yeah, right.

So I stayed in the bedroom, just like I had the first two days in this place—only venturing out for food and bathroom breaks when I was sure they weren't around.

Gah! I was going stir crazy.

I was my own jailer, and didn't know what was worse, being cooped up in this house—in this bedroom like a prisoner, or being on the run from killers. None of it had merit. But I certainly couldn't hide in here any longer.

At least neither man bothered me. While I kept to the bedroom, the guys did whatever they were doing downstairs. I didn't know, and frankly I didn't care...

Alright, that was a lie. I was bored and lonely sitting in the room, without conversation—without any interaction with them. I was talking to myself like a frickin' loon. I felt touched starved and my brain hungered for connection.

There was no television, and Decker had taken my phone away, *so no one can track us*, his words.

I hated the fact that I'd put myself in this corner. I was the one who'd made it damn clear that I didn't want to be bothered. And they granted me my wish.

Then the nightmare—the one with Teke hurting me, woke me from my afternoon nap. That familiar sick feeling clung to me like a wet woolen blanket, and the desire to be touched drained from my body. Those moments of desperation to escape drove a frantic rush to pack my bags.

I talked myself out of that impulse because I was certain that Decker and Krew would come after me, and my decision to run could ultimately lead to our deaths.

Nonetheless, I had to get out of this room. And the aromas creeping through the undercut of my door made that decision infinitely easier. I sniffed and my mouth watered as I identified meatballs, tomatoes, and garlic—some of my favorite foods. When I opened the bedroom door, the smell intensified, and my stomach growled.

The robust ambrosia filled the air with the scent of rich ragu as I crept down the stairs. My senses were bombarded with goodness when I took the last few steps to the main floor.

In the open kitchen, Krew stood in front of the stove, lowering a handful of angel hair pasta into a pot.

He turned, grinned, and then twisted back to whatever he was frying in the skillet.

"Is that meatballs?" I asked, slowly approaching him. I focused on the frying pan before looking at his face. Krew was relaxed, like he was in his element.

"I had a taste for Italian."

"I..." I cleared my throat. "Is there enough for me?" I would understand if he didn't make enough or didn't want to share with me, since I had been so horrible to him.

"There's plenty," he said, as he turned the meatballs in the pan. "I remembered that meatballs used to be your favorite food. Are they still?"

A lump formed in my throat and a sour taste laced my mouth.

Krew was still a genuinely sweet person. Whereas life had turned me into a cynical bitch.

"Yes," I admitted with hesitation.

"I figured that." His smile evolved into a smirk and I recognized his underhanded tactic. Krew clearly remembered, whenever my mother made spaghetti and meatballs, I went straight home after school and did my homework in my bedroom until supper time. It was the only time I hadn't hung out with the guys.

"Trickery." I mean-mugged him.

Krew's grin widened as though he knew he'd won this battle of wills. "I had to figure out a way to get you out of that room."

I shook my head and folded my arms across my chest. "What if it hadn't worked?"

"I knew you couldn't resist spaghetti and meatballs." He raised one meatball with a metal tong, dipped in the bubbling sauce and waved it in my face. "Want a bite?"

"I'd rather bite something else," I blurted out with no thought of what my words might do to Krew.

Krew's eyes went liquid as he slowly lowered the meatball. "Like what?" His voice dropped to a husky whisper.

There was lust and want in his depths, and instead of taking those closing steps and kissing his sensuous mouth, I swallowed down my own need and stepped back. I couldn't afford what my body and heart craved. "A candy bar."

Candy bar? Really, Regi? Stupid.

Krew returned his attention to the frying pan. "Decker and I are playing Spades after dinner. Want to join in?" he asked, his posture stiff—like if he moved, he'd break in half.

That was it? No questioning on why I put a halt to my blatant flirting and the stupid candy bar? His voice conveyed casual, while his body told a different tale.

"Umm." I didn't know what to say. And I was somewhat confused. Either he wanted me to play the card game we used to play together but he knew I'd say no to the offer—or he didn't want me to play but was too polite to not ask. I didn't think it was the latter.

I concealed my nervousness with a weary smile; this was my chance to apologize for being such a shrew. "Krew—"

"That smells great." Decker strode into the house and his presence totally obliterated the speck of courage I'd scraped together to apologize to Krew.

He went up to Krew and kissed him like they were in some sort of domestic bliss—minus me in the picture. I got it. *Messaged conveyed loud and clear, Deck.*

A tiny note of jealousy reared up, but it wasn't because Decker was kissing Krew. It was that I wanted a kiss too. Decker was true to his last words—he didn't look at me or acknowledge my presence, like I wasn't even standing there.

My chest hollowed out at his disregard. But I straightened my spine, and bolstered my take-no-shit attitude. Showing Decker any weakness was like giving catnip to a feline. I'd rather starve than expose more of my emotions to this jerk. I'd done enough of that.

"Is it ready? I'm starving," Decker said, rubbing his flat stomach. My eyes dropped to his hand, then down to his bulge, before I quickly looked away as the memory of my wet dreams filtered in.

"Almost. Just waiting on the garlic bread," Krew announced, then turned to me. The tension evident in his stance moments before was gone. "Do you want to set the plates?"

I opened my mouth to tell him yes, except Decker butted in. "I'll do it." His brisk tone and sharp stare were aimed at me now.

At least he's looking at you.

He grabbed three plates from the open shelving by the window, and placed two at one end of the table and the third dish on the other side. Not once did he talk or glance again my way. I knew what he was doing and it was pissing me off even more.

Instead of pasta, Decker wanted me to eat crow. And I would, for being such a bitch to Krew. I could give less than a shit about Decker. He'd made it clear that he was done with me.

I ignored the knot of pain corded tight in my chest at that notion, and stood there, unblinking, as I watched Decker set the table.

His cold, calculating blue eyes—eyes I'd once thought beautiful, had a threatening glint in them. And it hit me then that this man—*this* Decker Moss, was dangerous.

When we were young, I had never seen the vicious side of Decker. Sure, the dark wickedness of his temper had been doled out from time to time to the kids that had deserved it. And to his asshole father.

Decker's comebacks were cruel—but again, never aimed at me... until our confrontation in the bedroom three days ago.

The impulse to scream at him grew with my frustration. Now, whenever we faced off, every word out of his mouth would feel like a balancing act—one misstep and I could either stand my ground or lose my footing entirely. I was poised on the knife's edge, waiting.

Decker's eyes sharpened as I watched him watching me. My heart kicked up as they pinned me in place, daring me to say something. This silent confrontation between us gave me a shot of adrenalin, and I sucked in a breath.

This is what you wanted, Regi.

But had I really? Had I wanted to be ignored? The longer I stood there, the faster my resolve crumbled to dust and I looked away.

"You know what, I'll take my plate upstairs," I told Krew, picking up the dish and walking it over to him.

"No, I'd like you to stay. Decker, stop being a dick, and sit down," Krew barked over his shoulder.

"What? She wanted to left alone. She doesn't want to talk to us. I'm giving her what she asked for." Decker shrugged before placing silverware next to the two plates and three glasses.

I clamped my teeth tight, shame burning through me. Decker was right—I said those words, but they were lies. Lies to protect myself from them—from the hurt I'd soon feel once this whole contract murder was over and we part ways.

Although, what I really wanted to do *right now* was to chuck my dish at Decker's head. Then maybe I'd get my old Decker back. Since the plate belonged to his friend, I held on to it.

"Hey." Krew nudged me with his arm. "Grab the garlic bread and the water, will yah?"

With reluctance, I juggled my plate, the bread and the water bottle, carried them to the table and positioned them close to where I was sitting. Krew placed the large bowl of spaghetti and meatballs in the middle of the table and sat down. I poured myself some water and passed the bottle to Krew.

Decker's eyes narrowed, but the familiar smirk on his devilish face cut through my inner turmoil and I was able to relax. We each took our respective places at the table and began eating in silence.

The food was fantastic. I didn't know Krew could cook. Looking back, my only real memories of the boys were of those lazy days hanging out at the Honey Pot near the reservoir. We talked and laughed the day away, swam at Lions Pool, or just drove around, happy to be together.

To rectify my mistake, I needed to stop fighting with them, and talk. Even be honest... to a point.

"Thanks for cooking, Krew. It's delicious," I said and dug into another meatball.

"You're welcome." Krew grinned. As he wiped sauce from a corner of his lickable lips, a flutter in my belly sent tingles along my skin.

Get a grip, Regi. Don't look at them. My eyes dropped to my plate and breathed.

"So, Krew. I work in a salon. Decker's a hitman, what do you do?" I asked and took a sip of the water. Decker snorted and my eyes shot to his face. "What's your deal?"

"Nothing," he said and shoveled in a forkful of pasta.

"No, I really want to know. You get pissed that I don't talk, and when I do, you give me attitude."

"Attitude?" Decker's eyes narrowed into slits. "Okay. Here's the truth. When we ask *you* to talk to us, you shut up like a clam—you don't let us in. When *you* want to talk about our lives, it's okay." Decker's knuckles on his right hand were turning white from gripping the fork so tightly.

He was right. Again. If he knew why I didn't want to talk about my past, why the blood I'd seen on him affected me, then we would be having a different conversation that would ultimately shatter my soul. Especially once I saw the disgust in their eyes.

"Shut up and eat your food," Krew cut in, his eyes on me.

Decker grunted and refocused on his plate of food. He wasn't eating it, just stared at it with honed concentration.

"I'm between jobs. But I want to tattoo. That's my passion. Been working on it for a while now—as you can see on my skin," he said with his arms wide.

I took in every image on his flesh. Black and grey to colored. Individually, they didn't tell a story, but looking at them as a whole book, his skin was an epic saga.

"I like them. Maybe one day, I'll get one," I admitted sheepishly.

"Just let me know, and I'll do it."

I felt heat creep into my cheeks, at the idea of Krew marking me with his ink, and quickly changed the topic. "How did you get into fighting?"

"I started seriously fighting while I was at Chillicothe Correctional. I had to learn to protect myself from the moment I was sent there," Krew confessed easily, as though he was talking about a walk he had taken in a park.

I dropped my fork, and almost choked on the bite of meatball. "What?"

Decker chuckled. But there was no joy in it. "You didn't know he went to jail after we were captured that night?"

"Neither did you," Krew shot back at Decker.

I shook my head, afraid if I opened my mouth, I was going to vomit all over the table.

Jail. Krew in jail. My sweet Krew who never hurt a fly had to fight to protect himself. Oh, God.

"You have no clue that my father pulled some strings and gave me two choices—either go to jail or enlist in the military?" Decker added to the insult, completely destroying my perception of how they had lived their lives after I'd fled from Elida.

"Again, you didn't know either, Deck," Krew huffed out.

"Because I thought you were going to juvie—not jail."

"I went to both," Krew said flatly, stood from the table and picked up his plate. "It doesn't matter anyway. That's the past."

"It does matter, damn it. Teke should have been in jail for what he did," Decker railed as he slammed his fist on the table and the dishes rattled.

The realization that I wasn't the only one who was affected by that monster's choices hit dead center of my chest.

"No," I croaked, but I couldn't look away from Decker.

The corner of Decker's lips dipped further down and he shook his head. "Neither of us had a choice when we got caught by the cops that night, Regi. But *you* did. Now tell us, why did you run from Elida—from us? Why didn't you keep in touch—at least with Krew?"

I swallowed hard, afraid I'd blurt out the truth about what had happened that night. My throat hurt, as if an invisible noose had been drawn tight around my neck, and I could hardly take a breath.

I grabbed my glass of water and managed to drink the entirety to ease the strain, but the cold liquid didn't help. "I didn't know what happened. Maya—"

"Fucking Maya," Decker spat out. "That bitch has done more damage than—Fuck!" He shot out of his chair and began pacing.

"Maya didn't tell you that she used to come visit me every weekend? Bring me things?" Krew questioned, his eyes wide with surprise.

It took everything in me to not scream. I wanted to track down my ex-friend and beat the crap out of her. Not only had she put me and Krew in this precarious dilemma, she had been lying to me for all these years about my guys.

"Did you know that, in school, she used to proposition us behind your back?" Krew landed another blow, and it felt physical, like his confession had literally punched a hole in my stomach.

"No," I uttered, my eyes brimming with tears. "Why didn't you tell me back then?"

"Would you have listened? She was your best friend, after all—really, the only one you hung out with, besides us," Krew explained as he reached out and tried to take my hand. And I let him. "Regi, I promise you that we never did anything with her."

"You got that right. She was the carnival ride that everyone got on, except Krew and me. We stayed away from that stanky cunt," Decker grated out. "I need to get the hell out of here—check the perimeter." Without another word, Decker took off, leaving me with Krew.

I didn't know what to do. To think that all this time, Maya knew what had happened to Decker and Krew, and she'd hidden their fates from me. That whole time in school, she had kept insisting that hanging out with the guys made me look like a whore. And that I should have asked her to come with us to the Honey Pot, to where Decker, Krew and I hung out without any of our classmates causing trouble for us—especially toward Krew.

She had sworn *on a stack of Bibles,* that, as my best friend, she was saving my virtue and reputation. When, in reality, the whole time, she had used me. She had wanted Krew and Decker.

Maya used me then, as she was using me now. I sat there silent and numb as the truth fully hit me.

I then turned to Krew. "Please, hold me."

Chapter Twenty
Krew

I dragged Regina off her chair and placed her on my lap. With my arms wrapped tight around her, I whispered into her hair, "I have you, sweetheart."

"I'm normally not a blubbering mess—hell, I don't usually cry—you know that," she confessed in a hiccup. "Lately, though, since I've been around you two, that's all I've been doing and I'm tired of it."

"Look at me." I tried to tip her chin up, but she burrowed deeper into my chest.

"I can't," she uttered, her voice strained.

Her confession gave me pause, yet I let it go. "Alright. Then listen." I squeezed her tighter to me. "You have every right to be upset. Maya was your best friend and she betrayed you."

"This whole time, I thought she had my back—we were best friends since first grade," Regina said. She was shaking in my hold. "And why does Decker piss me off so much?"

"You know how he used to be. He liked pissing people off—especially if he got any satisfaction out of it."

"He's never done that to me, or you—"

"Hella ya, he did. You just never took his bait," I admitted, brushing her bangs out of her eyes. "Eventually, he stopped goading you."

"I don't remember... I'm sorry for putting all this on you." She wiped her eyes.

"*I'm* sorry that we didn't tell you sooner about Maya, but Decker and I thought we had it handled," I admitted regretfully.

"I've been such a bitch. This whole thing is just a mess. Still, Decker doesn't need to be a dick," she added.

"I get it. We're all under a lot of stress. This isn't a normal situation that we're in," I said with regret. "It's been years since the three of us have been together. Maybe we should do a restart."

She snorted. "I think that's a good idea, but I'm not so sure about Decker."

"You said it yourself—we have changed. We're not the people we once were. And on top of it, we've been thrown into something we have no control over—*Decker* has no control, and it's killing him. He hasn't been sleeping, and he barely eats. While you're in that bedroom, he's constantly doing perimeter checks, cleaning his gun, contacting Sabrina and running down new leads, just to make sure we are safe."

Regina finally looked at me. "When did you become so philosophical?"

I carefully wiped the tears from her cheeks. "I don't know. When I was in jail?"

"You were in jail," she whispered, more tears trailing from her eyes. "I should have looked for you—called—something."

I tightened my hold around her. "I don't know what drove you away from Elida, but it had to be big, in order for you to leave your parents—leave us, with no word. Whatever you're holding back, I'm patient and willing to wait until you are ready to tell us.

Anyway, I'm kind of glad you didn't see me in there," I said, cupping her face. Looking into her beautiful brown eyes, her dilated pupils swallowed up the gold flecks in her irises. "I truly missed my Regi."

"Krew." She leaned in, closed her eyes, and kissed me. The touch was so gentle—not like the one we had shared in the hallway upstairs or back at the motel in Chicago. This was innocent, like she was testing her boundaries for the first time. I remained still, giving Regina the time she needed to explore me with her lips.

Her hands skimmed up my chest, and in that moment, I cursed at the t-shirt I had on. She smoothed her hands over my hard nipples, up my throat, and along my jawline until her arms wrapped around my neck.

Regina deepened the kiss, her tongue probing the seam of my lips and I opened for her. She swept her tongue inside, and I was a goner.

I took over the kiss, delving my tongue deeper into her mouth like I was possessed. Because tasting Regina was a welcome refuge from the loneliness that had been my constant companion. My dad and my asshole brother were alive, but I was still very much alone.

Now, after having Decker and Regina back in my life—as fucked up as this week had been, I wasn't going to give them up. She could fight me all she wanted, but Regina was mine, and Decker's. We had claimed her the day we found her at the park, while she had waited for Maya to go to the pool.

"Krew," she uttered against my lips. "Please."

I quickly pulled away, but kept an arm around her body. "I'm sorry."

"No, I'm sorry. It's just that... I can't explain it."

"I understand," I lied, my heart aching for an explanation.

"No, you don't. I don't want to do anything down here." Regina got off my lap and took my hand. "Come with me."

She led me upstairs to her room and closed the door. When Regina turned around and faced me, her eyes trailed down my chest to the bulge at my crotch.

My dick was straining against the zipper, aching to be touched, stroked—anyway Regina wanted to handle me. I remained still and waited for her cue as she stood still and took in every inch of my body.

It was torture, but at the same moment, the anticipation only heightened my need to be with the girl I had fallen in love with back in school. I'd waited for so long to be with her, I wasn't going to do anything to mess it up.

"You are so beautiful, Krew," she confessed to me, and it felt like a stroke against my cock. I was so hard that it was nearing painful.

"You're the one who's beautiful," I gruffly said, as I reached out and caressed a finger along her jawline. "I want to kiss you so bad."

She smiled tentatively, before uttering, "Then kiss me."

I didn't hesitate, just scooped Regina up and kissed her. She wrapped her legs around my waist, as I took her mouth with a hot and hungry desperation. We were all mouth and dueling tongues before I gently laid her on the bed.

"I need to taste you," I admitted, kissing down her jaw, along her neckline until I reached the apex of her full breasts. I tugged up her shirt, and without further prompting, Regina sat up and quickly removed her shirt, along with her black lacy bra.

I relished the sight of Regina laying on the bed, spread and exposed for me. Her breasts full—enough to fill my hands. Her dusky nipples were taut and begging for my mouth. I gently glided my hand between them before cupping her right breast and pinching her tight bud. She arched her back and moaned, "Krew—yes."

Her reaction didn't disappoint. I trailed my hand down her

torso, enamored with her silky skin. I began pulling down the snug pants she had on. "Take them off."

She lifted her hips up and ordered, "You do it."

So, I did. Along with the underwear that matched her bra. And when she spread her legs open for me, her glistening cunt turned my want into a desperate needy monster. I quickly removed my jeans and tank to be skin to skin with her.

A gasp fell out of Regina's mouth as she studied my body—my large cock that jutted skyward—which only reacted for her and Decker.

"Don't be afraid," I said as I climbed onto the bed.

"I'm not." The trembling of her voice said otherwise.

"We don't have to do anything you don't want to, Regi." I hoped to ease the tension in her body, but she was lying there so still that I was afraid to move.

"I know. I trust you," she conceded, biting her lower lip as her eyes remained on my cock.

"If all we end up doing is snuggling, I'm fine with that. Just tell me what you want," I assured her, hiding the fear that she would turn me away again.

"Let's take it slow... And see." She finally met my eyes and a shadow of worry was still visible in them, even if her dark pupils were blown wide with lust.

"Slow," I repeated and took her mouth again. Our kiss was languorous and gentle, until Regina tugged on the back of my neck and drew my body on top of hers.

That skin-to-skin connection had my heart hammering in my chest, and the way she ground against my hard shaft, I almost came right then.

I pulled slightly away and dipped my head down, taking a taut nipple into my mouth. Fair game and all. I sucked hard, then laved the sensitive bud while cupping her other breast and pinching the nipple.

Another moan left her parted lips, which gave me a hint of satisfaction.

But I needed more—more of what I'd tasted on Decker's fingers when he had shoved his digits into Regina's wet heat and then pushed those same fingers—coated in her juices, into my mouth.

"Krew." Regina arched her back, and it took every bit of restraint in me not to shove my dick inside her wet heat, and claim her as mine.

Even though being with Regina felt right, I was coming to realize that loving her with my cock without Decker being here with us... It didn't sit well with me. Not for our first time, anyway.

"Regi," I began to say, hoping she wouldn't be upset that I didn't want to love her without Decker.

She touched my cheek. "I know. I want him here too. But..." A tear slipped out of the corner of her eye and I understood what she hadn't said.

Regina was afraid of Decker. His belligerent behavior around her made it hard to trust him. Still, I silently celebrated. She, too, felt the missing piece of us—that we were more than just childhood friends. That we had reconnected to what we three had all those years ago. My Regi was finally seeing us as a whole.

I relaxed and focused on loving her in my own way.

I slid down her body, until my knees were bent and on the bedroom floor. I spread her legs wider and smiled, inhaling her sweet heady scent. Without a doubt, despite her previous lies, Regina wanted me.

I didn't hesitate to dive into her slick folds. I licked from her clit down past the slit, lapping up her liquid heat. Then I clamped down on her bud and drew it in gently at first, then I sucked harder.

"Oh—Jesus—yes," she groaned. If I had hair, Regina would have yanked at it.

Releasing her clit, I trailed the tip of my tongue around the bundle of nerves while I coated my fingers with her nectar. "I'm going to eat you until I get my fill, Regi," I declared.

"Krew!"

I clamped my mouth around her clit again and with one finger, I slid into her slowly and then withdrew, repeating the movement until a loud wanton moan left her lips.

"More." She dug the heels of her feet into my back and drove herself upwards.

At her insistence, I glided a second finger inside her, then three. Pumping in and out while I sucked and laved her until she needed to come.

Regina began to tremble and I knew she was close. "I want you to come on my tongue. I want to taste you—lap you up—and get off, knowing I'm the one that sent you over the edge, Regi."

My teeth clamped onto her clit while I reached up and pinched both her nipples, hard.

"Krew," Regina screamed, and a familiar sizzle at the base of my spine went straight to my balls. I came right along with her, while my fingers kept plunging into her slick pussy. Not once did I pull my mouth off her cunt as I drank up her essence.

I slowly stood, went to the tiny bathroom and cleaned myself up. After wetting a washcloth, I gently cleaned her, then the side of the mattress where I'd spilled my seed, and then tossed the cloth into the laundry basket.

When I returned, I found Regina languid, her eyes fluttered closed and her breathing slow and even. Damn, she'd fallen asleep on me. A smile crested my lips as I watched her.

Carefully, I eased in beside Regina, about to pull her close, when a soft ping came from my phone—in the back pocket of my jeans lying the floor.

Thank Christ Regina fell asleep. If she knew I still had my phone, she'd be pissed. Decker took her phone away for safety—so it couldn't be tracked. The real reason was she threatened to call Maya to find out if she was involved with Jess's dealings with Kane.

The phone pinged again, then rang. Damn it, I knew that ring tone. It was Teke's. I debated for a moment if I should ignore it, except knowing my asshole brother, he'd either keep on texting or calling until I answered the phone.

I got up from the bed, covered Regina with the blanket and grabbed my jeans. I stepped out into the hallway, closed the door and retrieved my phone from my back pocket. As I slid my finger across the screen, I got another text message.

Teke: *Where are you motherfucker?*

Teke: *You better answer me!*

Teke: *Dad's sick. I had to bring him to the hospital.*

I wasn't sure if I should believe him. Teke had used that excuse before to get me to respond. Was he telling the truth this time?

Me: *What happened?*

Teke: *Where are you?*

Me: *Don't worry about it. What's going on with Dad?*

Teke: *He fell trying to get off the sofa, and I had to call an ambulance.*

Jesus. I rubbed my hand over my face in frustration. My father had always been a large man, and his mobility had long been limited due to his weight. Over the past few years, he had gained several more pounds, which worsened his immobility.

However, the notion of him falling off the sofa while trying to get up proved that my brother was a scheming dumbass. My father had lived on that sofa for the past ten years. He slept on it, ate on it, and every once in a while, he peed on it when he couldn't get his dick into the piss bottle. But get off the sofa? Teke was lying. Why?

Me: *You're lying. Now tell me what you really want.*

I waited a good two minutes before texting him again.

Me: *Teke. Answer me.*

Teke never answered me back. My only conclusion; the bastard was probably drunk. I shook my head, shoved my phone back in my pocket and went back into the room. As I glanced down at Regina, peacefully sleeping, my heart hitched up and I was a happy man.

For the first time since we got caught and I took the blame for Teke's stolen car, my life was finally coming together. And once Regina and Decker worked through their issues, we could finally be the family we were meant to be.

Chapter Twenty-One
Decker

I had been a real bastard to Regina. In fact, from the wariness in her eyes, she didn't trust me, and that was something I never wanted to see on my girl's face. But I couldn't help it. Whatever she was hiding was the big reason why she had fled Elida and cut off all communication with us. It had been years since we'd been together, and her silence felt like a betrayal.

Raking my fingers along my scalp, I realized I was no better than her. I had never reached out to either of them, because I was so far up my own ass with problems that I had solely focused solely on myself. "Jesus, Jeromy. How did I get myself into this shit?" I stared up at the stars, wished he heard me.

Damn. This was the first time since his death that I'd said my ex's name out loud. And it hurt. Genuinely pained me to the point that the initials I'd long-ago carved into my skin, on the inner part of my arm, ached.

I rubbed my fingers over the raised scarring and cursed. Needing to get out of my head, I started running. And since I hadn't fully cleaned up the cabin where those two hitmen had been hiding out, I headed back there to finish the job.

Relieved to find the dwelling dark and quiet, I gathered what little food and supplies they had brought with them. Since a fire was out of the question, and I didn't want to dig another hole, I decided to take everything back with me.

Once I knew no traces of either man remained, I climbed onto the ATV and started the engine.

Right as I pulled up to Merrick's home, my cell phone buzzed with a text message. I glanced at the screen and it was Sabrina.

"It's been a week. Give me good news," I said, while glancing at the upper windows, and wondered what Krew and Regina were doing without me.

"I have some—and some that's not so good."

"Just lay it on me." I dropped into the wicker chair on the porch, tipped my head back and stared up at the dark sky, which was littered with millions of stars.

"I had to do a deep dive on this shit. Eventually, I traced the original contract you completed," she said with some dread. The clacking of keys stopped and the silence had me on the edge.

"You found out who took the hit out on Maxwell?" I asked, keeping my voice low tone, in case Krew or Regina was sleeping.

"Not a who, but a what."

"Sabrina," I growled, dragging out her name in warning.

"It's not one person, it's a group called the Agonas Associates," she explained quickly.

"Never heard of them," I admitted, while glancing around the area, staying alert for movements. Two killers had already camped out this close to us. I wouldn't be surprised if more showed up.

"It's a syndicate that runs the underground fight circuit in the Midwest, but the powers that be want to branch out toward the East Coast. No one knows who is involved—or who gives the orders. The group keeps a low profile, while their low-level scumbags do all the work."

"Low-level. Meaning, Kane Maxwell?"

"Yes. And Jess Duncan."

"Okay. If they took out the hit for Maxwell, then I'm assuming they did the same for Duncan and Maya."

"Yes," she said.

"Then how do we contact them to clear the shit up for Krew and Regi? We need to make sure the hitmen are focused on Jess and Maya."

Sabrina chortled. "Dude, you're not understanding the words coming out of my mouth... Sorry, I couldn't help myself. But truth, you're not understanding me. You can't just call these people up. They are like ghosts in the network. I told you no one knows who's a part of the organization, or how many pieces are on that chess board. I wouldn't even know where or who to ask—and even if I did, I wouldn't ask it. Not without repercussions."

"Fucking Christ, Sabrina. I thought you're on my side."

"I am. Calm your damn jets, bossman. I didn't say I was giving up."

"Then how do we clear this shit up?"

"First, I went as far as to cover the trail you three left. Then, I need total clarity. I'm putting feelers out in the dark web about the confusion with these contracts. But I'm telling you, Decker, this group isn't going to give a crap if your Krew or Regi get dead over a mishap of names. All they want is to eliminate Jess and Maya. Everyone else is collateral damage."

"I get it about Jess. And I need to ask this, but why Maya?" Normally, I wouldn't give a fuck about that bitch. Except, my instincts were warning me that she was far more involved than what the surface showed.

"Through the dark grapevine and a bit of hacking, I found out that Kane Maxwell was in deep with the Agonas Associates, working small bouts here and there. However, about three years ago Kane and that Jess guy became partners, and started a low-level fight ring in Chicago. Agonas heard about it, wanted in and started supplying the money and secure locations, and all Maxwell and Jess Duncan had to do was fill the rosters with fighters."

"They wanted a cut of the profits."

"Yes. And Kane and Jess got a much smaller cut than what they wanted."

"I see where this is going," I admitted, rubbing the back of my neck.

"I'm guessing that Maxwell and Duncan weren't satisfied with their portion and so they started skimming larger chunks of cash off the top to add to the percentage they were supposed to take. And guess who was keeping the extra for the boys?"

"Maya," I hissed her name like it was poison on my tongue.

"Right again. But somehow Agonas found out about the money and took the hits out," Sabrina said with a hint of excitement.

In the two years I'd been working with Sabrina, I'd discovered that she had a strange fascination with chaos. In that respect, being a handler in this business of murder was a perfect fit for her.

"Maya is a bigger player than just being their bank," I said, and something settled in my gut. Resolve? I wasn't sure. "How are we going to rectify this? Contact them?"

"These people are powerful. They aren't going to listen to you. They aren't going to care."

My anger rose, flooding my veins with venom. "I'm not going to accept that excuse."

"Trust me, this is out of our hands," Sabrina argued.

"Then I'm going after Maya and Jess and I'll put an end to this shit once and for all."

"There's more, and you're not going to like it," she warned.

I closed my eyes and sucked in a breath, preparing myself for the news. "What is it?"

"As of yesterday, someone took out two more contracts. One for Regina K. Morton and the other is for Krew Matthew Gatlin."

"Motherfuckers—There's four contracts now—who did it?"

"Sorry bossman, the only person who has their hands in everything is none other than Maya Darvy."

Rage exploded in my mind like an atomic blast. Even though I had always thought she was a jealous, manipulative cunt, I never thought Maya had the brains or the balls to do something so devious. She took out a hit on her best friend. Why? Did she do it to save her own ass, or was there more? And why did she want to take Krew out? None of it made sense. Again, it didn't matter. She'd get hers, from my bullet.

"Hey, are you still there?"

"Yeah," I growled out. "I want you—"

"Already called shot on the contracts. But I swear I'm going to track that Maya bitch down."

"Call me back as soon as you find her location—and that Jess." I hung up and blew out a frustrated breath. The deeper this shit went, the farther down the black hole we three were falling.

Now the big question. Should I tell Regina and Krew about the new contracts and who took the hits out? Or let them be oblivious until after I tracked down Maya and Jess and eliminated those two?

I entered the house and noticed that the half-eaten plates of food were still on the table. As I picked up the dishes, I heard Krew's name screamed out in ecstasy. Every cell in my body was telling me to go up and join them. Instead, I dropped my chin and clamped my eyes shut, as pain lanced through my heart. I couldn't fault Krew and Regina for being together.

Maybe it was for the best. Regina hated me—she certainly didn't trust me. And without trust, we had nothing. The three of us had nothing. But her and Krew? They fit. Not like me. I was too fractured to be whole for them. Too much darkness overshadowed the person I once was.

I stood there as quiet descended on the space. No wind gusts, not even the typical creaks and groans of the house, reverberated against my eardrum. It was eerily silent. The night made me think

—hard and long on what I truly wanted out of my life. Merrick did it. Could I have the same happiness?

Could I have both Krew and Regina? Make a life with them, like I had tried with Jeromy? He would want me to—try—at least.

A tear trailed down my cheek and I quickly wiped the existence away with the back of my hand.

Broken or not, right then, I made a decision. I was keeping Krew and Regina forever... If they'd have me.

Since going upstairs to bed was a no-go, I went to the sofa, and crammed my body onto it. No doubt, it was going to be a long night. At least it was better than sleeping in the truck.

Regina's Diary

May 9ᵗʰ, 2018

Dear Diary,

I thought I didn't need to write down my feelings anymore since it's been three years from when I last picked you up. But here I am again, hiding in the bathroom, staring at a bottle of pills—trying to fight my need to just end this.

You're the only one I can talk to—tell my innermost feelings, while I fight off the demons that are still haunting me.

It's not all happy days for me—not since I tried looking for Krew and Decker this past year. No matter how many different searches I did on social media, their names didn't show up. I need to accept the notion that they simply don't have any profiles. Which means they don't want to be found. I also have to give up the dream of ever seeing them again.

I still miss them so damn much. My heart won't quit aching for them. I thought of calling Decker and Krew's fathers, but I nixed that idea immediately. Decker's father would hang up on me because he was a bastard—and I bet he still is. And I wasn't about to call Krew's dad in case...

I even went as far as calling Maya again for details, and she actually answered on the first ring. I hoped she'd offer to make the calls for me, but she didn't. All she told me was that both Decker and Krew left Elida and she didn't know where they went to.

I don't know what to do Diary. I want the hollowness in my heart to go away. I want the nightmares gone from my dreams. I want the memories of that night to be wiped clean from my brain so I can live again. So I can love again. So I can be me again.

I just reread what I wrote tonight, and I want to thank you, Diary for being here for me. Because if I can write that I want to love again, and be me again, I have a reason not to take these pills.

Regi

Chapter Twenty-Two
Regi

I slowly woke, sprawled across the bed on my belly like a starfish, contented and relaxed.

I turned my head, blinked and stared over at the night-stand and froze. The digital clock displayed five after seven in the morning.

Holy crap. For the first time in a long while, I had slept through the night with no nightmares. No waking up with my shirt soaked in sweat as screams tore from my throat. It was all because of Krew. He had kept my horrible dreams at bay.

I closed my eyes, and pressed my face into the pillow.

Krew.

Memories of last night had my stomach all fluttery and a slow thrum started between my legs. Krew had made me come so hard with his mouth and fingers I passed out from absolute bliss.

However, I thought he crawled into bed with me. Or was that my imagination? I looked around the room, but there was no sign of him or the clothes he discarded on the floor last night.

I nuzzled the pillow, inhaling the musky scent he'd left on it as I remembered how his talented mouth—his tongue, had made my body sing.

For years I imagined how he'd be in bed, yet I would never have fathomed the emotions he pulled from me, or the moans. And we didn't even fuck. A pang of regret settled over me that I took pleasure from him, but didn't reciprocate.

The sound of the shower pulled me from my thoughts and I immediately pictured Krew's muscled form, all wet and soapy.

I turned onto my back, stretched, and caught sight of the scars on my wrist. As I remembered the bloody night my demons won, a shiver ran down my spine. If it weren't for a counselor named Thomas and his life partner, James, who'd found me in the shelter's bathroom, I'd be dead right now.

Surprisingly, Krew or Decker hadn't mentioned my old scars on my wrist and thighs, or the bandage covering the fresh injury on my right leg. Although, I didn't advertise them either, which was a good thing. There was no way of lying through my teeth about how I had gotten them. I didn't think they would believe my lies any way. And talking about the scars would only open a can of worms. I'd rather the whole situation stay dead in the past.

I peeled back the bandage and examined the half inch wound on my thigh. Thank goodness it wasn't bleeding and the wound sealed up nicely.

After I covered my cut, I took a quiet moment, and promised myself to never pick up a blade of any kind again.

I lay in bed for another few minutes until my stomach growled. I thought of Krew's spaghetti and meatballs, and how he'd given me a taste of home. So why couldn't I do the same?

Scrolling through my memories, I recalled only one thing Krew loved. My mother's chocolate cake. While, I never made it, I remembered the ingredients and how Mom put it together.

"Why not," I uttered to myself, and got out of bed. And since I was baking a cake, I decided to make breakfast, too. If nothing else, it would get me outside.

As I rummaged through the meager supply of clothes I'd brought, I realized that most of my apparel—especially my underwear, needed washing. I decided to search the small closet and found a light blue, flowery summer dress with short capped sleeves. It wasn't my style but it would do until I washed my clothes.

I stepped into the dress, and was elated to see that it fit me. However, I wasn't going to wear someone else's underwear, so I went pantiless. I didn't have the same luck with shoes. My feet were a half size too big for the shoes I found. Instead, I compromised and grabbed a pair of white flip flops, not caring if my heels hung over slightly.

With a final glance in the mirror that hung on the wall, I carefully opened the bedroom door and made sure the hallway was clear. The shower was still running, which made me wonder if both Decker and Krew were in there.

Lust shot through my core at the image I conjured up.

Focus, Regi.

I crept down the stairs to the main floor, one quiet step at a time.

The moment my feet landed on the solid tile I saw Decker sound asleep on the small sofa.

Well, that answers my question of who's in the shower.

An automatic smile edged my lips at how Decker's sinewy frame didn't fit on the couch. One arm partially covered his rugged face, the other was bent and tucked under the small green pillow his head rested on. No matter how uncomfortable he appeared, Decker's breathing was deep and even.

This was a rare chance to study him without talking to the jerk. He must have been hot during the night, because his t-shirt and a blanket were tossed onto the floor, leaving his sculpted chest exposed.

I took in every muscled curve and his tattoos—not as many as Krew had, and etched this new Decker to memory. He wasn't the boy I knew. He was a man now, fully grown, and dangerous.

A flash of need prickled along my skin as my eyes trailed down his bent legs and then back up to the soft, denim-clad bulge at his crotch.

Hmm... I know what he's packing in there. How would it feel to get fucked by him—

Heat bloomed across my face, and I swiftly darted my eyes away.

Thinking of such things would only bring heartache and make me yearn for a dream that could never come true—no matter how temping either man was to me and to my wayward libido.

Not sure what to do, I quickly glanced at the kitchen. It was open to the living room, and I knew I'd make noise while cooking. The last thing I wanted to be confronted with a grumpy Decker.

Before I did anything stupid and woke up the grouch, I silently tip-toed out of the house, closing the door as softly as I could.

The sun was cresting the hillside, and the sight was stunning. Despite the brilliance of the early morning, there was a chill in the air, but it also eased the tension inside me and I let out a calming breath. There had to be something in the cool Vermont breeze because I felt soothed, like a gentle hand was caressing my skin, and combing through my short hair.

The single wicker chair beside the black, wooden front door looked welcoming, but I was a little too antsy to sit. I headed around the back of the house, breathing in deeply. The summer was nearly over, and I could detect the scent of fall in the air.

Autumn was my favorite time of the year. I could imagine the tall oaks and maple trees that stood sentry on the property, proudly displaying a kaleidoscope of colors. Burnt oranges and reds barely peeking between the tawny tones of brown. It had been ages since I last took a moment and enjoyed what was around me.

It turned into a bad habit of mine to never stop and smell the proverbial flowers. Even though I loved living in Chicago, the hustle and bustle of city life was nothing compared to the unhurried cadence of country living.

I could seriously see myself living simply. Alone? That part I wasn't so sure about.

Ever since I'd met Krew and Decker, fallen in love with them, my dream had been to build a life together—as a family. A messy, loud, beautiful kind of family. I could see it so clearly—one with late-night chats and breakfast on Sunday mornings. If only we'd been able to make that dream a reality. Sadly, it was too late for us. Too late for me, with only shattered dreams to look back on.

Get over it, Regi.

I shook off the illusion and rounded the back of the house. There, I discovered a small garden, fenced off by a short, white picket fence. How perfect.

So picturesque.

As I approached the garden patch, to my surprise, it wasn't as small I had believed it to be. To grow my own vegetables had been another dream of mine, ever since I'd been living in the city, where the price of groceries wasn't cheap. But I quickly learned that my thumb wasn't as green.

I stepped past the three-foot barrier to get a better look at what was growing in the ground. Then an idea hit me. An omelet fit for two men, and me.

Spotting a small basket by the gate, I picked it up and began gathering the veggies I needed. There were several varieties of tomatoes, planted in two rows. Cucumber vines crawled up and over a tall white trellis, and I twisted a ripe one off.

An arch made of chicken wire stood tall enough for me to walk under. Leafy plants crawled up it, anchoring themselves with tendrils, and they were bursting with long green beans. I snapped one off, stared at it for a second, and took a bite of it. Fresh. Crispy. And so damn good. I gathered a few of those.

There were sprawling zucchini plants, and I grabbed one and placed it inside the basket. Frilly carrot greenery ran in a neat row, and beyond that were peppers of different shades, along with other vegetables I couldn't identify.

My stomach rumbled, thinking of the hearty omelet that was going to satisfy my hunger, and I began gathering the rest of the veggies I needed. I'd bake the chocolate cake after I ate.

When I turned around, I startled—almost dropping the basket. Decker was standing silently by the house, watching me with such intensity.

"Jesus. You scared the crap out of me, Decker. Next time, make some noise." I glared at him, planting a hand on my hip. "It's creepy."

His eyebrows winged up in surprise before they furrowed. "I did, but apparently, you were too busy playing with the plants."

"Vegetables," I corrected. "And I wasn't playing. I'm going to make an omelet." I bent down, both to ignore the man and the irritation radiating off him and to snag a carrot. I gently pulled up a dirty, four-inch orange rod out of the dark soil. "Perfect."

"Are you done yet?" Decker growled, opening the gate. "We need to talk about your lack of sense on your safety, especially *if* you come out here, *alone*."

"Then talk." I still didn't bother looking at him.

"I told you *not* to go outside in case there are snipers."

"Umm... What?" I straightened and turned to him in confusion. "You said no such thing to me."

"I know damn well what I said to you," he snapped. "Again, you're not listening. It's dangerous out here—or did you forget everything I told you in the truck? Jesus, Regi. When did you become so—"

I shot my arm out, and raised a finger to stop him from saying anything further. "Whatever you're about to say, better think twice." I glared at him.

"Care-less," he emphasized with a snarl.

"When did you tell me all these rules? When I was asleep in the back seat of the truck?" My chin tilted up in defiance.

Anger radiated off Decker as he glared at me. I swore if he clenched his teeth any tighter, they would crack.

"I haven't been out here that long, Deck. Now if you will excuse me, I'm going to make a vegetable omelet that could save lives."

Decker wouldn't move. "You have a death wish or something?"

Or something.

Decker eyed the dress I was wearing and the full basket clutched in my hand. "Is your life worth these vegetables?" He picked up the carrot and tossed it back in.

"Why are you being such a prick to me?" I countered, trying to be brave, but my stomach began to churn. "You haven't told me anything about safety or that I couldn't go outside. I'm cooped up in this house with nothing but to stare at the walls for entertainment. You took my phone away in case someone might track us."

"It's all for your safety." He ground out.

"Yeah? Well, what about the blood from the other day? How did that happen? Do you expect me to stay in the house the whole time while we're here? You go out and do whatever you please— and I know damn well Krew does too. So why can't I—Oh wait, is it because I'm a weak woman—because I'm not strong? Well, get this through your head, Decker Moss. I. Am. Strong." I punctuated each word while pointing at myself.

"It takes more than strength to be strong. You have to listen too. Damn it, your strength isn't going to stop a bullet."

I was so pissed that I couldn't see the point Decker was trying to make. "You know what? You don't get it. I'm going inside, and you can just go fuck off," I shouted and tried to move around him.

"Fuck off?" In a flash, Decker was inches from me, so close that his hard puffs of breaths fanned across my face. "Did I hear you right?"

"Yes, but I'll say it again. Fuck off." I refused to back down. He wasn't going to intimidate me.

"You want to know where the blood came from? Alright. Listen up, princess. There were hired *killers* out there wanting to shoot you dead. The blood came from them. They came here to put a bullet in your and Krew's heads, but I got rid of them—for you and him." He pointed a finger toward the house, before he moved it to my temple. "Is it worth all these vegetables now?" He shot a hand out, smacking the basket out of my hands.

Decker was hulking over me like some snarling dog, ready to take a bite. I stumbled back, both from what he said and the enraged look in his eyes.

Fear and something foreign trickled into my body, and I was terrified and excited at the same time. God, I was sick. The need to run was followed by a shot of lust as an image of Decker hunting me down and fucking me in the garden had my pussy slick and ready.

Before I did something utterly stupid like taunting him into chasing me, I shouted in his face. "Step back, Deck."

Decker moved, giving me room to escape. I quickly raced to the front of the house, but I heard him following close behind.

"You're not going to shout in my face and then take off like a coward, Regi—not after you spouted so much about being *strong*." His taunt and maniacal laughter added layer of mortification to my now sour attitude.

"Leave me, alone." Damn it, I was whining. But Decker was right. I was a coward, and I wasn't strong. No amount of strength was going to stop a bullet aimed at me.

It was foolish to stand up to him, knowing full well that I'd never be tough enough to face any man, least of all Decker. I wasn't before, and I'd just proven that fact again.

"I can't believe my girl had the balls to tell me to fuck off right to my face." He chuckled, like he approved of my verbal retaliation, which was all confusing. One moment, he was raging at me about safety, and now he was acting like this was all funny.

I barely made it around to the front of the house when Decker's words hit me like a sledge hammer. Did he call me *his* girl? Because I wasn't. I was nobody's girl, especially not his.

"What do you think, Krew?"

I nearly tripped over my feet, halting in front of the door, where Krew stood, arms folded across his bare chest.

"Are you being a dick again?" Even though he glared at Decker with open hostility, Krew made no move to shield me.

"No," Decker said.

"Yes," I countered at the same time.

"I think you two need to work this out on your own." Krew spun around and strode back into the house, closing the door—leaving me open mouthed and shocked. He had left me with this jerk.

I took a step toward the door, when Decker's fingers gripped my upper arm and spun me around. He almost made me trip in those damn flip flops. My back was pushed against the clapboard house, and his body pinned me in place.

I gulped, realizing Decker's sizable erection was pressing against my lower abdomen. I stood there, attempting to ignore him and the escalating excitement coursing through my veins. He was turned on as much as I was.

Gaa! Stop this before it's too late.

"Do I have your full attention now?" Decker clipped out as he ground his hips into me. His granite shaft was a contradiction to his lips, dipped into a deep frown. They were a inch away from mine.

My heart was racing from the rush of heat that pooled in my

core. I didn't want to be turned on by his aggressive touch. My body didn't seem to care, which made me even angrier—*at me*, for being all hot and bothered by this jerk treating me this way.

"Step back, Deck," I repeated. My eyes never looked away from his fiery blue ones.

"No," he snarled in a whisper. "I want to know what the hell's going on with you. And why aren't you taking my precautions seriously?"

"There's nothing going on with me," I said, wanting to knee him in the balls just to make him back off. But I'd be lying if I said I didn't want him even closer. His mouth on me, his hands all over my body, his—

"Liar." Decker angled his head slightly, his eyes narrowed, like he was trying to read my mind. Then the tip of his tongue slipped passed his lips, and I followed the trail until it met one corner of his sexy mouth.

My breaths heaved in and out of my lungs, aching with exertion. Another shot of lust slammed into me, like Decker was some new-fangled drug being pumped into my veins.

What that angry mouth could do to my body—*Stop thinking of what his damn mouth can do, and run.*

"Back up," I hissed, but with a lot less bravado. I'd do anything to squash the desire pooling at my core. Even lie, so he could hate me. "I don't want you to touch me."

He didn't listen. Decker was so damn stubborn, and so overpowering, he was boggling my mind. When he leaned in even closer, I reacted without thought or consequences—biting his lower lip purely on instinct.

Decker's head wrenched back, and he quickly stepped away from me.

Did I run? Hell no. I stayed plastered against the house, shocked that I had actually bitten him. My eyes zeroed in on the blood seeping from the bite mark. I licked my lips, tasted his blood, and panic filtered in. Yet, it certainly didn't extinguish any desire swelling inside me.

He licked at the bitten area and smirked. "Damn, princess, is this how you like to play now?" He swiped his thumb against his lower lip, and it came away red before he stuck the digit into his mouth. "I'm all for playing hard."

Decker anchored his left arm around my waist as he pressed roughly into me. "Damn it Deck, release me." I couldn't wiggle out from between his hard body and the house.

His right hand slid down until he had a grip on the hem of my dress. "You wanted to play." The moment his hand was at the junction of my thighs, his eyes went molten. "No panties," he moaned.

Of all the days I decided to wear a dress with *no* underwear, I picked the wrong day. *Or maybe it's the right day.*

"Decker, please," I pleaded.

"Please what? Please you want me to let you go? Or please you want me to touch you. Fuck you. Make you scream out my name as you come around my cock?"

"Please," was all I could say, because I didn't know—yes, I knew what I wanted but I was afraid to verbalize the desire growing in my belly.

Decker slammed his mouth over mine, his tongue conquering, and igniting the lust within me until it blazed like a fiery inferno. His fingers were in my wet folds before his digits slid inside me. I tipped my head back, closed my eyes, and whimpered out his name.

The moment I lost his mouth, my eyes blinked open.

"Now tell me, is this what you needed?" He drove his fingers deeper in and out, then he curled his digits until they pressed the part of me that made me see fireworks.

Then Decker did the most unthinkable thing. He pulled his fingers out of me and stepped back.

I was suddenly left feeling bereft, until he stuck his fingers into his mouth and sucked up all of my juices. "Still sweet."

"Not fair," I moaned.

"Absolutely fair. Now are you going to finally tell me what's going on with you? Why aren't you listening to what I say? And why you are acting like a shrew toward us—toward me?"

"Fuck you, Deck. You deserve it because you're being a total prick."

He erupted into laughter. "Fine. Yeah, I've been an asshole—but for a good reason."

My hackles lowered, because he was right. All he'd been doing was keeping us safe. However, I didn't want to admit that to him.

"Regi." His tone more serious as he moved closer. "I'm trying to protect you and Krew."

"I know," I finally admitted, but no less frustrated.

"Good." He smirked. "Now that you understand, are you going to tell the truth and confess that you are ours—have been—and always will be? Or are you afraid of what could be between the three of us? Afraid of me and what I do?"

"Are you kidding me?" Irritation rattled near the brink of my common sense, and I got into his face. "Understand this, Decker Moss. You might be right that I should be more cautious, but remember my words. I'm not afraid of you. I'm no damn princess and I'm not your girl. And you won't touch me again."

He leaned in even closer. "You can lie all you want to yourself, but I see how much you want me. And you *are* my girl—and Krew's girl. *Our* girl. Just like we are yours. And the sooner you get that through your head, the better."

I shoved him back as hard as I could, desperate for the distance. "I'd rather kiss a toad than your ugly face," I growled out the outrageous lie.

Decker flashed a wicked smile, a single dimple teasing from his left cheek. I wanted to hate him—really, I did—but that flicker of boyish charm sent my heart fluttering like a schoolgirl's and I didn't stand a chance.

He leaned in closer, and I assumed he was going to kiss me. Instead, he bypassed my mouth, and his lips grazed my ear. "I thought you liked my ugly mug." His undertone was rough like heavy grit sand paper and the flutter in my heart shifted into a full-blown gallop.

When I turned my head and met his eyes, I was consumed by the carnal fire in them and my knees went weak. I knew that look. Decker regarded Krew with the same hungry intensity. Now, he was aiming that desire at me with equal fervor.

"I'm not sure if I'm ready to be intimate with you," I confessed. My body yearned for him, yet my mind and heart refused to believe Krew and Decker belonged to me—to cherish, to love, to keep.

"I heard you and Krew last night," he said with raw conviction. My breath hitched, and my heart dropped at his confession.

His question staunched the growing hunger in my belly. "We didn't…"

"Don't lie to me."

"I'm not lying. Krew and I didn't have intercourse."

"I heard you two," he hissed.

"He got me off with his mouth and… fingers." I closed my eyes, feeling utterly disgusted with myself.

"Look at me." I couldn't ignore him. I opened my eyes and barely glanced at him before I dropped my attention to his chin. "You did you let us touch you in Chicago?"

Why had I let Decker and Krew touch me? Loneliness? Out of desperation? Maybe both. Or maybe, they were a convenience—a need to satiate my sudden impulse to be touched. No. That wasn't it.

As the thrum between my legs eased and the fear that shad-owed me lessened, the reason why was clear. I was afraid to be alone and I missed them so much. However, I certainly couldn't tell him the truth.

"Curiosity," I finally said. Though true, and a safe answer, it was still a partial lie. The least amount of resistance on the path to the actual fact.

But that was my issue. What my heart wanted versus what was safe.

"Bullshit. You're lying, again," Decker called me out.

This push and pull between us was draining, and I had no more mental energy to fight with Decker—no matter how much I wanted to force him away from me. I wanted him—just as much as I had needed Krew last night.

"Fine. Tell me what you want me to say so I can go in and make breakfast." I finally looked at Decker in the eyes and saw the hurt I placed there.

Why couldn't I just say it? I needed Decker. Needed the way his presence anchored me. Even though he had been nothing but a loose buoy in the middle of my storm.

Right now, everything in me was unraveling. The emotions, the mess of my life—they were swallowing me whole. No safe place to land. Just open water and the weight dragging me down, straight into the darkest corners of my mind. The ones I never let anyone see. The ones where my nightmares lived.

Decker's left hand gripped my hip, grounding me as I spiraled in doubt. A shudder ran through me at his touch. His blue eyes, steady and intense pulled me back to the present.

Without asking, he lifted me up and tossed me over his shoulder, striding back toward the front of the house.

"Decker, put me down," I shouted, and slapped at his ass.

"You were forewarned, princess." Then he slapped my ass hard.

"That hurt," I screeched, as he carried me through the front door and into the living room, where Krew was sitting on the sofa. "Krew!"

"He isn't going to help you." Then Decker slapped the same ass cheek again.

"You're an asshole."

"You love me." He smacked my ass again. "Now you know how it feels to be lied to."

The sharp bite of pain across my butt lasted only seconds, then a burn seeped into my skin, and re-ignited the ache between my legs.

"Damn it, Deck—"

He took the steps two at a time until we reached the second floor, but he didn't stop. Decker hauled ass into the room I was sleeping in and tossed me on the bed.

I quickly scrambled backwards until my back hit the head-board. "Don't come near me."

"You think that's going to stop me from bending you over my knee—better yet, I'll shove something inside your mouth to teach you a lesson to not lie to me, or to Krew."

Yes, fucking please was what I wanted to say, but I remained silent, my lips pressed tightly together, as I glared at Decker with indignation. What was I thinking? I wasn't a masochist... I didn't like being hit—much less be roughed around.

"Okay. If silence is your answer, and this is what you want." Before I got a chance to deny his words, Decker dived at me and wrangled me up into his arms. I tried to fight him, using all of my strength, but I failed miserably.

When I saw a chance to escape, I went limp in his arms instead. Tired of fighting him, my desires, and stopped denying the love I had for this man. I wanted Decker with every molecule in my body.

Decker turned me until my ass was up and I was bent over his legs, with my hands rooted to the floor. "I don't think..."

"Hmm. I need to see you," Decker crooned as he slid the dress over my bare ass inch by slow inch, like he was savoring the moment. And so was I as the fabric grazed along my sensitive skin.

"You know what?" He squeezed one of my butt cheeks. "I think you want me to spank you, mark your skin pink. Mark you as mine and Krew's.

I wanted to deny everything he said. But his light touches along the crease of my ass sent tremors throughout my body. Then his words gave me clarity. No more denying myself of the pleasures these men could give me. And no more denying the fact that I was very much still in love with both Krew and Decker. With that, I had to tell them the truth about the past. At least to Decker. He deserved to know what had happened to me.

I couldn't chicken out—not this time.

"Decker..."

He slid a finger along the crack of my butt and I tingled with desire. Wetness pooled at between my legs, I groaned and squirmed to get more friction.

Nevertheless, I tried telling him about Teke, but Decker placed a finger across my lips. "Shhh," he whispered and grazed his hand along my sore ass cheek he had slapped earlier.

Jesus, was he serious? He wasn't going spank me. Was he?

I was wrong. Decker was playing with me this whole time.

Now Decker had me where he wanted, he landed a solid, hard blow across the fleshy part of my right ass cheek. I cried out in pain as my core clenched in anticipation.

For a long three beats, I waited for the panic to strike—waited for it to sink its teeth into me. Surprisingly, it didn't. I even expect the air supply to my lungs be cut off. Or the fear to claw its way up my throat, which had me running for my life in the past.

No. This new sensation raced across my skin, finding every nerve ending in my body, and I was drenched at the apex of my sex. My clit thrummed even more than before, aching to be stroked, pinched, and sucked on.

Decker chuckled, running a hand over the area he had slapped, and another ripple of electricity skated across my skin. "That's it, Regi. Now you know that this is what you need, and it will keep you focused on me."

I shook my head, denying the truth. How crazy was it to want Decker to spank me, then fuck me out of my mind until there was only him and me in my head.

And yet, I kept my teeth clenched and my body coiled tight, trying to breathe through the riot of emotions he was evoking in me.

"Not ready to admit your feelings yet?" Decker moved his hand to my other cheek, slapped it equally hard a few times, and then stroked the skin, sending another rivulet of pleasure up my spine. I groaned, swimming in a pool of trepidation and yearning so profound that it scared me, and wished Krew was here holding us. Holding me.

To be so intimate with not only one man but two...

"Say it, Regi. Admit that you want me, just as much as you want Krew." He demanded a confession.

If I did confess, would I lose what little I had left of my heart when we parted ways?

Another sting of pain pulled me out of my downward thoughts. My resistance lasted about a nano-second before my defiance crumbled to dust and a ravening hunger took over.

"Yes, Decker," I finally admitted in a whisper. "I want both you and Krew."

My ass stung, but Decker carefully turned me around in his arms like I was a fragile piece of glass and sat me across his thighs.

I was about to protest until I saw the wealth of emotion in his blue depths, which made my breath catch in my throat.

"Then tell me you trust me with your heart and your body," Decker insisted, a hint of vulnerability in his voice.

Could I trust him? Did I trust him? I reached deep into my memories for that boy I once knew—the boy I fell in love with, and the answer was there, tangled in with the thorny vines of my trauma. I pulled, ripped, and tore through every dark corner to retrieve those pieces that were precious to me.

The hours we had spent at the Honey Pot, filled with laughter and joy. The times we had hung out after school, and the confessions of our feeling for one another. I hugged those memories tight to my chest and stared into Decker's eyes.

"I trust you and Krew, but I'm afraid, Deck," I confessed, my eyes filled with unshed tears. "I'm so afraid."

"I have you." How ironic, that he said the same thing Krew professed to me last night. Once I divulge the truth, would they say the same?

I wrapped my arms around his torso and kissed Decker like I was giving my last breath to this man.

The kiss wasn't gentle or sensual by any means. It was rough— all teeth, lips, and tongue. There was no comparison between the sweet, innocent first kiss we had shared on my sixteenth birthday and this kiss—how his mouth and hands were strumming my body to life. I was engulfed by the scorching desire that flowed from him into my veins and I relished the heat his body gave off.

The tight hold he had on me was comforting, until he pulled back and stared intently into my eyes.

"I need to be inside you, Regi. Tell me yes." Decker dipped down and nipped at my neck, my collarbone, hard. I knew there was going to be a bruise. It made me heady thinking he had marked me. I waited a beat, expecting the familiar panic to rise again. Except there was none. No fear surging forth. No need to run. Only the hunger that filled me to the brim.

Decker kissed me once more—sweetly this time as though he was giving me time to mull over what he had asked. And I wanted to agree—so badly, but something was preventing the yes from leaving my mouth. Should I tell him that I wanted both men? That having both Krew and Decker here made me complete?

"What is it?" he asked in a whisper.

Just say it, Regina.

"I need Krew too." I couldn't look into his eyes, for fear I'd see disapproval. The guilt I had felt over the years for wanting to be with both of these men—for that level of depravity, I was sure I'd be consigned to the pits of hell.

"Christ," Decker hissed, and my eyes darted to his. But it wasn't censure I read on his face. It was happiness. "Krew!" Decker's bellow echoed off the walls of the bedroom.

Chapter Twenty-Three
Krew

The moment Decker shouted my name, I raced up the steps as though a swarm of hornets was after me. I opened the bedroom door, my chest heaving, and my eyes riveted on Regina reclining on the bed, and my best friend was lying next to her.

"She needs us both," Decker professed in a throaty rumble.

I walked to the bed and dropped to my knees beside it. I reached out and ran a finger over the fresh mark on her collarbone, then tenderly cupped her cheeks. "Are you sure, sweetheart?"

There was so much raw emotion roiling across her face. She leaned her head into my touch, and nuzzled against my calloused palm. She then reached out and touched Decker's cheek. The turmoil I saw in her eyes calmed, like someone had flipped a switch in her head.

"There's no past, or future. Just here and now. Just us," she whispered.

Decker began kissing her, slow and unhurried.

"Deck," Regina protested, her fingers gripping the back of his head.

"What do you need, baby?" he asked against her lips, then dipped down to the sensitive flesh of her neck, and began sucking hard, like he was marking her again.

The need to do the same had me get on the bed, next to them.

"I need more," Regina confessed. "Please."

I leaned in, kissing my way up to the crook of her neck—opposite to Decker—and sucked, leaving another mark. A loud moan escaped Regina's lips, which amped up my desire to touch and taste these two people I'd loved for so long.

I trailed my hand down Regina's arm to her exposed sex, then paused, my gaze catching on several thin, white scars on her thighs—along with a small bandage—and what the meaning behind them.

Decker straightened, his eyes zeroed in on her legs too, but remained silent on the subject. I knew there was going to a conversation in the near future and he'd demand a reason why she had done that to herself.

My soul ached at seeing Regina's self-inflicting wounds. The pain she must have endured to harm herself like that was unimageable. I knew she was carrying a heavy secret—something so profound, something she wasn't willing to share with us. But those battle scars, and the fresh bandage, proved one thing clearly; she was still fighting those demons.

Instead of demanding an explanation, I didn't want our connection broken, I ran a finger down the small patch of curls. "Part your legs for me," I said, before sliding a digit between her slick folds. "You're so wet for us."

Decker wrapped his hand around the back of my neck and pulled me close. Our lips crashed together. The kiss was scorching, like we were making up for loss times.

Then we refocused on Regina. Our mouths met her's at the same time. Our tongues danced and played, while our hands touched and caressed each other.

My desire ignited into a blazing pyre. I was near combustible. Just their lips alone had the potential to make me shoot a load.

Decker pulled away. "Let's take the dress off," he said with a grin. But his eyes were on me, and mischief sparked in them. I knew that look. He was in the mood to tease—to play with our girl and I was all for that.

With my help, Decker and I slowly glided our palms up Regina's legs, skimming the dress higher until her breasts were exposed. I sucked in a breath. "Bare."

"Surprise," Decker chuckled. "Lift your ass for us, baby."

Regina raised her hips and Decker skimmed the dress further up, past her ribcage, above her full breasts where her nipples were taut. They were begging to be touched.

"Sit up and raise your arms, sweetheart," I said while admiring her naked form. My already engorged shaft thickened even more as she lay back down and waited, completely still. "So beautiful," I hummed, staring at her radiant skin—the opposite of mine, which was covered in ink. I'd love to ink her skin with one of my tattoos. Decker, too, if he had room on his skin for me.

As Regina's eyes were fixed on my cock, she sucked in a breath. "You're bigger up close."

"What do you mean by that?" I asked, trying to recollect when she saw me naked, and I couldn't recall one instance. I was still clothed last night when I made her come twice. Then Decker chuckled, which drew my attention. "What?"

"She watched us that first night."

My eyes shifted to Regina; her skin blushed pink with embarrassment. "You two woke me up with your moaning. I had no choice but to look in on what you were doing."

A smile sliced across my face. "And you got off watching us?"

Her cheeks went from pink to crimson. She nodded.

"Well." I glanced down and looked at my dick proudly. I was

above average in length and thickness. "It's all yours, sweetheart. And Decker's."

Decker tossed his clothes, and climbed back on the bed. "I'm no chump either." Which was true—while I had more girth, Decker's impressive length was longer than mine.

"No, you are *not*," Regina finally spoke. She swallowed hard as her eyes bounced between our pricks. "All mine."

There it was. The easy banter between the three of us. It was back, like we never lost touch.

"Now spread your legs for me wide so I can see your pussy, baby. I'm hungry," Decker insisted. I met his intense stare with excitement as we waited for Regina to do as he instructed. It was her choice. Decker might be the one who was directing this three way, but Regina had all the power to say no.

She slowly spread her legs further apart. With her pussy fully exposed, Decker leaned close and asked once more. "Are you sure you want this, from us?"

He slid his hand slowly across her stomach and down to the apex of her sex, where my hand was already massaging her inner thigh.

"Yes," she whispered huskily. "I'm aching for your fingers to touch me—for the two of you to be inside me."

Decker took the lead and his fingers glided between the lips of her pussy before he leaned down and clamped his mouth around her small bundle of nerves.

As much as I loved watching them, I wanted—needed more. I leaned down and sucked her left nipple into my mouth while I pinched the other taut bud with my free hand. Perfection.

"Oh, my god," she gasped, as Decker and I explored her body.

"So wet," he said as his fingers came away glistening. "Taste our girl." I moaned as he offered them to me.

He stuck his fingers into my mouth and I sucked them clean. "So damn sweet," I confessed with a smile.

"Kiss our girl, while I taste her pretty cunt and get her ready for us." Without preamble, Decker's mouth was on her clit.

I hungrily took Regina's mouth like I was a starving man. But our moment didn't last before she said, "I want you in my mouth." How could I say no to her? I got on my knees and moved toward her head.

She licked her lips, reached out and gripped onto my hard shaft. "Come closer."

I shifted some more until I was hovering over her, my balls nearly touching her chin. She angled her head and then dragged her tongue along my shaft. I shivered on contact.

"Mmm." Regina then slid the tip of my dick into her warm mouth and sucked as she slowly stroked.

"Open your mouth more and take more of him," Decker instructed, his face still between her legs.

Regina's lustful gaze met mine before she guided more of me inside her willing mouth. She never stopped stroking me, and there was a rhythm between us. I was already on the edge, ready to shoot down her throat.

"Fuck yes—you two look so damn hot together—Don't come, K," Decker ordered. I shifted a pleading gaze to him, as he slid two digits into Regina's pussy. "I want some of that."

Decker leaned over and licked the exposed section of my shaft, while his fingers were stretching her open. When he pulled away, Regina swallowed my cock down the back of her throat.

She gagged and pulled away, her eyes tearing and spit dribbling from the corner of her mouth. Regina couldn't be more perfect— lying there, staring up at me with passion reflecting in her gaze. Then she went right back to sucking my cock eagerly.

Pressure began to build in my balls, and with a few more sucks and strokes from Regina's talented mouth and hands, I was ready to come. "Regi," I crooned. I pulled out of her mouth and covered her lips with mine. I kissed and licked and tasted—her and me—on our tongues.

"Are you ready to take us, Regi?" Decker asked, as he grabbed the condoms from where he had tossed them earlier.

"Not both—I don't think—I'm ready for that—my body isn't ready—for the two of you together." Regina was tripping over her words. And I understood her apprehension, Decker and I weren't small.

"Hey—hey, look at me," I said, cupping her face with both hands. "If you're game, how about Decker fucks me while I'm inside you?"

Her eyes went wide and her mouth dropped open. "Can we do that?"

"We can do whatever you want," Decker added, as he glided a hand down my back to my ass and squeezed.

"Don't stop," I moaned in reverence.

"Demanding. Just you wait." Decker reached over and stroked my length before he gently pushed Regina back down on the bed. "Regi, don't move. Krew."

My name was an unspoken order. I moved between Regina's legs, my ass in the air and began eating her out like a never-ending feast, while Decker prepared me. He wasn't gentle as he stretched my asshole, and the little sadist in me relished the bite of pain.

"We're going to love you, Regi," Decker admitted as he pulled his fingers out of me.

Decker shifted and then he handed me a condom. Then I heard the rip of a foil wrapper, before I felt cool liquid coat my pucker and I shivered.

"I can't wait until my cock sinks into your tight hole," Decker whispered to me. The tip of his rigid shaft was rubbing against my balls, and I knew he was ready. And so was I.

With one last lick of Regina's clit, I sat up on my knees and rolled the condom down my shaft. Then I positioned myself over our girl, my cockhead at her entrance. I met her eyes, and said, "Tell me again, this is okay."

Regina tenderly smiled up at me, her fingers gently gliding up my arms. "Yes, Krew."

I didn't waste time and slowly sunk into her hot, tight heat. We both moaned in pleasure.

"My turn," Decker declared. The moment I was balls deep in Regina, he slowly guided his dick inside me. "That's it, open for me."

There was no way to describe the sheer euphoria of fucking while being fucked at the same time—no, we were making love to each other.

"Deck." I groaned low, and shivered over the fullness in my ass and the anticipation of the dicking I was going to get.

My eyes snagged onto Regina's, as she tried undulating her hips. "I trust you. Now move, Krew."

That was all she needed to say to me. I didn't ask for those words, but Regina gave them to me as if she knew I needed to hear them again. My heart was fuller than ever, and I was ready to claim her as ours.

I began to move slowly, pulling away and then sinking back into her pussy while Decker remained still until I was adjusted to his length.

Then a cyclone of whirling desire moved through my body, kicking up my need until I couldn't control the steady rhythm of my thrusts.

Decker angled my face and took my mouth in a brutal, hungry kiss, as he savagely pounded into me.

Our intimate joining—Decker to me, me to Regina—felt like we were one.

Regina moaned in pleasure, while Decker pistoned his hips, matching my frantic pace, as my cock drove into her.

"I love you both," I confessed, and drove into Regina with ruthless determination, while Decker did the same to me. Our bodies slapped together, and our mingled moans and grunts echoed off the walls, and I splintered.

Regina screamed out her ecstasy, as her womb clenched so tight around my cock that sparks flashed in my vision, and tears of happiness trailed from the corners of my eyes.

I grunted, my balls drew tight and my hips faltered. I slammed into Regina one final time and came.

"Now you're both mine," Decker growled. "Fuck-fuck—yes. He pulled out of me, ripped off the condom and came all over my back, before he collapsed on top of me and Regina.

Watching the two people I loved taking pleasure from me stirred a feeling so profound that I had no words to share it with Regina and Decker. The raw beauty of this man and this woman coming apart above and below me was a magnificent achievement.

Our bodies shifted, Decker was now next to Regina, and they were kissing and touching each other. These two people were the ones I treasured most in this world, and a quiet torment stirred in my chest for their full connection—their touches, their kisses.

Was I jealous that Regina and Decker were giving each other their full attention? I had to admit, yes. For the first time ever, I was envious of my best friends, and I didn't know why. Not once had I felt this way when we were kids, or even when we three shared a moment in the nasty motel room in Chicago. And what we had shared moments ago was beautiful.

Then why was the giant green monster in me demanding my turn? I shook off those dour thoughts and got up. "I'm going to shower."

"Wait, Krew," Regina called, her hand out to me. "Come back here."

I leaned in, greedily took her mouth while avoiding Decker's eyes and then left the room.

I stepped into the bathroom and shut the door, locking it behind me. Morning light spilled in through the small window—enough to see around me. I twisted the shower handle, cranking it to cold. Maybe the icy water would clear away these negative thoughts in my head.

"Krew," Decker shouted as he knocked, expecting me to open the door.

"I'm going into the shower." I switched the water to the shower head and climbed in.

"I want to talk," Decker said, knocking harder this time.

"We can talk after." I pulled the white plastic curtain around me, wishing it block out Decker's ranting.

I didn't even get my head under the cold spray before the door smashed open. I knew who it was, so I didn't bother looking.

"Don't ignore me," Decker growled as he whipped open the curtain. I turned my head slightly and eyed him, seeing that he was dressed in only his jeans. "Now what the hell is up with you? We had a great time, and then you're..." he circled his fingers, "Like this."

I stood there, naked and wet, and glared at him for the intrusion. "Can you give me five minutes to clean up?"

"No. You're too much in your head. I saw how you looked at us and it wasn't good, K. We need to talk—all of us," he demanded.

"Bossy motherfucker," I seethed between clenched teeth.

Regina came into view just outside the bathroom. Her eyes were wide, watery, and remorseful, like she was the one who was at fault for making me feel like shit.

"Decker's right," she finally said with a trembling lower lip. "We do need to talk."

Her eyes roved from my face, down to my cock. My very erect cock.

Jesus. We just fucked. I should be flaccid. However, my dick didn't get the memo that we were done.

I might have been jealous, but I wasn't numb—even with the freezing cold shower, I was still so turned on; I still wanted them both.

"Krew," she said breathily. The way Regina ravenously sized up my cock and slowly licked the corner of her lower lip made my jealousy vanish, and I was able to breathe. She too lost that panicked expression.

"What's going on in that brain of yours?" Decker asked, his aggression ebbed.

"Come out here and talk to us," Regina said with a smile.

I dropped my chin to my chest, and let the water sluice over my scalp and down my back before I shut it off. "Alright." As I stepped out of the tub, I reached for the towel hanging on the rack, but it slipped off and fell on the floor.

As I bent down to pick it up, red hot pain lanced through my shoulder a split second before Decker dove onto me and knocked all three of us down to the tiled floor.

All at once, a riot of bullets hit the bathroom wall, leaving holes the size of large grapes in the plaster wall. Regina screamed, and Decker roared, "Stay down, Regi!"

I lay there, slightly disoriented after knocking my head against the tile floor, while Decker hovered over me like some dark avenging angel. His face was marred with a fierce frown and a deep crease formed between his brows.

I glanced up at Decker and then at Regina, who was next to me. I reached out, she quickly grabbed my hand and squeezed it tight. "I'm okay," she admitted and trembled.

Not entirely sure whether she was reassuring herself or me, but it eased my worry that she hadn't been hit by one of those bullets.

"You're hit," Decker said, his voice firm but void of emotion.

"My shoulder," I uttered, peering at where the throbbing radiated from. "I'm okay, Deck."

Still in a crouched position, his eyes fixed onto the blood seeping out of the wound, before he turned his narrowed gaze back to my face. "Don't move from this spot." I nodded as he turned to Regina. "Regi, I need you to put pressure on his wound."

"With what?" Panic seeped into her voice. Her dark eyes were wide and centered on my wound.

"I can do it," I said, but Decker shook his head.

"*She* can do it." Decker disappeared from my sight, returning a moment later with two blue towels. "Regi, listen to me. I need you to press on the wound and don't stop until I come back, or Krew will bleed out. Understand?"

"I—I…"

"You can do it," his tone brooked no argument.

"K, lift up your shoulder."

I did as he directed, assuming that Decker was checking for an exit wound.

"Through and through. Good." He then proceeded to place one towel under me, and then pushed me back down. "Press here, Regi," Decker explained in a throaty whisper as he pressed the other towel over the bullet wound. "I'll be back. No matter what, don't leave this spot. Don't stand. Don't move. Don't do anything other than what I told you to do. Understand?"

He peered into Regina's eyes then mine, wanting confirmation that we wouldn't be hauling ass out of the house.

We both nodded. Then Decker took off. I wanted to call him back, and from the stricken look on Regina's face, she wanted the same. To ease her fear, I said, "He'll be back."

"How do you know?" Fat tears streamed down her face as she pressed hard against my gunshot.

I groaned from the pain, then breathed through it and said,

"You know Decker. When did he ever break a promise that he'd made?" My question had Regina dropping her eyes.

"I don't know Decker, or you, anymore. I know I sound like a broken record, but it's been years since we've seen each other—I don't even know if I should have slept with you both," she confessed.

"What do you mean by that?" I didn't mean to be harsh with her, but the sting of her words was like taking several more bullets—this time to the heart. "What did we do to make you question us?"

Her eyes went wide again. "It's not you or Decker, damn it." She wiped her trailing tears with the back of her hand. "There were things that happened in the..." She gulped; her spine straightened like she was steadying herself before telling me one of her secrets. "The past messed me up. And I don't know if bringing it up will help any of us."

It was my turn to be surprised. "Us? What happened in the past, Regina?"

She opened her mouth, but more gunshots echoed off the battered walls. I wrapped my good arm around her and brought her flat to the floor, and covered her with my body.

My injury made my movements awkward, yet her hand never left my shoulder. If anything, she put even more pressure on the wound. Or was she trying to push me away?

As I looked down at her, utter terror overtook her face. Her skin went pale white, like she was staring at a ghost. Her mouth gaped opened, ready to let loose a scream.

I clamped my hand over her mouth to keep her from exposing our location. And I wasn't going to give the shooters any indication that we were still alive.

Regina began to buck—she was fighting me—her fisted hands flung about and knocked me in the face a few times, catching me in the left eye. For a second, I pulled back and she screamed like her soul was torn out of her body. I felt her anguish down to my own soul.

From the crazed look in her eyes, I had no doubt someone had physically hurt Regina—hurt her bad. I recognized that bleak terror staring back at me. I'd seen that same look in the infirmary's bathroom mirror after I was assaulted that first week in prison.

More gunshots pelted the already battered walls. It didn't matter, because Regina had all my focus. I hovered close, but didn't touch her. "Regi, it's me. It's Krew. Look at me, baby."

Another shrill wail came out of her as she covered her head with her arms. And what she shouted next had me frozen. It was the last thing I expected Regina to say to me.

"Teke, stop!"

Chapter Twenty-Four
Decker

I scrambled to the bedroom I used to store my rifle and the rest of my gear. Once I gathered my nine mil, the ammo and two of my knives, I quickly crept down the stairs, keeping my body low.

I didn't bother with a shirt or shoes and carefully avoided the windows. Judging by the bullet trajectories and the damage to the bathroom walls, I figured the hitman—or hitmen—were positioned somewhere eye-level to the second floor.

Which meant they weren't experts. For one, they used too many bullets. And two, if they were real aces, their aim would've been true and Krew would be dead. That was how I would've done it. Quiet and clean.

I shuddered at the thought of losing Krew—or Regina, for that matter to a bullet.

When I found the asshole who'd shot Krew, putting a bullet between their eyes was going to give me great satisfaction.

As I reached the bottom of the stairs, I heard more gunshots going off.

I chanced a glance to the ceiling, and sent a silent plea. *Please stay alive.*

On the main floor, by the fireplace, I found more bullet holes. Jesus, it looked like the hitman had brought the big guns to the party. I'd fix that the second I located the bastard and killed the motherfucker.

Jesus. Merrick was going to have my balls for lunch when he found out what happened to his house. Hmm. Maybe I should tie up the hitman as a gift and leave him for Merrick to torture the asshole.

But I couldn't worry about Merrick right now.

Since the damage was on the west side of the house, my only conclusion was that the assassin was somewhere on the west end of the property. A quick study of the holes, gave me a direct route to where the shooter was set up.

Avoiding the front entrance, I went out the back door where the storage shed hid my exit. I crouched behind the ten-by-ten shed and took a measure on which direction I needed to crawl. In order to get the shooter, I needed the element of surprise.

I studied the gun in my hand, and realized I couldn't use it. Stealth was the name of the game.

Close combat, I thought to myself, before hiding the gun behind the shed and pulling out my knives.

I kept both K-bars in my hands and began to crawl through the overgrown field to where I suspected the shooter was. About half way across, more gunfire hit the house and a scream ripped through the air. I stilled as all the oxygen left my lungs, because I knew that scream. *Regi.*

I debated for all of two seconds when a slight movement ahead and to the right caught my attention. *Bingo.*

More bullets showered the upper floor of the house—hitting the exterior wall, turning the clapboard into Swiss cheese.

Wait until I get my hands on you.

Right as I started to move, a flash of metal caught my periphery to the left. Sunshine glinting off metal. I ducked, knowing there were two hitters in the game now. I wasn't sure if they were working in tandem, or whoever killed first, but the sniper in front of me was closer, so he'd be the first to die.

I moved, slow and methodical, until I was ten yards from a pair of booted feet partially covered by underbrush. Closer. And closer, until I was six feet away. Then three.

I took a long silent breath, held it, then launched myself. I didn't give the shooter time to turn or utter a single word. Before the hitman realized I was there, I'd already shoved my knife into his neck, then wrenched it upwards and freed the blade from muscle and bone. It was a quiet death. Too quick, though for my liking.

Then I released the air from my lungs and breathed in the faint metallic scent of his blood. I wiped the blade on the back of the dead bastard's shirt, and grabbed a hold of the man's hair and lifted his head so I could see the hitman's face.

My stomach dropped as I stared down at... "Shit. Jay—man," I uttered before I let go of his hair. And I thought... I guess there really were no honorable killers out there. I wanted to believe Jay when he said he wouldn't come after me and mine.

I took a deep breath, and released the subtle annoyance. No matter. One down and one to go.

I back tracked, then crawled toward where I'd seen that flash of light, taking my time until I was several yards away.

"I'm leaving, man," a deep voice called out. "That money isn't worth my fucking life."

I wanted to laugh. What? Did this bastard think he was playing with a novice? Someone who didn't know tactics? First rule of the game. Never trust a word coming out of a killer's mouth. *Jay just reaffirmed that one.* And second? Never show your hand until you see the whites of their eyes, and then you pull the trigger. Apparently, this guy didn't get the memo.

I stayed silent. Watching. Waiting for the guy in front of me to move. A good three minutes went by and he still didn't show his location.

"Okay. You got me. I'm not leaving. But since this is a stalemate and I'm guessing you got Jay—he's dead, isn't he?"

I remained silent but inwardly chuckled.

"I don't want to die. Let's call this even. How about it?"

Okay, asshole. Keep talking.

Unbeknownst to him, I was an expert at stealth recon—one of the few good things I'd learned in the military. I could be inches from the enemy and they would never guess I was right up their ass before I ended them. And as he kept talking, I moved silently like a snake.

This douche bag would learn how good I was soon enough. I inched in until I was close enough to see that it wasn't a person, but a fucking walkie talkie.

"Surprise?" The hitter cackled from behind me.

Shit. That's genius. No sooner had that thought entered my mind, a bullet nailed my thigh. Pain exploded from the entry point and spread like an electric charge from the center of the damage, up my leg.

Then another bullet hit the knife blade and the force of the impact jerked the now broken weapon from my hand. Damn, this guy was good—maybe almost as good as me.

"Thought you were a smart one, huh? But I got ya. I'm the smarter mammal. Now, you got to understand, this is only business. No hard feel—" A gunshot rang out, then silence ensued.

Were there three killers?

"Fuck," I quietly hissed, as pain lanced through my leg.

Krew—Regi. My thoughts were now centered on them, and how I was going to stay alive to protect them.

Then I saw a figure in head-to-toe camouflage gear emerged from behind a cluster of trees to the east—and headed straight for me. As he got closer, I tagged a FN Ballista slung over his right shoulder and Sig Saur Rattler in his left hand.

He got to about three yards away from me before he stopped. "The bastard in the tree is dead," he called out before he tucked the gun away. "I'm glad I got here in time to help."

"Who the hell are you?" I calmly asked, as I lifted the second K-bar and pointed it at this new comer, but wished I had my gun. I didn't care how someone came at me; I didn't trust them until I was sure they were an ally.

Since I was at a disadvantage, I tried getting up—be eye level with the man. It took two attempts before I got my footing and stood, but I never looked away from the stranger.

The asshole laughed like a hyena. "Merrick sent me."

Merrick? Jesus.

"Why would he send you?" I asked, while trying to get a better sense of what the hitman actually wanted.

He glanced at the house and winced. "Sorry I didn't get here sooner," he said with a smile that didn't reach his narrowed eyes. "But I'm here now to save your sorry ass."

As he cautiously approached, I immediately recognized his face.

Bonner Kelly. Most people called him Boom, because he liked to play with explosives.

"Am I staring at a ghost? I heard you died." Relief coursed through me, now that I knew the man standing a yard away.

I'd only come across him one other time—several years back in a dusty back alley in a small Iraqi town, before either of us became assassins for hire. Two different units with two different missions, but one objective. In the end, this man wouldn't be walking around if it wasn't for me saving his ass when an enemy sniper wanted to use Bonner's head for target practice. And in the end, my unit completed the mission, got to the militants first before more women and children were taken and imprisoned in a rape house.

"Nope," Bonner said as he approached until he within spitting distance.

"Some said you were killed. Others said you ran away like a coward from a mission and left your unit to die." I kept my voice neutral.

He stared unblinkingly at my face. A deep, dark rage filled his green eyes, before the shadows cleared and he smirked once again. "I know you. Mosul. The rape house. Did you get them?"

"Yes." It was all I said, not needing to explain further, or expect a thank you from the guy for saving his life.

"Good. I hope those fuckers rot in hell for what they did. And all that other shit you've heard about me are lies. I didn't run away, and I didn't leave my unit. They left me for dead after I saved their asses."

"You said Merrick sent you. How did he find out about the hitters today."

"I caught wind of a few individuals who want you and your demented throuple dead. Now, you do you, boo—I'm the last person to tell anyone how to live their life. But dude? You have a perfectly good pussy in that house, why would you go after ass too?"

"Really? I'm standing there, bleeding out from a bullet hole in my leg, and you're asking me about my sex life," I said flatly.

A single eyebrow winged up before he shook his head. "You're standing." His eyes focused on my bloody leg.

I nodded. "Okay. Now why did Merrick really send you here? I could have handled things on my own."

Bonner chuckled. "Yeah right. Merrick told me that you'd need back up. And from the looks of it, I got here in time—but you have to let Merrick know that I didn't shoot up his home. It was those other fucktards," Bonner said as he kept staring at my leg.

Then it hit me. It wasn't the other killer who shot me. "Why did you shoot me?" I growled.

"Because it was the only way for you to hear me out before you put a bullet in my head," he explained with a shrug.

He was right. I would have shot first—then asked questions—if I'd had the chance. I still didn't believe him... But then, why would he lie? Bonner currently had the advantage over me.

"Alright."

"Call him. Merrick won't lie," he insisted. "He sent me here knowing you needed help. And tell him I didn't shoot his house up."

"You want me to call Merrick right now?" I was slightly put off. "If I don't, you're going to shoot me? Again?"

A scary yet genuine smile slid across his face. "If I wanted you dead, Moss, you wouldn't be breathing right now." He extended a hand. "My friends call me Boom."

"I know." I glanced at the extended hand—like I was going to take it.

"I get it. You don't trust me. Yet." He pointed to the bullet wound in my leg. "Got to say, from my vantage point, I'm glad I didn't nick an artery."

"At least it's clean through—" A roar tore through the air, and my heart ratcheted up at the anguished cry coming from the house.

"Krew." I limped back toward the house, leaving Bonner standing in the field. I wasn't usually so careless, turning my back on a killer, but there was a good sixty percent chance that the man was talking truth and wouldn't shoot me in the back.

When I finally reached the back door of the house, a naked Krew stumbling out, defeat cresting his face. His skin was ashen and his eyes were filled with tears. The blood from his shoulder wound left tracks down his chest.

"Krew," I uttered, fearing the worst. "Where's Regi?" I glanced around, but she hadn't followed him out. "Talk to me."

He blinked. Then again. More teardrops streamed down his

face. "She's... But now I know why she hates me," he whispered, his voice taut with agony.

"What? She doesn't hate you."

Krew's eyes were filled with such anguish and heartbreak that the news had to be horrific. "The day we took that joyride with Teke, and he..." Krew sucked in a harsh breath and let it out. "We separated from Regi."

"Yeah, so we could lead the cops away from her, so she wouldn't get into trouble with them, or with her parents," I added, knowing by heart how that day had gone irrevocably wrong, and how it had changed our lives forever.

"Teke followed her and—" Krew dropped to his knees. "I'm going to find him and kill him myself, Deck." And a bellow tore from his mouth.

"Baby, slow down. I'm not understanding you."

My words penetrated and Krew finally looked at me. His eyes scanned my body before they widened in shock. "Oh fuck—you're shot." His hands covered the top of his head and he crumbled to the ground. "I'm sorry, Deck—for everything. My brother—everything."

"You're not making sense, Krew. What did Teke..." My mind quickly replayed what Krew had said about why Regina hated him... And then it hit me. "Teke did something to Regina, didn't he." Rage laced my words as hellfire burned in my gut.

The moment I got clarity about what Teke had done to our girl hit me, I saw red. This entire time, I had assumed she was safe and away from the cops. It was that scumbag we should have worried about.

"Teke Gatlin is a dead man walking," I seethed, never looking away from Krew.

"Need a hand?"

I whirled around, fisted my knife and pointed it at Bonner. "Why are you still here?"

"I think you need my help," he said nonchalantly, but his attention was on Krew. "Besides, your... man looks like he's about to crack."

"I got this handled, you can go." I somehow found the strength to put aside my wrath and focus back on Krew. Even though my insides were being pummeled like rocks in a dryer.

Jesus. I needed to check on Regina to see if she was alright. And here Krew was, on the ground, still bleeding from his wound, looking ready to pass out.

"I think someone is trying to take off with your truck, Moss," Bonner snorted, then folded his arms across his chest. "If you want, I'll watch this big boy while you go retrieve her." I opened my mouth to say no, but he raised a finger. "I won't touch what's yours."

"I heard that before," I said gruffly.

"Probably. But I know how to keep my word," Bonner clipped out with ferocity, as he tapped his chest. "Besides, I don't want to be on Merrick's bad side."

I rarely trust anyone in this business—no one, actually, least of all a hitman. But something in my gut was telling me to trust this hitman... To a point.

"Be right back," I grated out, never looking away from Bonner's face. "If one hair—"

Bonner tipped his head toward Krew. "He doesn't have any. Get moving before it's too late and she's gone." His keen stare was enough confirmation for me to leave Krew with this hitman and get Regina before she took off with my truck.

Regina's Diary

August 17th, 2019

Dear Diary,

It's been just over a year since I last picked you up. I thought I was good, focused on my career and my life. I thought I was over the fear and the nightmares of my past. I was wrong.

I went on a date for the first time in my adult life—imagine that, Diary. A twenty-three-year-old girl, going on her first date. Truthfully, it was absolutely horrible.

The asshole was all handsy and that was before he took me out to dinner. He did all the talking, and didn't take a breath to give me time to respond. Then at the end of the night, when he drove me back to my apartment, he wanted to come up. He wanted in my pants instead of wanting to get to know me.

Diary, I have another confession. The entire date, all I thought about was Krew and Decker. I wished they were the ones to take me out on my first date. I wanted their hands to touch me. To love me like I have fantasized about.

God, Diary, I miss them so much—even to this day my love for them has never left my heart. I know I can't have them in my life—not after what happened, but still, a girl can hope. A girl can dream. The tragic thing about memories—especially mine, is that they keep me grounded in anxieties and more nightmares. I will forever be alone.

Maybe it's for the best that I stay single. Celibate... except for my trusty vibrator.

Yeah, that's what I'm going to do. It's for the best.

Thanks for letting me vent.

Regi

Chapter Twenty-Five
Regi

"Jesus Christ, why won't this damn thing turn over." I slammed my palm against the wheel and tried the ignition again.

I glanced over my shoulder, looking through the back window of the cab to see if either of my boys were coming after me. Nope.

Guilt clung to me. I had to get the hell out of here before Krew told Decker what Teke had done to me all those years ago.

I hadn't meant to spill my guts, but when Krew covered me with his body—trying to protect me from the bullets some asshole was shooting at us, my panic reared like a dark specter and I couldn't fight the living nightmare of the past.

I was back in those woods. Teke was on top of me, ripping through my virginity as if it were his God-given right. I screamed. I fought. But this time, it wasn't Teke I pushed away. It was Krew.

By the time his voice penetrated my mind and cleared away the waking nightmare, it was too late. I shouted Teke's name, and Krew —who was far from stupid—figured out without further confirmation from me, what had happened.

"He touched you," he said sternly, yet his tone was one of confirmation rather than accusation.

I opened my mouth to deny it as tears streamed from my eyes, blurring my vision. I couldn't hide this secret any longer and slowly nodded.

"*How* did he touch you?" he asked, but from the way the muscles along his jawline jumped and his nostrils flared, it was obvious that Krew knew. His gaze pierced me with such dark intensity that I flinched. "Tell me!" he roared.

I couldn't hold onto the past any longer—not when I was vulnerable, naked, and still bathed in the scents of my men from the beautiful connection we had made. I had to expel the poison that flooded my veins before Teke corrupted of what was left of me.

If I wanted that beautiful life with Krew and Decker, I had to tell the truth.

"Tell me, Regina," Krew uttered in a guttural plea.

I sucked in a deep breath and held it in for a beat before I let it out with the words. "He raped me."

Krew dragged in an audible breath like it was his last, and tears fell through his thick, dark lashes. "That's why you hate me so much." He then began to punch the tiled floor repeatedly, causing lacerations on his knuckles.

"Krew," I cried, but he shook his head, stood and walked out of the bathroom, leaving me kneeling on the plaster-littered floor.

Dread weighed me down. But I stood, knowing I had to leave. I had to fix this for us—for me. I raced to the bedroom, quickly dressed, and began throwing my things into my backpack. I grabbed my purse, found my phone and the truck keys in Decker's room and hauled ass through the front door.

Every second, I kept telling myself that I had time—time before the boys found out that I was leaving. I was ashamed for taking Decker's truck and not being able to tell them what my plans were. Nonetheless, they would try to stop me and I couldn't let them or my guilt from ending what had been long time coming.

"Regi!" I heard Decker's voice.

"Come on, damn it." I turned the key once more, and the engine revved to life. "Yes," I screeched with relief, before shifting into drive.

I chanced a glance over my shoulder and saw Decker rounding the house, and I jammed my foot down onto the accelerator. As I tore out of there without looking back, I heard Decker shouting my name again.

"I'm sorry," I whispered as Decker screamed. I looked in the rearview mirror and saw him—limping? He was hurt, and still he tried to reach the truck. I shook my head, ignoring his pleas for me to stop, and I kept driving.

Call me a coward for taking off, but I had no doubt that Decker would take care of Krew and his wound. I was also certain that once Decker found out what had happened to me, he would look at me in the same disgusted way Krew had. Tainted and no good.

I returned my attention back on the road and drove.

I had no idea which direction I was going, and since my phone had no bars in this back country of Vermont, I had to trust my sense of direction. But that was my superpower. I never got lost. And sure enough, after a while I saw signs for a highway.

I drove until the gas light blinked on. Since I had no clue where exactly I was and this state had apparently banned billboards, I focused on getting to a gas station before the tank hit empty.

Thankfully, there was a sign at the next exit, and I coasted in to the station right as the engine began to sputter.

It was dark now, but the area was well lit and I was the only vehicle at the pumps. It seemed safe enough to use the mini-mart's bathroom as the tank filled.

I glanced at my face in the mirror while I washed my hands. Tears were streaking down my ruddy cheeks. I hadn't realized I was still crying. Disappointed in my lack of control over my emotions, I quickly wiped the wetness away with the paper towel I'd dried my hands with, and walked out of the bathroom.

I grabbed a few snacks and a bottle of water, I paid for them, and headed back to the pump. I returned the gas nozzle to its cradle and got back in the truck.

After I opened a bag of chips and swigged on some water, I checked my phone and saw that I finally had full bars. I typed in where I wanted to go and got the hell out of there.

The moment I merged onto 90 West, my cell phone rang. At first, I was going to ignore it, assuming it was either Decker or Krew. Then I glanced at the name on the screen.

Maya.

A knot lodged in my chest, and a bitter taste formed in my mouth as I thought of my ex-best friend and her betrayal. For a moment, I debated on answering her call. But if I wanted answers, there was only one way to find out. I tapped the green button on the screen and answered her with, "Hey, bitch." I couldn't hide the anger in my tone.

Silence.

"Regi?" Maya's trembling voice gave me pause, and I almost asked her what was wrong. Then I remembered her tactics. She played the victim well.

"What do you want?" My tone was sharp and unbending.

"What's wrong?"

"Tell me why you called, or I'm hanging up," I threatened, not caring one bit if she was laying in a ditch and dying. Even if my old friend had pulled *me* from one all those years ago, she had broken my trust. Maya was no friend of mine anymore—not after how she'd lied to me and schemed to have me killed instead of her.

"My dad died four days ago. I'm home for his funeral tomorrow," she said tearfully and my gut clenched, sorrow sliding in for her loss. Her father was a good man—at least, he was good to me.

Were Decker and Krew wrong? Was Maya a victim too?

"I'm sorry that your dad died. I know you two were close," I admitted, less acidly.

"Where are you? I went to the apartment, but when I walked in there yesterday morning, I saw that someone had ransacked the place. I tried calling you several times. Why haven't you been answering my calls and texts?"

"Long story. Since I'm heading home too, we can talk there," I said, surprised at the calmness in my voice.

More silence.

"You're coming back to Elida?"

"As we speak."

"Oh." Was that trepidation in her tone?

"Yes, oh. I'll see you at your dad's funeral. And after, we're going to have a chat. Gotta go." I hung up, feeling a hint of satisfaction.

I was able to breathe a little better, knowing I'd have the chance to confront her. Hopefully, she could clean up her mess and then Krew and I would be safe.

However, the further I got from Vermont, the ache in my chest intensified, like someone was carving my heart out with a dull spoon. But the pain also gave me clarity. Clarity to see that I'd be better off by myself. Better off to clear this mess with Maya—and hopefully put Teke behind bars.

First, I *needed* to go home and see my parents.

Chapter Twenty-Six
Krew

I didn't hear a word Decker said before he took off around the front of the house.

I couldn't—not when my ears were still ringing from Regina's confession, the terrible truth she'd been holding onto all this time. The day we got arrested... Teke had raped her. Now the truth was rotting in my chest, heavy and foul.

All this time, I had thought she was safe, away from the cops, away from the danger my brother had put us in.

This cold, dead weight where my heart used to be was rage that burned bright. I let out another roar of fury and dropped to the ground. All I saw was red and I began pummeling the dirt. The small bits of stone in the dirt cut into my knuckles, adding to the bloody mess. I wished the entire time I was punching Teke's face.

"Hey-hey." Decker was on his knees beside me, and he caught me mid-punch. He took my face into both hands. "Stop."

"Regi?" I was hoping Decker stopped her from leaving.

"She's gone. And she took my damn truck."

"It's all my fault." I wrenched my face away from his touch. I didn't deserve his affection or his solace. "If we hadn't gotten into that car—Teke—if I had only said no..." I barely got out the words before I pushed Decker out of my way and I started punching the ground again.

"Stop, damn it." Decker got in my face, his hands gripped my neck and he pressed his forehead against mine. "Take a breath," he demanded.

I sucked in a breath, but I wanted to rail at the injustice of what happened to Regina—to Decker—to me.

He pulled back and peered into my eyes, his glare steely and exuding strength—everything I wasn't in this moment. "Hear me. It's not your fault, K. It's Teke's for stealing that car—it's Teke who hurt our girl—not you," he lectured, but his words weren't penetrating the shield I put up.

As I stared into his beautiful blue eyes, my vision blurred, as if I were viewing them through a layer of guilt. "If I had known Teke was going to follow Regi, I would have gone after her. Protected her."

"Me, too," he growled. "But we didn't know. We were kids, Krew. I never thought Teke had it in him to..." His frown deepened; I swore his face would crack. Then his scowl disappeared and resignation stiffened his jaw. "Teke's fucking dead. I don't care if he's your brother, K. Do you understand that?" he barked.

"Damn. Family drama." A man's voice cut into the tension.

Decker and I swiveled our heads to the man who was standing several feet from us. "Who *are* you?" I glowered at the stranger, my eyes riveted on the gun in his hand.

He shrugged, tucking the weapon behind him. "I'm Bonner Kelly. You can call me Boom. I wasn't one of the guys who tried to kill you or who shot up the house. I came to help." He smirked, like what he said was a joke.

My watery eyes widened and I turned to Decker for answers.

"Merrick called in reinforcements. And he didn't shoot at us—

or so he says. Well, you and Regina, or the house." Decker grimaced as he looked down at his thigh.

"We need to look at your wound," I said, finally getting up from the ground. "Then we have to go after her."

"We will." Decker stood and glanced at my shoulder.

"I have honor, you know," Bonner boasted, but I had no idea what the hell the guy was spouting about. "Most of the time of time anyway." He looked back at the house. "Shit, Merrick's going to lose it. You'll tell him it wasn't me. Right?"

Decker turned back to me, ignoring Bonner—Boom—whoever this guy was. "Let's clean up."

"Alright," I admitted, my attention dropping to my bloody knuckles.

"Do you have a clue where she's running to?" Decker asked.

"I don't," I replied, though the weight of Regina's words still lay heavy around my neck like a chained noose.

"Jesus Christ," Bonner murmured as he pinched the bridge of his nose.

"What?" Decker snapped, but his eyes remained on me.

"You can track your girlfriend by her cell phone—I mean if she has one. Or do you have a tracker on your truck?"

"What?" Decker and I said in unison, our attention on the man who now looked perturbed.

Bonner shook his head, before he narrowed his eyes on Decker. "Jesus, I thought I was working with a professional. Like the one you should put on your truck in case someone steals your vehicle."

"No, I don't." Decker clenched his teeth before turning to me. "I'll call Sabrina."

"You *will* call Merrick first..." Bonner's words trailed off as Decker glared at him. "Fine. You can call Merrick after."

Decker studied Bonner before he finally grumped out, "I will." He then turned toward the house.

"Alright. You go do that while I bury the bodies," I heard Bonner say as I followed Decker to the house. "Oh, by the way, I'm taking the ATV over there. I parked my vehicle way too far and I don't feel like walking."

I glanced over my shoulder and watched the strange man—who was a killer like Decker, climb onto the ATV and drive away, disappearing into the adjacent woods, before I put him out of my mind.

We took the stairs slowly up to the destroyed bathroom. I washed up while Decker grabbed the first aid case. I followed him to the bedroom where we'd made love to Regina. As I sat on the edge of the bed, pain was finally leaching all my energy.

Decker cleaned and bandaged my shoulder and his leg, then grabbed his phone. "I'm calling Sabrina," he said and handed me the first aid kit.

As I bandaged my hands, the words Regina confessed to me were on repeat in my head. She was raped. Teke raped her. Teke—my brother couldn't get away with this atrocity. He had to pay.

"Yo, Bossman." Sabrina's voice pulled me out of my spiraling thoughts. "I take it Boom was there," she announced over the speaker.

"Yeah, Kelly was here. Listen, I want you to track Regi's cell phone. Can you—"

"Give me a sec," Sabrina said, as tapping sounds echoed off the phone. "So... How's Boom doing?"

"Who cares—he left." Decker glared at the phone.

"What about the tracker on the truck?" I mouthed, thinking it was easier than tracking her cell phone. But what did I know.

Decker tapped the mute button, glanced at me and shrugged. "There's no tracker. I checked my truck yesterday and there wasn't any. I doubt Jay and that other dead idiot would have tagged it."

I nodded in understanding and then offered, "I'm sorry about your friend."

"He wasn't my friend," Decker said with indifference, then unmuted the phone.

"You know muting your phone doesn't do anything. I can still hear what you're saying," Sabrina said with a chuckle, her fingers still tapping away.

My eyes widened, but Decker rolled his eyes. "If I wanted you to listen in on our conversation, I wouldn't have pressed mute. If you do that again—"

"Got it, bossman. Now, I, have," a few more taps, "got her. She's heading along Route 87. Her Waze app is marked for Elida, Ohio."

"How do you know that?" I blurted out.

"It doesn't matter," Decker said. "Sabrina, can you get a rental car out here as fast as you can? Something non-descript."

"Can't Boom give us a ride?" I asked, but Decker glowered at me. I guessed that was a no.

"No worries. I got you, boo," she snarked. The rapid sound of keys being tapped drowned out her chuckling.

"Why is she heading to Elida?" I questioned.

"I don't know," he hissed, limping away. "We will soon find out."

Out of all the places Regina would run to, why back home? She had made it clear that she would never step foot in that town again.

"Krew." Decker's voice cracked like a whip—sharp and commanding.

I froze. My fists clenched tight before I even turned. I wasn't some dog he could order me around. Baring my teeth, I spun to face him. "I know you're pissed, but don't take it out on me."

"I'm sorry," Decker said with a hint of remorse. "I'm fucking riled up and worried that Regi is going to do something stupid, and we won't get there in time to save her ass."

The glimpse of the tired man in the doorway and I recognized the fear on his face. I strode up to him, leaned my forehead to his, and pulled him into me. "I know we have to get to our girl before she does something reckless. But babe, don't bark at me again."

"I'm sorry." He kissed me, and we held each other for a little while.

Knowing Regina, she was going to confront Teke. And that was the last thing either of us wanted for her. Regina would lose, especially to my monster of a brother.

It took almost an hour before the rental car showed. It was a black 8 Series BMW Alpina Gran Coupe.

I whistled. "That's not keeping it on the down low."

"Fucking Christ. Sabrina," Decker hissed before getting into the driver's seat. "Get in, K. We've wasted enough time."

I got in, and Decker took off like the proverbial bat out of hell. I just hoped that we got to Elida in time—before Regina set the town and Teke on fire.

And from the last messages I had with Teke, he was on a hair trigger. It wouldn't take much to make him explode, and Regina would be the casualty.

Chapter Twenty-Seven
Decker

"She can't be too far ahead," Krew said as he riffled through his bag, pulled out a hoodie, and slipped it on.

"Maybe two hours ahead of us since we had to wait for the damn rental car," I hissed, though I appreciated the soft leather and comfortable seat under my ass. Krew probably did too, with the way I'd pounded his ass this morning.

"So, we're doing this?" The statement came out more of a question.

I glanced over at Krew, who was looking at me with a mix of anger and trepidation, before I returned my attention to the highway. But I knew what he was asking. "We are. He's not getting away with it, K. By my hand or yours—it doesn't matter, he's going to die for what he did to Regi."

He let out a long breath. "I know."

His tentative resignation was pissing me the fuck off. "It doesn't sound like you do. K, your douche bag of a brother raped our girl. He took what wasn't given. Teke ripped my family apart—and before you say anything, you and Regi were always my family. My life—your life—Regi's life, they were all crushed to dust because of what that bastard did."

"I know—damn it—I know." Krew rubbed a bandaged hand on his forehead in frustration. "I just thought jail would be better, since he could suffer long term."

"Do you believe that?" I snapped, but regretted it immediately. "Sorry."

Krew leaned his head against the window, and a pained resolve raced across his face.

In that moment, I took in his appearance. The dark circles under his eyes and the sallowness of his skin. Even with the blond stubble coming out on his scalp, which matched the scruff along his jawline, Krew was still beautiful to me.

"Deck, how come you never looked for me—I know I asked this question before but you never answered. I promise I won't be mad."

I met his eyes, and I had to give him the truth. Many truths, if I was honest with myself. And if I wanted Krew to open up, I had to do the same. With a calming breath, I told him.

"By the time I got a chance, my life was a mess. I was nearly court-martialed for punching one of my drill instructors. Granger was a fucktard, and he got off on picking on me and one other guy from my unit. From day one, he was in my face and in Jeromy's."

"This Granger was a bully," Krew confirmed.

"That asshole did everything he could to get us kicked out. One night I had enough," I admitted with a chuckle.

"Did you try to report him to his superiors?"

I chuckled at Krew's question. "I did talk to my other drill instructor. That asshole told me rats don't belong in the Marines. So, I kept my mouth shut and put up with Granger's abuse."

"What was your breaking point?"

Krew knew me well enough to know that it would have been only a matter of time before I blew my shit. "It was three weeks before we were to graduate from boot camp. It was past midnight, and my unit was asleep as usual. That bastard woke Jeromy and me up and ordered us outside. It had been raining all day and was cold as hell, but he refused us clothes. We had to go out in our underwear and t-shirts. Anyway, he made us do calisthenics for a while—which wouldn't have been horrible, except he turned to Jeromy and told him to strip naked and stroke his dick."

"Jesus," Krew growled. "I hoped you punched that motherfucker hard."

I sliced a wicked smile Krew's way. "I broke the bastard's nose in two places."

Krew winced but a smile crested his face. "He deserved the pain."

"And more."

"So, what happened next?"

"I guess Jeromy paused a little too long for Granger's liking and he kicked at Jeromy's legs out from under him and he dropped to the ground. Then Granger proceeded to kick his face. I stopped him before he did any more damage. When Granger turned and swung at me, but I caught his swing and knocked him on his ass. He kept getting up. Finally, he took another swing at me and I countered and punched his face."

"Why did you get arrested?" Krew asked, red-faced with anger. "You were only defending your friend and yourself."

"Jeromy wasn't my friend." No, he was so much more, but I couldn't tell Krew that—not yet anyway.

"Sounds like he was special to you," Krew admitted.

I couldn't look at Krew, because he might see just how true his words were.

"Jeromy was such a small guy that it wouldn't take much before he was seriously injured. We were taught to look out for each other —to rely on each other, especially when we were out in the field. Anyway, I got caught mid-act, punching Granger, when the military police arrived."

"How did you get out of it?"

"Apparently Granger had been doing this for a while to recruits, and the Staff Judge Advocate had already started to compile a list of recruits he'd abused, which in turn had Granger court-martialed for Article 133."

"What's that?"

"Conduct Unbecoming an Officer and a Gentlemen and I think there were a few other charges, but I don't remember them."

"Shit," Krew uttered before he leaned his seat further back. "That still doesn't explain why you didn't come looking for me when you got out."

I clenched my teeth tight before I let go of the tension flooding my body. "I thought you'd be better off without me, K. That's all. I just... Figured you were with Regi and had made a happy life. And I didn't want to fracture anything you two had."

"You were wrong, Deck. None of us had any happiness in our lives, especially Regi." Krew shifted in his seat until his back was facing me. "Wake me when it's my turn to drive."

Krew had said I was wrong, but it was *him* who was wrong. For a brief period of time, I did find happiness, but then Jeromy died and I became lost again.

Regina's Diary

April 2nd, 2023

Dear Diary,

April fools on me. Guess who showed up on my doorstep yesterday—you will never believe it.

It was Maya. My best friend from school—the same one that ghosted me for years, suddenly shows up at my apartment with no warning.

I'm still not sure how she found me—and I'm not sure how I feel about seeing her after all this time. But I let her in and we talked. She said she was sorry for not staying in touch. She sounded remorseful but something was telling me that there is more to it than she's letting on. She's hiding something, but in the same sense, I am too.

I don't know how she talked me into it, but she's moving in with me. I don't know if that's a good or a bad thing. One thing is for sure, sharing the rent won't be a hardship, since the rental prices are going up in Chicago. It only means I will have more money in my bank account.

I did break down, though, and asked if she'd seen Krew and Decker. Maya told me that she hadn't seen them in years, and that they had moved away from Elida—the same thing she said years ago. So no news there.

My heart is still broken, Diary. But this is just another sign that it's better for me to stay away from home and the memories the town holds.

Other than that, I've kept my vow of celibacy for nine months now. I'm good in my life. Happy for a change.

Write to you soon.

Regi

Chapter Twenty-Eight
Krew

We were about three hours shy of reaching Elida. After filling up in Euclid, Ohio, Decker relented and I took the driver's seat—for first time. The man had to learn to relinquish control or he was going to grind himself down until there was nothing left.

Once we got back on the road, Decker fell asleep and I was too focused on the road and keeping my bandaged hands on the steering wheel to worry about Regina. I just hoped she didn't do anything stupid like confront Teke.

I knew my brother well. He wouldn't hesitate to hurt a woman. If he had the balls to assault her, there was nothing holding him back from using his fists.

That thought had me pressing my foot to the gas pedal harder.

I'd never guessed when I left home for that fight in Chicago that I'd be going back home with Decker in tow. And with Regina probably there already, all three of us will finally be back together where it all started. Something in my gut told me that our days were going to be limited. That our time with each other—our connection, was over once we found Teke.

I quickly shook my head, clearing away those dour thoughts.

As we approached Cairo, a few towns before Elida, Decker's phone rang and the car's Bluetooth picked up. The screen read Badass Bitch, and I knew it had to be Decker's handler, Sabrina.

I pulled over to the side of the road and answered the call. "Decker's asleep," I whispered, lowering the sound.

"No, I'm not." Decker sat up, rubbed his eyes and adjusted the seat back. "What do you have for us?"

"Your truck thief is at 5124 Surrey, in Elida," Sabrina said as steady taps echoed out of the speakers.

"She's home," breathed.

"She's home," I repeated the sentiment, then glanced at Decker. "Now what?"

"Your place. The sooner we take care of Teke, the better." The sneer on Decker's face sent chills through me. As much as I hated Teke, I still wasn't sure if my brother should die. Have the shit beaten out of him? Yes. Go to jail for sexual assault? Hell yes. But die? "Deck—"

"You're not changing my mind, Krew." The finality of his tone made me grit my teeth, but I didn't argue—not with his handler on the phone, listening in.

"Before you two lovebirds get into it, I have info on that biotch Maya."

"What do you have?" Decker asked, his eyes remained on me.

"She was last seen in the south suburbs with that guy Jess. The latest intel has her on the bus to guess where?"

"Elida?" Decker and I responded at the same time.

"Wrong. Vegas," she chirped. "I love doing that."

"Why would they go to Vegas?" Decker muttered to himself.

"Not *they*, bossman. She. Maya was on the bus alone. Or so I thought."

I wondered about Sabrina's last words, but Decker was still

focused on Jess. "Where's the guy, if he's not with her?" Decker asked, as he chewed on the inner part of his lower lip.

I automatically reached out and touched his mouth with my finger. He paused, looked at me and then kissed it. The easy smile he gave was a boon, although the grin left his face as fast as it had arrived, and was replaced with a frown.

"From my contact, Jess Duncan is still holed up somewhere in the south side of Chicago." More taps. "I don't think he has long. Another contract just went out, this time a quarter of a mil is on his head. Damn, the Agonas Associates aren't messing around and they're blatantly advertising that they want him gone," she explained with a bit of excitement. "There's even a poll on how long he's going to stay alive."

"Jesus," Decker said, then his eyes widened, like an idea struck him.

I leaned in closer to him and asked, "What are you thinking?"

"I'm thinking we need to keep Jess alive to find out how Maya got Regi and you involved in this. Because I'm beginning to think there's more than just mistaken identity. I can feel it. Sabrina, reach out to Bonner Kelly. He still owes me a favor. Tell him to bring Jess Duncan to Elida alive. After we get done with him, he can collect the payout."

"You got it," Sabrina said with giddiness. "Also, before I hang up, this is where it gets delicious. Remember I said that Maya's on the bus to Vegas? Well, your girl got a call from her dear best friend. Maya is actually home, because her father died. The woman on that bus was a decoy."

"Christ," Decker spat. "Regi is going after Maya—I know it."

"That's bad," I said. Then an idea struck me. Hell, a two for one. Teke first, then that lying bitch. "Why can't we take down both Teke and Maya?"

"Teke, definitely. But we need Jess to clear up some shit before we go after Maya. In the meantime, we need to take care of our girl, before she gets hurt. Or before your soon-to-be-dead brother gets his hands on her."

I pulled back onto the road, heading straight to Regina's childhood home, hoping Decker's plan worked. Because after wishing so hard and long for a life with the two people I've always loved, nothing was going to hold me back from securing that future.

Even if *I* had to kill my brother myself.

Chapter Twenty-Nine
Regi

It took me almost ten hours to cross the border into Ohio. I still had another four hours to go until I reached Elida. There was a twinge in my gut that felt like a warning. A warning to stay away. To keep driving until the miles I'd gone were far more than what was already on Decker's odometer.

The moment I drove past the Elida city limits, memories of my childhood crashed down around me like a tower of blocks. Good and bad, mixed into an amalgamation of happiness, tears, and then heartbreak.

The note Maya had written to me about my feelings for the two popular boys in our school. The day I met them at the park. How our friendship had bloomed. Our times at the Honey Pot. My parents—who I loved dearly—no matter how they felt about me spending time with Krew and Decker. Or how they would feel about me once I told them the truth.

I turned down my street; the place I still thought of as home was in the distance. The front porch light was lit like a welcoming beacon. Or I wanted to believe it was.

Should I have trusted my instincts and stayed away? No. This had been a long time coming. My parents, who'd done their best raising me, had been left wondering what happened to their only child. Because I had left them without a word. Vanished without a thought for their feelings or whether they'd miss me or not. They needed to know the truth. And it had to come from me, and me alone.

I slowly pulled into the driveway, put the truck in park, but left the engine on. *Just in case...* I thought to myself, as I stared at the single-story, vinyl sided house. I closed my eyes and found I could still recollect every inch of my home as I'd known it. Three bedrooms, two bathrooms, and a combination kitchen and living area that had seen so much in the sixteen years I had lived there.

Did they remodel it since I've been gone? What did they do with my room—my stuff?

As I glanced out the windshield, fireflies sparked to life. They danced about in the growing dark, flashing their glow on and off, urging me to get out of the truck to catch them, like I used to when I was a kid.

I was so immersed in watching them that I didn't see the front door open and someone step out. At first, there was just a blur of movement in my periphery, until I focused on the person standing on the brick stoop.

"Daddy?" I whispered, afraid to talk louder. Afraid I'd scare him back into the house.

Bob Morton didn't get off the stoop, just stood there staring at the idling truck. He was probably wondering why it was in his driveway. His tall bulky frame was stiff, and his honed attention was aimed my way.

"Who is it, Bob?" I heard my mother's soft voice come from behind the partially opened door, and I wanted to cry. The last time I heard her voice was when I had first arrived in Chicago. I had called, but I was too chicken to respond to her *Hello*. I'd hung up and didn't bother to call again, because my emotions were still a jumbled mess at that time.

"I don't know, Lidia. Stay in the house." Dad stepped off the stoop and strode to the end of the walkway. "Can I help you?" he called out. His gruff tone made me chuckle. He always sounded tough, but I knew better. For a giant of a man, he was a teddy bear in my eyes.

Tears that I had held onto for so long began to trail down my cheeks. "Courage, Regi," I told myself and finally opened the truck door and got out.

I stood there, silent, while I stared at my father, who looked so much older than his sixty years. Was it my absence that spackled all those wrinkles on his face? His hair had changed too. It had been thick and full. Now, it seemed much thinner. I couldn't tell in the dark if was gray too.

"Bob." I heard the screen door open, and I looked around my father and saw my mother standing on the porch.

"Hi, Dad. Mom." I swallowed down the large lump in my throat before I continued. "It's me, Regina."

"Regina?" my father croaked out and stumbled toward me.

"Sweetheart, is that really you?" My mother raced past her husband and collided into me. Her arms wrapped tight around me like a vise. I could hardly take a breath, because she was holding onto me so tightly. "Regina." She was crying.

She pulled back, not to release me but to take a good look at my face.

My father came around, "Give her to me. I need some squidges from my baby girl," he said with wet eyes.

My mother barely moved before my dad engulfed me in a hug. He picked me up and then put me down, before he broke down into tears.

"Turn off the truck and come inside," my mother said, a lilt of authority in her tone.

"Okay, once Dad lets go of me," I squeaked.

"Sorry—not sorry," he said with a watery smile before he released me.

As I shut off the truck, a chill raced up my spine. I darted a look down the street in both directions and spied an old beat-up Charger parked five houses down. It was running—I could tell by the rumbling sounds coming from the tailpipe. But that wasn't what raised the hairs on the back of my neck. It was the way the vehicle was parked, against the flow of traffic, with the driver's side next to the sidewalk.

"Come inside, we have some catching up to do," my mom said after I locked the truck.

"We need answers," Dad corrected.

"I'll explain everything once we're inside," I said, before glancing once more down the street. Right as I stepped onto the stoop, that car passed the house, with the interior light on, and going much slower than it should.

I stared at the driver, with shock and fear flip-flopping my world. I gripped the front door for balance and sucked in a breath.

Teke.

He'd purposefully had the interior light on so I could see his face—his unhappy face. But I wasn't elated to see him, either. I refused to look away. I stared back at him with utter disgust until he was completely gone from my sight.

One thing at time, Regi.

I had to deal with Maya first. Then Teke. One way or another, the torture I'd endured for so long would end. Either by my hand or by Decker or Krew's. Before I left this town, everyone would know who Maya really was and what that son of a bitch Teke had done to me.

Mom and Dad didn't take the news of the rape well—no parents would have. And, they didn't understand why I hadn't confided in them to help or asked them for help.

They were hurt by my lack of trust and was confused on why I thought they wouldn't have taken care of me.

Even though Maya had insisted that runaway was my only option, my decision to leave was solely on my shoulders.

I went through the last several years of my life as we sat at the kitchen table. I didn't have the heart to tell my parents that I changed my name, but maybe... I'd eventually change it back. Maybe.

Through it all, we cried. We argued. We laughed. We ate dinner—meatloaf, mashed potatoes, corn and homemade gravy. How could I have forgotten it was Thursday.

But something felt missing. Like a key piece—or pieces, of who I loved wasn't with me.

Too exhausted to talk any more, I hugged and kissed my parents, then went to bed in my old bedroom, shocked they'd kept it ready for me all this time.

There was too much to unpack in my head—everything that happened in Chicago and Vermont was still swirling around in my thoughts. And now, with what my parents told me about the town, the people I once knew and the life they'd led without me.

I finally went to sleep only after I settle my thoughts on what I was going to say to Maya and the mess she put me and Krew in. Tomorrow.

Chapter Thirty
Regi

The funeral service for Joseph Darvy, Elida's ex-mayor and the owner of Darvy's Tech Repair & Solutions, was standing room only. The townsfolk packed the Lutheran chapel off Pine Street. My parents and I sat in the back pews, since I didn't want to be anyone's focus.

I'd seen Maya and her mother, Briney Darvy, along with several other family members in the front pews. We never made eye contact until the procession out of the chapel. Even then, our glance toward each other lasted for less than a second.

The whole time I sat there, I was on the edge of my seat. For one, I'd expected Decker and Krew to crash inside, causing all sorts of ruckus. But no, they hadn't shown up... Yet. And two, Teke had arrived, dressed in dirty jeans and a jean jacket that had seen better days, and he sat kitty-corner from us.

My mother forcibly restrained my father from jumping up from the pew and beating the hell out of Teke. "Bob. We're in church." It was all she said before my dad settled on sneering at my attacker, with an unspoken promise of retribution.

After the service at the chapel and interment at Memorial Park

Cemetery in Lima, most of the mourners headed over to the Darvy's home in Lima for a luncheon. My mother contributed a broccoli casserole in her favorite fish-shaped dish. It was one of my favorites of her foods.

Not a half an hour in from talking to people I hadn't seen in years, and I was anxious to confront Maya about the past, the lies she had told, and the kill contracts on my and Krew's heads.

I looked for Maya in the kitchen but quickly scooted out of there, because nosy Ms. Gina Smith was the last person I wanted to chat with. She'd make all sorts of innuendos about where I'd been all these years. And she'd keep on digging until she was satisfied with the answers. No thank you.

I diverted to the hallway that led to Joseph Darvy's den and the powder room. Half way down, I heard voices coming from the den —Maya and her mother were arguing.

Without thought, I slipped into the powder room and partially closed the door so I could still hear what the mother-daughter duo were fighting about.

"I still can't believe you'd invite all these people back here, Mother," Maya huffed.

"We have to keep up with appearances—your father would have wanted that—"

"You have no money! Your husband gambled it all away. There's nothing left, except what Grandma Katie left me and he couldn't..."

The next thing I heard was glass crashing—like someone had thrown something through the window, and then Maya was screaming. "Are you fucking kidding me? How in the hell did he get his hands on my money, Mother?"

"Quiet down. And you're going to pay for that window and have my Persian rug cleaned."

"I think I already did," Maya shot back in a hiss.

"I'm sorry but I needed that money or I would have lost this house."

"Maybe you were better off without it," Maya grated out in rage.

"I said quiet. I don't want rumors—"

Maya started laughing maniacally. "You've got to be kidding me, right? Everyone in this fucking town knows your husband had a gambling addiction."

"Stop calling your father that."

"Joseph wasn't my father, was he? Or did you forget that tidbit about sleeping with Frank Moss?"

Holy shit. Did I just hear Maya say that she could be Decker's sister?

"I told you those rumors are false. You are your father's daughter. Always criticizing. Always listening to others when I've been telling you and your father the truth all these years. You are Joseph Darvy's child."

"I don't fucking believe you, Mother."

"I told you that I won't tolerate swearing in this house," Briney groused in a schoolmarm tone. "Now that you're done making my day the worst, I'm going back and see to the guests."

"You know what, I'm done, too. After today, I'm fucking out of here and you won't have to see me again," Maya warned.

"Maya, you don't have to tell me that. I already know you're leaving for good." Briney's words were cold and impassionate. Nothing like how my mother treated me last night.

I almost felt sorry for Maya, until I remembered why I was here in the first place.

Then I saw Briney Darvy stride past the powder room, toward the main part of the house. This was my chance, and I didn't care if Maya was in a foul mood.

When I stepped out of the bathroom, I found Maya standing in the den's doorway, watching her mother stride away.

"I want to talk to you," I demanded, and without giving her the chance to deflect, I strode up to Maya and pushed her back into the den.

"What the hell, Regi," Maya grated out, but back-peddled into the room.

I closed the door behind me and leaned against it, purposefully blocking the only exit from the room. I whirled around and faced her, not trusting what she'd do if I gave her the chance to physically hurt me. Then I got the full scope of what I heard. The shattered window, the broken vase and the glass all over the Persian rug.

"Regi—"

"No Maya." I cut her off. "I need answers from you."

"Fine." She dropped into a leather side chair, folded her arms across her chest and glared at me.

"You've been lying to me all these years."

"What are you talking about?" She narrowed her eyes on me, but I knew my best friend—or ex best friend, and the games she played.

"You lied about Decker and Krew. They got caught by the cops that day with Teke. You knew Krew went to jail and Decker had to enlist in the military. This whole time I thought they were okay and together, but they weren't." I raised a hand in front of her face— palm out—I didn't want to hear any bullshit out of her mouth. She needed to listen. "You also lied about how you were never inter- ested in my men—and yes, they were my guys. Even back in high school, you wanted them."

"Whoever told you all this is a liar. I only wanted what was best for you and your reputation."

"Don't lie to me anymore," I shouted and took a step toward her. "I know for a fact you were jealous of me and my relationship with Krew and Decker. You even went as far as trying to break our friendship up by making up shit—I know this to be true."

"Fuck you." Maya jumped up and got in my face. "You had to

be a greedy bitch and take the two best looking guys all for yourself."

"They were my friends," I defended. "We were kids."

"Don't accuse me of making up rumors. Who do you think saw you and the boys heading into the Honey Pot—like all the fucking time? Other kids—our classmates. I was the one who protected you—made sure no one called you a whore, or a slut."

"I don't—"

"That's your problem, Regi. You always think about yourself. I was your best friend—I looked out for you and when those cunt-lickers came into the picture, I was shoved to the side. I was a second thought to you."

"I can't believe I'm hearing this shit. Krew and Decker told me you were a manipulative bitch and you'd tried numerous times to sleep with them. Krew said you even tried when he got out of prison. All this damn time, I could have been with them."

"Krew and Decker—when did you talk to them?" she asked in a growl. Something flickered behind her cornflower blue eyes and I stepped back, because I suddenly became wary of being near her. But nothing was going to stop me from getting to the truth.

"The morning after the fight in Chicago. This whole time we've been hiding from killers who want us dead, Maya. Did you know we had a hitman in our apartment? Did you know they were looking for you, and thought *I* was you?"

"That's not my fault they got the wrong person." The casual-ness in her voice sent signals to my brain that screamed *Run now!* And still, I didn't listen to those warnings. I was too pissed off to think clearly.

"You purposefully changed your looks to mimic mine a few days before the fight, knowing whoever was after you would come after me instead. You and Jess set Krew and me up for the fall. Tell me I'm wrong."

"You're wrong." Maya smiled, and casually walked around her

father's desk, and then picked up the letter opener that was an exact replica of the sword that hung over the fireplace in the living room, only much smaller. She flipped the knife around in her right hand like an expert sword wielder. "You know, I could use that hundred grand about now."

I gasped—there was only one way she knew the amount, and I stepped backward until my back hit the door again. "Maya—" I said cautiously as I reached behind me for the door handle.

Before I was able to twist the knob, Maya launched herself at me and she held the blade against my throat. "Don't fucking move. Now *you're* going to listen. I didn't think I had to do this, but I don't have a choice now."

"You always have a choice," I uttered, then swallowed hard as she pressed the edge of the blade harder against my jugular. I flinched as I felt a slight sting across my skin.

"Oops, I cut you." Maya's eyes were glued to my neck as she pulled the blade back enough for me to see my blood on its edge. "I'd suggest you don't move."

"What happened to you?" I asked, trying to distract her from focusing on the knife.

Maya chuckled, tilted her head back slightly and I knew—cut or not, this was my chance to get the letter opener away from her. I had only a second to get the advantage and use what I'd learned in the self-defense classes I took.

I grabbed her right wrist with both hands and twisted it to the left at the same time I moved away from the door. I had her bent over, her right arm—and the knife, pointing away from me.

Maya started fighting me. "Bitch," she hissed and tried to wrangle her wrist out of my hold. I dug in and tightened my grip.

"Drop the letter opener, Maya." I twisted her wrist more, which had her screaming.

"Fuck you, Regi. You're dead to me." Maya twisted, and

punched my stomach with her free hand. I gasped in pain, but I still didn't release her right arm.

"Let go of the knife," I grated out, feeling my grip begin to loosen. "Maya!"

I wrestled with her until we were by her father's desk. Without a second thought, I slammed her knife-wielding hand down onto the desktop twice. Maya screamed and released the letter opener. It dropped to the floor and we fought against each other to get to the weapon.

I was there first and got a hold of the handle. Maya was on top of me and started punching wildly—not caring what part of my body her fist landed on. My head, my back, my arm—anywhere she could do damage, while a litany of curses and excuses flew out of her mouth.

"This is for all the times I had to protect you." Punch. "This is for taking what I wanted the most." Punch. "This is for Teke." *Teke?* "This is for my father. This is for the hatred I have for you, Regina Morton. My best friend—not."

No matter what she said and did, I was determined to not relinquish the letter opener. I finally got to my knees—ready to stand to defend myself, when Maya flipped around. We were face to face— so close that I saw her pupils swallow up the brown. Her eyes went wide—wider than I'd ever seen them, and her mouth was a gaping maw of silence.

I slowly looked down and realized that the letter opener was embedded her left shoulder and blood began to seep out.

"Oh my god," I uttered, releasing the handle and stumbling backward.

There was a loud thud, then the den door flew open and crashed against the wall. My eyes darted that way and I saw Krew and Decker storm into the room.

"Regi," Krew shouted.

My eyes riveted back to the still-silent Maya, who was now

looking at the embedded letter opener protruding from her shoulder. Then she looked at Krew and Deck before her eyes shifted to me. "You tried to kill me."

"I didn't—I swear," I said in a shudder. Decker and Krew, who were squatting beside me nodded. "I was defending myself and she came at me."

"I'm calling the police," I heard Briney Darvy declare.

"Come on," Decker urged, and he and Krew grabbed my arms and lifted me onto my feet. My eyes dropped to my hand, which somehow become covered in Maya's blood. My attention shifted to Maya, who was laying on the floor, clutching at her bloody chest, screaming that I was trying to kill her.

The world around me turned into a cyclone. My vision spun and spun until everything went black.

Regina'a Diary

September 5th, 2025

Dear Diary,

It's me again. It's been a while—more than two years.

Where do I begin? I think I want to pick up where I left off with you when Maya showed up on my doorstep.

Life with her as a roommate was actually pretty normal, if you can believe it—at least until she started dating Jess a few months ago. It's been insane since then. Last month Maya took me to an illegal fight organized by Jess and his friend Kane. And Diary, you would never guess. KREW was one of the fighters! I was so happy to see him again, until his brother stepped into the ring. I was so terrified, I ran out of there and locked myself in my apartment.

I'm ashamed about this next part, Diary. But since you know all of my deepest secrets, I'm going to confess one more. I was so upset about seeing that monster again, that after I got home, I cut myself. I'd been doing so good—it had been years since I'd picked up a razor blade. But I did it. Just one cut, and it made me feel at peace for a few seconds, until the realization of what I did came rushing in.

Okay, I'm back. Sorry those last few sentences—my hand was really shaking from remembering my lapse. But I'm good now. Got a drink of water and repeated my mantra to settle myself.

I'm alive. I'm safe. I'm here.

Ready for more shocking news, Diary? I'm just gonna lay it all out—it's pretty much a clusterfuck. After I took off from the fight, Kane was shot dead. Maya saw the whole thing happen.

But get this, when I woke up the next morning, Maya was gone and a huge thug broke into the apartment and tried to kill me. If it wasn't for Krew AND DECKER!! Yes, I said Decker, I'd be dead. Decker killed the meathead, and I passed out.

I woke up in a crappy motel all freaked out. I still can't believe the guys kidnapped me and brought me there!

But wait. There's more, Diary.

Someone shot at the motel room's window because—get this, there are contracts out on me and on Krew!! Decker said so. He's a hitman now. To keep us safe, he hid Krew and me up in fricking Vermont, but even there we were attacked by other hitmen.

I escaped and came back here to Elida to see my parents. On the way, I learned Maya was home for her father's funeral. I decided I was going to confront Maya, about everything that happened since the fight.

Seeing my parents was okay. They had a lot of questions, tears and hugs. Overall, I'm glad to be home.

Now the for the Maya part.

After the funeral, I went to Maya's house to get some answers—we fought—and I accidentally stabbed her. Or Maya purposefully pushed herself onto the letter opener I was still holding—I'm still not sure on that part. But Krew and Decker were there. And they saw everything, including her lying through her teeth.

Anyway, the police were called. I was led outside by a deputy and we stood on the sidewalk—him, me, my parents, Krew and

Decker—and watched Maya get put in an ambulance. After they drove away, all of us saw Teke standing by his car.

Condensed version, Diary. Decker took off after Teke. Teke saw Decker, and the bastard got in his car and sped away. Decker got in his truck and was right on his tail. And I haven't seen Decker since.

Soon after, the sheriff read me my Miranda rights and hand-cuffed me like I was a criminal. Who could blame him, when I was standing there, covered in someone else's blood. Krew started to argue, and so did my parents, but it was no use.

Believe me when I say that being arrested and taken to jail wasn't the worst of it. No, the worst was being interrogated. I swear I could feel the trauma from it piling onto my PTSD.

At every turn, the cops tried to discount my version of that disaster, believing what Maya told them before she was taken to the hospital instead of what I described. That bitch is just like Krew and Decker said—only out for herself.

In the end, I was set free nearly twenty-four hours later, because Maya didn't file charges against me.

What's strange about all this, Diary? Maya disappeared from the hospital without a trace. No discharge from care, no word to anyone —poof. Gone. Was it her own doing or did someone else make her disappear? I couldn't say. And I'm not heartbroken about it.

What is breaking my heart? Decker hasn't come back. And Krew hasn't either.

I've spent most of the time at my parents' house, waiting for them. My mother is elated by their absence in my life, which irritates me.

I attempted to reach out to Krew's father, but he hung up on me the second I told him who I was. And Decker's dad was no better.

Without a word from either of my men, and with Maya missing in action, I assume my life can go back to normal. As much as I love my parents, I have to leave, head back to Chicago, where my life is and try to get my job back.

What do you think, Diary? Is leaving the right thing or should I wait a few more days for them? Should I move on with my life? Maybe even start dating again. Please disregard that part. The second I wrote those words I realize that I can never date anyone—not when I'm still very much in love with Krew and Decker.

No matter what, my love for Krew and Decker will always be with me. Even if I never see them again, that time in Vermont (and here's a delicious confession, Diary) will be my Best Memory Ever, because I was finally able to be with them—the three of us loving on each other. It will be enough.

This is the most that I have ever written to you, but I had a lot to tell you.

Diary, Krew just showed up and he said we needed to leave—like now. I gotta go. Sorry...

Love, Regina

About the Author

CJ Warrant is a Best-Selling Author for dark romantic thrillers, suspense, Contemporary Romance. A lover of strong coffee, baking and family, but not always in that order—She's a wife, a loving mother of three and worked in the beauty industry for many years until writing—which is her other passion took over. Now is a full-time author, CJ is happy being home and writing dark gritty stories to life.

https://linktr.ee/cjwarrant
www.cjwarrant.com

More Books by CJ Warrant

<u>Morally Grey</u>

Protecting Delaina

<u>Dark Romantic Thrillers</u>

Forgetting Jane

Mirror Image

Dance of the Mourning Cloak

<u>Boba Book Babes Mystery Series</u>

Pandemonium in Peoria

Silenced in San Antonio (Coming Soon)

<u>Contemporary Romance</u>

Deacon

<u>Chance At Love, MM Romance Series</u>

Four Days

One Kiss

Two of Hearts

Three Times Lucky

Five Seasons of Love

CJ Barlowe Books

<u>Warrior Black Series, Road to Rocktoberfest World</u>

Killer Notes

Beyond The Stix

Tone Deaf (Coming October 29th, 2025)

What's to come in 2026

CJ Warrant

Romantic Thriller Series (Title Coming Soon)

We All Fall Down Series

Fractured Soul (Date Coming Soon)

Ravaged Heart (2026)

CJ Barlowe

The Beckett Cousins, Bear Shifter Series

Warrior Black Series, Road to Rocktoberfest World

Book 4

Book 5

Not the End

www.ingramcontent.com/pod-product-compliance
Lightning Source LLC
Chambersburg PA
CBHW070622300726

48975CB00006B/1900